D1435003

MURDER
on the PIER

BOOKS BY MERRYN ALLINGHAM

MURDER
on
the PIER

Merryn Allingham

bookouture

Published by Bookouture in 2021

An imprint of Storyfire Ltd.
Carmelite House
50 Victoria Embankment
London EC4Y 0DZ

www.bookouture.com

ISBN: 978-1-80019-886-9
eBook ISBN: 978-1-80019-885-2

ONE

Flora Steele stood gazing at the buffet table, admiring its plentiful display but longing to be elsewhere. Anywhere, but at Bernie Mitchell's wake – a man she'd so disliked. Tucked up in front of the fire at her cottage, perhaps or, even better, at the All's Well, unpacking the latest parcel of books to arrive at her shop.

'He was one of the best. A great chap, don't you think?'

The man who'd spoken was unknown to her and standing uncomfortably close. His black funeral suit, cut a little too tightly, seemed barely to contain his six foot of muscle, and she could feel the warmth that emanated from him. Desperately, she tried to edge further away but, seemingly oblivious to Flora's discomfort, the stranger leaned across to snaffle a plate of sausage rolls, a solid column of flesh trapping her against the trestle.

Shuffling to one side, she fudged a response. 'Any premature death is sad,' she said.

In her opinion Bernard Mitchell hadn't been a great chap. He was a man who'd never been out of trouble and the worst kind of husband, but his funeral was hardly the place to voice such a sentiment.

She wasn't here for Bernie Mitchell, she reminded herself. She was here for Kate, his widow, a girl she'd barely known when they'd sat in the same class at school but who, in their twenties, had become one of her very best friends. Owning businesses in Abbeymead and working hard at making them a success – Kate in her café, and Flora in her bookshop – had brought the two of them together and cemented their friendship.

Kate, now, was standing only feet away, bidding a fellow guest goodbye – even more reason for Flora to watch her words.

'You haven't met Frank, have you, Flora?' Kate turned to ask her. 'He was a good friend of Bernie's. He's come down from London for the funeral.' Her eyes, red-rimmed from tears, expressed a wariness and Flora wondered why.

'Frank Foster.' The man shot out a hand and Flora found hers crushed in its grasp.

'Miss Steele owns the village bookshop, Frank. The All's Well.'

There was a wobble to Kate's voice, Flora noticed. She had held up well during the service at St Saviour's, and even at the burial that followed, but the wake appeared a trial too far. The cloying air in the ancient hall didn't help. The Priory Hotel had been unlived in for months, and the general mustiness, mixed with the smell of cooked food, was unpleasant.

The man Kate had introduced stared at Flora, his gaze sweeping her from head to toe: long coppery hair, hazel eyes, pale face, dark green fitted woollen dress. Flora could almost see him ticking her off, item by item. Appraising her, she thought furiously.

'Funny kind of a name for a shop,' he said at last, flashing a set of very white teeth. They were grimly fascinating, like teeth Flora had once seen in a childhood picture book. Sharks' teeth.

'Not funny at all, if you know your Shakespeare,' she said a trifle curtly and turned back to her friend. 'Kate, you should go home. You've done enough. Most people have eaten and Alice and I can clear up between us.'

The buffet was now looking sparse, but the original spread had been generous, the long trestle filled with an array of Scotch eggs, sausage rolls, sandwiches, and half a dozen plates of small cakes, courtesy of Alice Jenner, Abbeymead's foremost cook. Alice had worked at the Priory from the day she went into service, first as a kitchen maid, then rising rapidly to become chief cook for Lord Edward Templeton, and when he'd died and the place had become a hotel, the chef in charge of its kitchen.

'I'll be round later to pick up my bags, Katie,' Frank Foster said. 'I'm catching the evening train.'

The pet name grated on Flora. 'He's been staying with you?' she asked her friend quietly, as they left Frank to continue his grazing.

'Only for a few days. I felt I had to offer him a bed. When he telephoned, I remembered his name. Bernie mentioned him as a friend and talked about him quite often. I've found him a bit over-bearing, but I suppose that comes with being an important busi-nessman. He owns a nightclub in the West End – the Blue Peacock, Bernie told me, a really expensive place.' She lowered her voice. 'He's keen to own a hotel as well as a club. He's talking about buying the Priory.'

Flora was astonished. Instinctively, her gaze travelled around the magnificent wood-panelled hall that, until a few months ago, had been the foyer of an exclusive hotel. Unoccupied, the Priory had already begun to look shabby. The beautiful oak floor, its high gloss once dazzling, was now faded and scuffed, the valuable Chinese vases brought to England as trophies by past Templetons were in desperate need of a wash, and the portraits of those very Templetons, their frames rimmed with dust, looked down on the scene with haughty disdain.

'He wants to buy this place? Really?'

Kate nodded wordlessly.

Before Flora could make any sensible comment, Alice Jenner bustled up to them, her cheeks pink from constant forays to the kitchen. Reaching out for Kate, her two plump arms encircled the girl and hugged her tightly. 'It's time you went home, my love,' she said quietly. 'Raymond is doing a last round with what's left of the beer, then we can call it a day. That crowd can certainly drink, I'll say that for them.'

A number of the hotel's former staff had attended the funeral,

more to support Kate than from any liking for her husband, and
had been enjoying the generous hospitality with some gusto. The
rising chatter was inevitable, people appreciating the company of
their fellows despite the sad occasion, but Flora was keenly aware
of how painful that must be for Kate.

'*We* can pack up,' Alice went on. 'And I'll call by later – see
how you're doing.'

'Go!' Flora encouraged her. 'Jack is here somewhere – he'll
help as well.'

Her eyes roamed over her fellow guests: the vicar, his housekeeper, Miss Dunmore, various ladies from the Mother's Union, a
nice irony, she thought – Mitchell would have hated that – Flora's
bloodthirsty pensioner, Elsie, and several of the Abbeymead shop-
keepers: the butcher, Mr Preece, and beside him Mr Houseman,
the greengrocer, with Leonard, chief baker at the Rising Dough.
But no Jack.

'Don't worry, he'll put in an appearance sooner or later,' she
said, 'and between us all we'll leave the place as shipshape as any
administrator could wish.'

The hotel's disgraced owner had left behind multiple debts,
and administrators had been appointed to sell the property and its
grounds. In the meantime, they were happy to recoup whatever
money was possible by renting out parts of the Priory. It had been
Alice's idea to use the reception area when it became obvious that
the numbers coming to the wake would be far too large to cram
into the Nook, Kate's small café.

'If you're sure,' Kate murmured, plainly relieved to be going.

Collecting her hat and coat from a nearby chair, she said hasty
goodbyes to everyone close enough to hear, and disappeared into
the wintry afternoon. Seconds later, the figure of Jack Carrington
emerged between a knot of people and weaved his way to Flora's
side.

'There you are!' she exclaimed, a trifle piqued that he'd been
absent for so long.

Were all crime writers this elusive? But she shouldn't be cross.

Rather, be glad that the recluse she'd met a mere three months ago, a man unwilling to step out into the world, seemed happy to mix freely these days. Jack had certainly come a long way since they'd first met in her bookshop – perhaps that was what happened if you found a dead body together.

'Have you missed me?' His grey eyes held mischief, but she ignored his teasing.

'We need another pair of hands,' she said practically. 'And they happen to be yours.'

'What it is to be wanted! The waiter who's helping out – Raymond Parsons? – tells me the drink's almost gone. And most of the food by the look of it. I've asked Charlie to start clearing the empties.'

'How much did you have to pay the boy?' Alice asked sagely.

Charlie Teague might be only twelve years old, but he drove a hard bargain, willing to turn his hand to most things as long as the chink of money was loud enough. For the last few years, he'd helped with bookshop deliveries and, until Jack had decided to venture further than his front door, Charlie had been the one to keep him supplied with the books he needed.

'I promised him a bit extra if he helped out today,' Jack said. 'He's already working for me after school. I must say, he's not a bad gardener. Better than me, at least.'

'That wouldn't be too difficult.' Flora's smile took the sting out of her words.

Jack spread his hands in a gesture of appeal. 'Alice, she's been nagging me for weeks to sort out the garden at Overlay House. And what do I get when I do? Praise? Enthusiasm? Not on your life.'

'Take no notice.' Flora waved his objections away. 'I *am* enthusiastic. I've already booked my seat under the beech tree – if summer ever arrives.'

'This winter's been real bad,' Alice agreed. 'Such a terrible amount of snow. Almost brought the village to a standstill. I don't know how many books your customers have been buyin', Flora, but since I've been workin' at Kate's place this last month or two, she's had hardly any trade.'

'It's been slow at the All's Well,' Flora admitted. 'Just a trickle of people most days, but I've been kept busy working on the new window display.'

The latticed windows of the bookshop were a focal point for passers-by and Flora was conscious of how important it was they looked fresh and attractive. The idea of featuring the Priory had emerged after her adventures last autumn. A display of local history books, she'd decided, along with several volumes on the Templetons, the local aristocracy, and an illustrated backdrop tracing the development of the Priory itself from an important religious institution to a fine country house, housing generations of Templetons, to an expensive hotel after Lord Edward's death. She'd stopped at that point. The building's future was too uncertain. It was sad to see it empty and discarded, awaiting whatever buyer the administrators could find. Someone like Frank Foster, she feared, who would care nothing for its history or its traditional links with the village.

'Where d'you want these, Mrs Jenner?' It was Charlie Teague, carrying a tray that was almost as big as him, brimming with empty glasses.

'You'll need to take them down to the kitchen,' Alice told him, 'but only if you think you can manage the stairs.' When the boy nodded over the top of the tray, the beginnings of a smile hovered on her face. 'You're doing a good job, young man,' she said. 'C'mon. I'll lead the way.'

'I wonder if he'll be as keen on the washing up?' Flora said, as Alice marched her young helper towards the flight of stairs leading down to the kitchen.

'I've a feeling that will fall to us. But it's good, isn't it, to get this business over?'

Jack meant the funeral. There had been months of uncertainty, months that must have felt like a living death to Kate. It had been last October that her husband's clothes had been found on the beach at Littlehampton. His death, though, had remained unconfirmed until two weeks ago, when his body was finally washed up in a Dorset bay, further down the south coast.

Flora had been at the café when Constable Tring had brought the news and was surprised that Kate had barely reacted. She suspected her friend hadn't really taken it in. Had refused, maybe, to believe her husband was dead, convincing herself that Bernie was simply missing. That he'd decided for his own reasons to disappear from Abbeymead, leaving a pile of clothes behind to confuse anyone who might try to find him. The funeral, though, had forced Kate to face the truth. Today must have been devastating for her friend, even though in Flora's view the man had been one of the most wretched husbands ever.

She stripped off the cardigan she'd donned against the Priory's draughts. 'We'd better follow them down and make a start,' she said to Jack.

It was as they were making for the kitchen and the gargantuan pile of washing up, that the iron-studded entrance door to the Priory was flung wide and two very late guests strode in. A general gasp travelled around the room as people realised who it was: Polly Dakers on the arm of the man said to be sponsoring her new career as a model.

Polly had been transformed. No longer the lovely but humdrum receptionist they'd known at the hotel, but a woman who would not have been out of place in Hollywood. Wrapped in a fox-fur coat, her hair a brighter blonde than ever, and wearing make-up fit for a film studio, she walked in, arms linked with a stubby middle-aged man.

'The sugar daddy,' Flora breathed. 'I do believe it's Harry Barnes. My goodness!'

'Just as well he's got money,' her companion said wryly.

She stole a swift glance at Jack's lanky figure standing close, the thick brown hair that never sat straight and the astonishing eyes, an ever-changing grey. There'd be no need of money for Jack to boast a beautiful woman on his arm. Not that he was likely to. It gladdened Flora that, for an attractive man, he seemed impervious to any of the lures he encountered.

'Flora, darling,' Polly called out in an extravagant voice, diamond earrings jangling as she bounced over to them. Behind her trailed the earthy smell of fox fur. 'And Mr Carrington. How wonderful to see you.'

She was actually blowing them kisses, Flora realised.

'You *must* meet my very good friend, Harry Barnes. But perhaps you know him already?'

'We've never spoken,' Flora murmured.

Polly tottered back to her escort on a pair of precariously heeled shoes, grabbing him by the arm and dragging the reluctant man to their side. 'Harry, this is Flora Steele – she runs the local bookshop – and this is Jack.' He was accorded her most inviting smile. 'Jack Carrington. He's a crime writer, so you better be careful.' She gave an artificial giggle.

Harry Barnes said nothing, his face moon-white and blank. He seemed uncomfortable in the suit he was wearing, fidgeting with the velvet lapels of its jacket. Velvet? Flora smiled to herself. The jacket must have been chosen by Polly. Almost certainly.

'Have you seen my uncle Ted?' the girl asked brightly. 'My cousin should be here, too. Sylvia said she'd come with her father. I'd like to say hello to them both.'

'I'd like to see Ted,' Harry Barnes said unexpectedly, his voice gruff. 'Haven't seen him for a while, but it's good to keep in touch with old friends.'

It was Ted Russell, Flora remembered, who had introduced Polly to the older man. The Barnes family owned a house a few miles out of Abbeymead, but both husband and wife had worked in London for many years and were not well-known in the village. As far as Flora was aware, they were still living at the same address.

'I'm to blame for that!' Polly gushed. 'I've kept you a bit too busy for friends, haven't I, Harry?'

Her hands flew to her cheeks as though she felt herself blushing. Which was highly unlikely, Flora thought witheringly.

Ignoring Polly's play-acting, she said, 'The last time I saw Mr Russell and his daughter, they were sitting beneath Lord Edward's portrait.'

Polly stretched herself as tall as she could, her head waggling this way and that.

'I can't see them. I knew I should have worn a higher heel.' She gave a crack of laughter. It was a laugh Flora knew well, one that belonged to the old Polly. For a moment, the girl had forgotten her new persona and it was refreshing.

'Your uncle is still there,' Jack confirmed, looking over the heads of the crowd, to the wall opposite. 'Still in his seat.'

'It must be wonderful to be so tall,' she breathed huskily, back in character again.

Her escort scowled, but Polly took no notice. 'Harry, darling, why don't you find Ted while I pop across for a quick chat with some of the people I worked with. I'll only be a minute, then I'll join you.'

She was most definitely in charge, Flora decided.

Polly had begun to move towards the group of young people when Frank Foster stepped in front of her, barring her way.

'Hello, Polly, nice to see you, girl.'

His reappearance took Flora aback. Should the man still be here? Wasn't he supposed to be collecting his bags from Kate's cottage and leaving for London? Polly, she noticed, looked slightly sick.

'Hello, Frank.' The two words fell flat, the girl's excitement draining away. 'Sorry, I can't stop. People to catch up with. You will excuse me, won't you?' she asked of no one in particular, before pattering away on the ridiculous shoes.

Harry muttered something inaudible, but it was Frank Foster's reaction that stuck in Flora's mind. He jerked forward as though he was about to start after the girl. Polly, though, had disappeared in a flurry of fur and was lost among the noisy crowd of youngsters. Frank's gaze, as he followed her with his eyes, was hungry. Rapacious.

Harry Barnes cracked his knuckles and Flora winced. 'I best go and find Ted,' he muttered, glancing angrily at Frank who was still staring after Polly. Giving their small group what passed for a nod, he thumped across the crowded space to the seats opposite, barging his way without apology through the chattering groups of people.

She watched him go, uneasy with the hostility that had sprung out of nowhere and was cloaking the air.

'Ready?' Jack asked.

'I suppose.' It might have been useful to stay a while. There was definitely something wrong and Flora's instinct was always to discover the hidden.

They were almost at the basement stairs when she caught sight of Polly again. The girl had detached Raymond Parsons from the group of young people she'd been talking to, and her face was flushed, her small fists raised. It had been Raymond that Polly had danced with at her leaving party. In this very room, Flora remembered. She wasn't dancing now. She was embroiled in what appeared to be a very angry argument.

Flora looked over to the row of seats that she and Alice had placed against the far wall, and saw that Harry had found his friend, and his friend's daughter. He hadn't taken a seat, though, preferring to anchor himself to the floor, his stolid figure seeming to have grown roots. He was glaring across the room at Polly and Raymond, his eyes never leaving them. And by his side, seated on a tapestry-covered chair, Sylvia Russell, her thin frame clothed in unflattering mauve, was glaring at the couple just as hard.

What on earth was going on?

TWO

It was nearly two hours later that Jack and Flora walked back to the village together. They were tired but satisfied. The Priory had been returned to its former state and Bernie Mitchell had finally been laid to rest.

Jack pulled a torch from his pocket to light their way along the winding drive.

'That was some afternoon,' he said wryly. 'And what looked to me like some very angry people. No one could call Abbeymead sleepy.'

Flora didn't respond. She was concentrating hard on avoiding the puddles. It had rained heavily during their time in the kitchen, and the driveway's potholes were a hazard.

'Polly Dakers made quite an entrance, didn't she?' Jack went on, adjusting his fedora against the drizzle that had just then started again. 'Though a bit late for the food.'

'I don't think it was the food she came for.' Giving up on the puddles, Flora tucked her arm in his, enjoying the feeling of companionship.

'No,' he said thoughtfully. 'The business with young Raymond Parsons. It looked a bad row.'

'That was strange, though to be honest, so was a lot of this afternoon. I always thought Raymond was a friend of Polly's. I remember them at her leaving party, dancing uproariously together.'

'Ah, yes, the party.' She felt him move closer and knew he was remembering what a truly terrible day that had been. 'They certainly didn't look much like friends today,' he said. 'Something must have upset them badly.'

They passed through the wrought-iron gates of the Priory, their heads bent. The wind had risen and the trees along the lane back to the village had begun to dip and bend in the sudden gusts. Flora tucked herself in tighter.

'Polly was already upset,' she observed, 'before she even spoke to Raymond. She made that spectacular entrance and then Frank Foster popped up. She definitely didn't like Frank.'

'And who is he?'

'You didn't meet him. Kate introduced me, though I got the impression she'd rather not have. I thought him a horrible man. Apparently, Foster was an old friend of her husband's, which tells you all you need to know. It seems that Kate has been forced to put him up at her cottage for several days. I didn't like him and, very obviously, neither did Polly. And neither did the mysterious sugar daddy who, it turns out, is Harry Barnes – someone living nearby. Extraordinary! They seemed to know each other. Polly and Foster. She must have met him in London. Maybe on one of her modelling trips.'

The lane they'd been following had widened and Abbeymead's main road lay ahead. Walking close to the fronts of the cottages and shops that lined the high street, they gained some shelter from a storm that was increasing in strength by the minute.

'You think the modelling stuff is going ahead?' Jack asked.

'It's why Polly's with that tubby little man, isn't it?'

'Don't be unkind. I thought she might be with him for the fur coat and the diamonds in her ears.'

'I'm sure they come in handy, but Polly has a knife-like focus when it comes to what she wants from life. And what she wants is to be a model. She won't let Harry Barnes off that hook, no matter how many fur coats he buys.'

'Bernie's "old friend" better not get in the way then. A knife-like focus sounds dangerous.'

Flora said nothing, thinking over the rest of the afternoon. When she broke the silence, it was to say, 'Kate told me that Frank Foster is hoping to buy the Priory. I hope he doesn't manage it.'

They were just then passing the post office – Dilys, the post-mistress, hadn't come to the wake, she realised, which was unusual. It would have provided the woman with gossip for weeks. In the faint light from the shop window, she caught a glimpse of Jack's face. He looked slightly stunned.

'I suppose someone needs to buy the place,' he said at last. 'Already, it's not in the greatest shape, and the longer it stands empty, the more decrepit it will become. I don't think Lord Edward would be happy with that.'

'I don't think Lord Edward would be happy with the hotel either, but I agree the house needs an owner. Not Foster, though. Definitely not him. I hope he caught that train back to London. Kate didn't complain, but it was plain she didn't want him around any more.'

'It was a miserable day for her,' Jack agreed, 'and Foster prob-ably made it worse.' He nodded towards the sign for Katie's Nook. 'She's kept the café going so far, but do you think she'll close for a while?'

'I'm hoping she'll be persuaded to stay home for a week or so. Alice is more than capable of running the place on her own.'

'At least until she gets another chef's job.'

'That doesn't seem likely.'

'What if the Priory is sold and reopened as a hotel? Would Alice take a job there again?'

'She'd have to, if it was offered. She needs to work and Kate can't afford to pay much. But poor Alice, if Foster were the one to buy the hotel. The old owner, Vernon Elliot, was bad enough but now this man...'

They had arrived at the white expanse of the bookshop door and she left the thought trailing.

'Why are we here?' Jack asked in a puzzled voice, taking off his fedora and ruffling a hand through hair that was damp around the edges. 'Why haven't we walked straight to your cottage?'

'I wanted you to see my window display. It looks particularly special at night. The shop lights pick out the book covers beautifully – see, they're a rainbow of colour. The colours of precious gems.'

Jack bent his head and peered into first one and then the other latticed window. 'Very attractive. Very tempting. Pity that none of the villagers ever venture out after dark!'

'It's there if they do,' she said cheerfully. 'And they can always take a look during the day.'

The drizzle had given way to heavy rain again, the wind sending ice-cold shards to lash at them as they stood looking through the bookshop window. 'You best get off home, Jack. This rain isn't going to stop any time soon.'

'I'm walking you back to your cottage,' he said firmly.

'No, you're not. I can find my own way home.'

But, as if to disprove her words, Flora's foot slipped off the pavement as she began to walk away. Jack grabbed her arm, supporting her while very gingerly she straightened up. Her ankle had twisted badly.

'I'm walking with you. Take my arm and don't argue – I'm the one with the torch.' He waved the light at her. 'And I have all the time in the world.'

'You're not writing tonight?'

'I'm a free man. I typed the last words of that dismal novel just before I dressed for the funeral.'

'You must be glad to see it done.' She knew how hard Jack had struggled with this last book. 'You've finished your novel and I've finished my window display. *And* the snow has gone – finally. Do you think it's time we offered Charlie his treat?'

Charlie Teague had been instrumental in saving Flora's life the previous autumn and, in a euphoric burst of gratitude, Jack had promised him a day trip to Brighton, complete with beach attractions, a theatre visit and a fish and chips meal. The inclement weather had so far made it impossible.

'I'm afraid it is.' Jack looked down at her, barely hiding a grin. 'Prepare to be exhausted.'

Still hobbling slightly, she walked on before saying thoughtfully, 'The pantomime will be on at the Hippodrome. It's *Aladdin* and supposed to be very good. Elsie's granddaughter loved it. Charlie might be a bit old, I suppose, but I reckon he'll still enjoy a live performance. Monday would be a good day to go. The shop is always quiet and with so few customers I won't feel guilty playing truant. I'll dig out the bus timetable this evening.'

'No need,' he said airily. 'I've bought a car.'

Flora stopped dead, causing him almost to trip. 'You've bought a car? You hate cars.'

'I hate telephones, too, but I'm thinking of getting one installed when my name comes up. I'm on the waiting list.'

She glanced at him, intrigued. 'What's happened to you?'

'Not a lot. I made a decision, that's all – that it was time Jack Carrington joined the modern world.'

'You mean it was time Jolyon Adolphus Carrington joined.' It had been a joy for Flora to discover that 'Jack', rather than being his given name, was simply his initials.

'Be quiet!' he commanded, the shadow of a smile accompanying his words.

They fell back in step again, turning down one of the many narrow twittens that led from the main street with Jack carefully aiming the torch at the road ahead. Despite a petition to the council, signed by most of the inhabitants, street lights had never come to Abbeymead. They were seen as contrary to rural tradition, apart from costing too much, which the villagers suspected was the real reason. The wartime blackout had meant little to Abbeymead – it was something the village lived with, before the war and since.

'But the car...' Flora pursued.

'It turns out that the new project – the one Arthur Bellaby is so keen on—'

'The one in Cornwall?'

'Among other places. The contract he persuaded me to sign came with a very nice advance. It arrived last week and was just enough to buy a small Austin. The car's a bit shabby, but it goes well. All I need now is to remember how to drive.'

She gave him a gentle poke in the ribs. 'You'd better. I must say I like the idea of travelling in style.'

'Only the best for you, Flora, only the best.'

A few yards further and they reached her cottage, its flint walls standing proud in the twilight. Limping slightly, Flora made her way up the red brick path to the solid oak front door. Fitting her key in the lock, she turned to wave goodbye. A thoroughly wet Jack, still waiting at the garden gate, raised a soggy arm in return.

THREE

Jack felt unusually nervous when, three days later at nine o'clock in the morning, he pulled up outside the All's Well bookshop. It was where he had arranged to meet Flora and Charlie for their big day out in Brighton. He'd dressed carefully, keeping his faithful fedora but abandoning an ulster that had seen better days in favour of the smart trench coat he'd worn years previously for New York winters. His clothes weren't too much of a worry. It was the car that concerned him. He'd told Flora the Austin was shabby, but in this morning's dreary winter light, it looked even worse. Still, the engine was sound, and it had to be better than waiting at bus stops in what was still very cold weather.

'Mr Carrington!' Charlie Teague burst off the pavement and into the road before the vehicle had come to a complete stop outside the bookshop's weathered brick and flint walls.

'You gotta car! I didn't know,' he gasped, almost ending beneath its still moving wheels.

'You don't know everything,' Jack said, extricating his long legs from the driver's seat.

'What do you think?' he asked Flora, as she turned around from pulling the shop door closed for the day.

She was looking particularly pretty, he thought, which was irritating when he hadn't slept well and his extra ten years were weighing heavily. It looked as though she had bought herself a new winter coat, bright red, which should have clashed with her reddish-brown hair, but somehow didn't.

Flora gave the car a swift inspection. 'It's got four wheels,' she said prosaically, 'and presumably it goes.'

'If you want anything better, you'll need your own sugar daddy.'

'What's one of them?' Charlie was already climbing into the back seat.

'Nothing you need worry about,' Jack said severely.

The journey to Brighton was slow but uneventful, and by the time they reached the seafront and parked outside the Grand Hotel, the sky had cleared to a piercing blue and a weak sun had begun to shine.

'It's going to be a good day,' Flora said cheerfully.

She'd perked up noticeably – as soon as they'd passed the Pylons, the sentinels that marked the gateway to Brighton. Perhaps, until then, she hadn't expected to arrive.

Collecting his hat from the back seat, Jack locked the car and looked at her expectantly. It was nearly six years ago that he'd moved to Sussex, but most of his time had been spent locked away at Overlay House. A recluse, Flora had called him, when they'd first met. Brighton was still an unknown town to him, an exotic town – he knew the Pavilion's oriental domes from photographs – but the Prince Regent's extravaganza was unlikely to interest Charlie. What would, though? He was hoping for Flora's suggestions.

'Tussaud's,' Charlie said, having his own ideas of how to fill the day.

'Madame Tussauds is in London,' Jack corrected. 'We can't go there.'

'Yes, we can.' Flora smiled at them both. 'We walk along the seafront and the waxworks building is near the Palace Pier.'

It set Jack wondering what exactly he'd let himself in for, but the saunter along the promenade was pleasant enough. There were few people around – one or two dog owners, several early-morning walkers, but mercifully none of the crowds that summer would bring to the town. A breeze was ruffling the water, the sun sending sparks of light dancing across the waves as they rolled into shore. Over the years, he'd rarely visited the sea but, breathing in the salt-laden air, hearing the splash and drag of the tide, brought back memories of childhood beaches, of buckets and spades, of ice creams and wet costumes.

In ten minutes, they were standing outside a pink-painted building. Louis Tussaud's, the sign announced. A cameo relief of a man's head appeared beneath and, lower still, French Waxworks, printed in large letters, made clear to waverers what they were missing if they chose to walk on.

Jack didn't think it looked much like the real thing, but Charlie's nose was already pressed against the glass frontage.

'Cor, look at that!'

The Tussaud's window featured a scene from *The Pit and the Pendulum*, with a man strapped to a table and a huge scythe moving backwards and forwards, getting lower and lower until it just missed the man's body, the machinery rewinding to start again from the top.

Jack stifled a sigh. He had a good idea what this visit was likely to entail and, after a traipse up and down the three floors of the building, he knew he'd been right. Celebrities of the day such as Max Miller were the highlight, with the effigies of politicians proving indifferent and various scenes from fairy tales artificial. The chamber of horrors was indeed a horror, but not in the way intended.

'Where next?' Jack asked glumly. He was already wishing himself back at Overlay House.

'Cheer up. It was fun.'

Flora's tone was too bright. Her coat was too bright and so was her hair. He could feel a headache developing and tried not to scowl.

'How about the aquarium, Charlie?' she asked.

Charlie nodded a little dubiously and it was plain, once they'd passed through the turnstile, that he had little interest in sea creatures. The visit was saved from total disaster by, of all things, two chimpanzees. Jack was unsure what chimpanzees were doing in an aquarium, but Charlie was utterly fascinated and that was what mattered.

'Why's this one called Gordon?' he asked.

Flora looked blank, but attempted a wild guess. 'The other one is called Steve, so maybe they're named after their keepers.'

'Try two famous jockeys, Gordon Richards and Steve Donoghue,' Jack offered, congratulating himself on a piece of quick thinking.

Neither of his companions seemed overly impressed with this information, Flora saying briskly, 'We won't wait around for the chimps' tea party. It will take too long. So where next, Charlie?'

Next proved to be a journey on the Volks' railway to Peter Pan's Playground and an hour in which Charlie slid, stumbled and otherwise fell around the roller skating rink on a 'one size fits all' pair of skates.

At least it had tired the boy sufficiently for an early lunch, Jack reflected, paying the bill for three large plates of fish and chips, with Charlie having eaten most of the chips.

'I'd like to call it a day,' he said quietly to Flora, as they walked out of the restaurant. 'How about you?'

Flora's morning bounce had dwindled. 'I never thought sightseeing could be so tiring,' she murmured.

'It's not the sightseeing. It's a twelve-year-old boy. How about getting into the car and pottering back to Abbeymead?'

'We can't, Jack. We promised him a visit to the theatre. You do have the tickets?'

He fidgeted. 'That's been a bit of a problem,' he confessed. 'I couldn't book the pantomime at the Hippodrome – too short notice. We'll have to make do with the show on the pier. A drama group from London has been in town for a few weeks, putting on their own panto.'

Flora grimaced. 'Doing what?'

'Something called *Harlequinade*.'

'I thought that was dead and buried before I was born.'

'It probably was, but someone must have decided it would make an interesting show for Christmas.' He hesitated, waiting for the traffic to clear before crossing over to the pier. 'I'm not sure that Charlie will think so.'

Charlie didn't and neither did Jack. *Harlequinade*, with its silly plot of lovers separated by a greedy father, aided by a mischievous clown and servant, and involving chaotic chase scenes with a bumbling policeman, made the boy yawn.

'Now you know why it's never performed these days,' Flora whispered.

All three of them were glad to emerge from the dreariness of the theatre, but a sky that had been bright blue when they went in was now looking ominous, dark clouds banking on the horizon, and a new chill in the air.

'That wuz rubbish,' Charlie opined, once they were clear of the building. 'Didn't you think, Mr Carrington?'

Without waiting for an answer, he rushed over to the pier's iron railings to watch a flurry of seagulls engaged in a major argument.

'Mr Carrington did think it rubbish,' Jack said heavily. He looked down at a silent Flora, huddled by his side. 'Are you still awake?'

'Awake and cold,' she said shortly.

'Miss Steele, Miss Steele.' It was Charlie and his cry was anguished. 'You gotta come, Miss Steele. And you, Mr Carrington.'

'What the—?'

Together, they rushed across the intervening space, careless of the icy patches still covering the pier's wooden boards. Charlie was hanging over the rail almost vertically, and Jack pulled him back to safety. A swift glance at Flora, and he saw her mouth open, heard a stifled cry on her breath.

Following her gaze, he peered down into the steel grey of the water. There was a body floating between the iron stanchions of the pier. A body, with glazed eyes, gyrating to the rhythm of the waves, up and down, side to side. Long, blonde hair spread itself across the water, like a fan in constant motion.

He recognised that hair. Recognised that face. They belonged to Polly Dakers.

FOUR

The next few minutes were pandemonium. Flora wrapped her arms around Charlie, trying to comfort him – or was it the other way round? – while Jack rushed back into the theatre in search of a telephone. What audience there'd been had melted away, but the two or three people on the pier for a walk rushed to the railings as soon as they became aware of something amiss, and were bunched together in a knot, their bodies bent nearly double as they struggled to catch sight of the drifting body.

Flora's stomach was pirouetting dangerously. She wanted to flee, to run at full speed along the promenade to the Grand Hotel, find the Austin and escape back to Abbeymead. But that wasn't possible. They were witnesses of a kind, though what they had witnessed was difficult to say. Grabbing Charlie's hand, she took shelter in the lee of the theatre, trying hard to swallow the nausea. It was Charlie she should be worrying over. After the first moments of adrenalin, he had fallen unusually quiet. It was a dreadful ending to the treat they'd promised him.

And Polly. Poor, foolish Polly. How had her young life ended in such tragedy? That would be for the police to determine, Flora told herself – this time she would not get involved. Yet, already, she felt the stirrings of wanting to know.

The police arrived twenty minutes after Jack had telephoned

999. It was Alan Ridley who led the posse of officers – the policeman Jack consulted from time to time to ensure he got police procedures right.

'This is a nice how d'you do, eh, Jack?' Ridley greeted him. 'You can't seem to keep out of trouble.'

'It's not me that's in trouble,' Jack said mildly. 'That poor girl—'

'Don't suppose you know her?'

'In fact, I do. Her name is Polly Dakers. She's from Abbeymead and worked at the Priory Hotel as a receptionist until a few months ago.'

Ridley strode to the railings to look for himself, passing Flora and Charlie huddled against the theatre wall. 'I've brought a couple of divers with me, though I can see they won't be needed.' His gaze was fixed on the grey waters below. 'Still, they can pull the lass to shore. Now, let's see...'

Questions followed, Ridley leaving his sergeant to take notes. Who had spotted the body? Where had they been standing at the time? Had they noticed anyone close by? Two of the other policemen had corralled the few spectators and seemed to be asking much the same questions.

At last, when Flora had frozen to an almost immoveable block, Ridley returned to tell them they were free to leave.

'Might have to get in touch with you later,' he said, 'but I doubt it. It's pretty clear the girl slipped.'

'How do you make that out?' Flora's question was sharp.

The inspector looked down at her, a benign expression on his face. 'None of you saw anyone hanging around. And all they saw' – he pointed to the small group of people now making their way off the pier – 'were one or two of the actors. They'd come out for a breath of fresh air but, during the performance, most of them were on stage or waiting in the wings. The girl hasn't been in the water long – I'd say the first half of the morning while the tide was coming in – otherwise she'd have been carried further out to sea. So who was here then? The only people we know for certain were the theatre group, rehearsing for the matinee. We'll be ques-

tioning them later, but I don't hold out much hope we'll learn a
lot.'

'You say Polly must have slipped. But how could she?' Flora
asked. 'The railings are waist high.'

'Ah, what you don't know, Miss Steele, is that the guard rail
doesn't go all the way round. Walk to the end of the pier and you'll
see a gap. Quite a big gap. It's for the pleasure boats, you see. They
tie up there in summer for people to board for trips along the coast.
There are still patches of ice all along the pier – I noticed as I
walked on – and they would have been more widespread this
morning. One of my men tells me that at the very end, it's even
icier. The girl must have slipped and not been able to save herself.
Maybe she was fooling around.'

'Fooling around. With whom?'

Ridley looked stuck. 'She could have been playing games by
herself. Showing off, you know.'

Polly was more than capable of that, Flora thought, but she'd
need an audience. She always needed an audience and, by the look
of it, there had been none.

'We'll do a post-mortem, of course, but I doubt we'll find more
than the cuts and bruises a body would get from being washed
against the stanchions.'

Flora flinched at the thought.

'The only other explanation,' he went on, 'is that she jumped.'

'Jumped? She had everything to live for,' Flora said indig-
nantly, then remembered how uncomfortable Polly had seemed
with Frank Foster at the wake, how angry she'd been with
Raymond. And the thunderous look that Harry Barnes had worn.
Not everything in Polly's life had been sweet.

'She's a young girl,' Ridley said in a tired voice. 'From my experience, there's a lot that can go wrong at that age. Problems can
seem insurmountable. It happens all the time.'

Flora couldn't believe it of Polly and, feeling out of sympathy
with the inspector, she detached herself from the group and
walked towards the end of the pier, taking care to avoid any

splashes of ice that remained. She felt Jack's eyes watching her progress. The gap the inspector had spoken of was certainly there, together with a particularly wide pool of ice, that had partially melted in the earlier sunshine. Threatening clouds were gathering overhead now and the water was growing darker. Flora felt a shiver. Was it really possible that Polly had slipped?

She heard Jack's voice calling to her and, skirting the ice, began to retrace her steps. As she did, her foot felt something soft underfoot. Squishy ice? A lost glove? She bent down. A red wool bobble. From a hat perhaps. It was a strange find and she picked it up and slipped it into her coat pocket. There was no point in mentioning it to Inspector Ridley. One of his detectives had been here, at the end of the pier. The man must have seen it for himself and thought it unimportant.

'Shall we go?' Jack was coming towards her, a concerned look on his face. 'We should get Charlie back to his mum. The boy's not saying much, but I think he's pretty upset.' He reached out and took hold of her hand. 'How are you?'

'Upset, too. Very upset. And confused – about Polly. I can't understand why anyone would want her dead. For all her brashness, she was well liked in Abbeymead.'

'We'll leave this one to the police, shall we?' he asked anxiously.

'If you say so.' That didn't really commit her and Flora was unsure if she wanted to leave it to the inspector. Seemingly, he'd already made up his mind.

Dusk was gathering as, with Charlie between them, they walked off the pier. Hands in his pockets, the boy trudged back along the promenade, his shoulders sagging a little and his expression unreadable. Not a word was said until they reached the Grand Hotel and the Austin parked on the road outside.

Opening the rear door of the car, Charlie suddenly broke his silence. 'I liked Polly,' he said. 'She wuz OK.'

FIVE

Everyone who came into the bookshop the next day wanted to talk about Polly. There were theories galore as to how the girl had died and why, though a consensus was building, particularly among the older members of the community, that she'd been asking for trouble ever since she'd left the Priory.

It hurt Flora to hear the village gossips. Polly had annoyed many of them with her boastfulness, shocked some with the brazen flaunting of her new-found wealth, and she had definitely not been sensible, but... She was barely twenty, without parents – she'd stayed to pursue her dream of modelling when they'd moved to New Zealand the previous year – and Flora doubted that Uncle Ted, with whom she'd been living, had exercised much influence.

By the time Jack put his head around the door two days after the tragedy, she was feeling decidedly angry. 'I hope you've come to buy a book,' she greeted him. 'No one else has.'

He took off his fedora and laid it on the front table where Flora displayed her most recently published books, masking from view Graham Greene's latest offering.

'No books today,' he said quietly, 'but something as important. Have you thought of Ted Russell?'

'Of course I've thought of him. He's Polly's uncle.'

'What I mean is, have you thought of calling on Ted? We were the ones to find Polly and I've been wondering if we should visit and say how sorry we are.'

Flora shifted uncomfortably behind her desk, rearranging the small pots of paper clips and rubber bands she kept by the till. It was a while before she spoke. 'I had the same thought,' she admitted, 'but I haven't had the courage. He'll be in a bad way. He loved Polly lots.'

'If we go together? It might be easier.'

She looked across at the Victorian station clock that hung on the opposite wall. It was one of the many possessions Aunt Violet had bequeathed her, along with the bookshop itself. Her aunt had been thrilled to find the timepiece in a jumble sale and every evening had wound it religiously before she locked the bookshop door. It was almost lunchtime and today was early closing. Flora thought of the work she needed to do with customers absent – culling books that no longer earned their place on the shelves and returning them to the warehouse – but if she made the call on Ted a quick one, she should still have time to finish. Her aunt would have expected it.

'I'll get my coat,' she said.

Ted Russell lived on the new estate that had sprung up on the outskirts of the village just after the end of the war, and it took them a good twenty minutes' walk to reach his house.

'What happened to the car?' she asked, as they turned into Mulberry Crescent.

'In the garage, being checked,' he said briefly.

'Not good news then.' She pulled a small face. 'Have you wasted your advance, d'you think?'

'The Austin still has four wheels and an engine, so hopefully not. What house number are we looking for?'

The car was evidently a sensitive subject and Flora said no more.

The houses of Mulberry Crescent were identical: terraced, with two windows top and bottom and a front door in between. In front of each house, adjacent to the road, was a tarmacked space.

For car parking, she imagined, though most of the spaces lay empty, the residents content to travel by bus – she'd noticed a stop at the entrance to the Crescent. The gardens were identical, too, a severe square of grass surrounded by a two-foot flower border. Flora found the street vaguely depressing, not that the houses weren't warm and easy to keep clean – they certainly appeared to be – but that residents had opted to keep them so much alike. No one had wanted to step out of line by planting an unusual shrub or painting their front door purple or finding space for a quirky statue.

Ted's daughter, Sylvia, opened the door to them, and rather grudgingly showed them into the sitting room. Flora could imagine that the death of a cousin the same age as Sylvia must be almost impossible for the girl to accept. As they passed through the hall, she saw the figure of Raymond Parsons hovering in the doorway of what must be the kitchen, but he made no attempt to follow them. Flora remembered now – Raymond was Sylvia Russell's boyfriend, or so she'd heard, which made his quarrel with Polly at the wake seem even odder, though it might explain Sylvia's furious expression as she sat watching them. The young man's face was pale and drawn and, yes, full of suffering. In the light of recent events, was he feeling guilty at the words he'd flung at Polly?

Ted was sprawled in an armchair so old that it sagged back and front, but he staggered to his feet as they came through the doorway.

'Don't get up, Mr Russell,' Flora said. 'We won't stay long.'

'Oh, but you must. Sit down, Miss Steele. And you, Mr...'

'Carrington. Jack Carrington.'

Ted Russell's body appeared to sag as badly as his armchair and his face was etched in sadness. Flora was shocked at the change in him and cast around for how best to begin. 'We thought that as we were the ones to call the police...'

'...you might like to speak to us,' Jack finished for her.

Ted nodded. 'It's good of you to come. Good that you were there for my Polly.'

'We were in Brighton for the day. We'd taken Charlie Teague to the pantomime on the pier,' she said, not knowing how that might help.

'Panto, eh?' Ted's attention was caught. 'I've been in some of those. In my younger days. Amateur dramatics, you know.'

'This was a drama group from London. The performance had just finished when...'

Ted nodded sadly. 'Like I say, good you were there. I've felt that wearisome, not able to do anythin', not knowin' what to think. My little Polly. How could she?'

'How could she what?' Flora shifted to the edge of her chair.

'Jump,' he finished, gulping down the word. 'That's what the police think happened. I had Constable Tring round here yesterday.'

'I've told Dad they're wrong, if they think that.' Sylvia had come unnoticed into the room. 'Polly wouldn't have jumped. I've been telling him over and over again.'

'It was one of the possibilities they mentioned at the time,' Flora admitted. 'But only a possibility. What do you think happened, Sylvia?'

'It's obvious, isn't it?' The girl tossed her hair, anchoring it behind her ears. 'Polly must have slipped. It was real icy that morning. I nearly slipped myself.'

'It would be a comfort to think it,' Ted murmured. 'Perhaps the police have got it wrong. If only Sylvie had gone with her cousin that morning...'

'I would have, Dad, you know that. I often went walking with her, but I had a hair appointment that I didn't want to miss. They're like hens' teeth at that salon,' she explained.

'Which salon is that?' Flora asked and, feeling Jack's eyes bore into her, added quickly, 'I'm looking for a new hairdresser. It's always good to have a recommendation.'

'Annabel's, d'you know it, down North Street? Carol's particularly good.'

'I'll make sure I phone and see if she can fit me in.'

The conversation was bordering on the surreal and an uncomfortable silence crept up on them. She was glad when Jack spoke at last with a question of his own. 'Did Polly go walking in Brighton very much?'

It was what Flora had been wondering, those very high heels in mind.

'She loved walking in the town,' Sylvia enthused. 'It's a lot more interesting than walking around here. And she loved the seafront – the promenade and the pier. Living in Brighton suited her.'

It was news to Flora that Polly had moved out of Abbeymead. Her attention sharpened.

'She loved the town,' Ted Russell confirmed. 'And I was happy for her to be there. She'd have been happy to stay, too, if that man had left her alone.'

'What man? Not Mr Barnes, surely?'

'Harry? No, he's a good bloke. I introduced them. Harry likes the girls, that's for sure, but I turn a bit of a blind eye. He and Evelyn have their differences. Well, to be honest, it's never been exactly a marriage made in heaven and what he does when he's not at home is between the two of them. But Polly was my niece and I wasn't having any funny stuff. I made sure it was all above board. I made sure of that,' Ted repeated.

'He wanted to help Pol, he said, no strings attached. I was a bit dubious at first, but then the girl was nagging me that it was what she wanted and Harry seemed sincere, so I agreed. I couldn't help her myself, that was the problem. I gave her what money I could but it wasn't enough. Nowhere near. That modellin' business is expensive and Harry had the cash. Set her up in a flat in Brighton – easier to get up to London from there, he said. Mind you, I insisted Sylvie went with her. I didn't want Pol livin' on her own. It wouldn't have been right.'

'So who wouldn't leave her alone?' Flora persisted.

'That Frank bloke, the one who came to the funeral. Supposed to have been a friend of Bernie Mitchell's, which tells you somethin'.'

'What did Frank Foster do?'

'Followed her around, that's what. Wouldn't leave her alone. The girl met him up the West End at some club or other and after that, she couldn't get rid of him.'

'Couldn't Mr Barnes have helped?'

'He tried warnin' him off, but the bloke was persistent. And a bit threatenin'. Harry didn't want to get involved in any fight with him, but it really put the wind up Polly. She was movin' back here, back to Abbeymead, she was so scared.'

'It wasn't only Frank Foster that scared her, Dad,' Sylvia put in. 'There was Evelyn, too.'

'Oh, yes. But we could have smoothed that over. I could have smoothed it over. Evelyn got a bit shirty about Polly,' he explained.

'More than shirty. She was furious. Really gave Polly a going-over.' Recalling the quarrel, Sylvia seemed to come alive. 'It shocked Pol. She'd thought Evelyn didn't care what her husband got up to. After that, she didn't want to stay.'

'Her bags are still in that flat,' Ted said gloomily.

'Mine, too,' his daughter said. 'We were getting a taxi that lunchtime, after I got back from the salon, but then Pol never arrived and I had to let the chap go. I came back here in case she'd been too scared to wait for me and gone ahead. Maybe caught the bus to Abbeymead, like I did – but Dad hadn't seen her either. Then we heard.'

There was a long silence, before Sylvia asked artlessly, 'D'you have a car, Mr Carrington?'

Jack gave a half smile. He was getting used to the village grapevine, Flora thought.

'I do. Would you like us to collect your suitcases? We could go Saturday afternoon, Flora?'

When she nodded, Ted staggered to his feet again. 'That would be champion. Sylvie, go and get the key to the flat and I'll write the address down. Rose Court, it's called, on the seafront.'

Once the key was safely stowed in Flora's handbag, along with the slip of paper, she saw Jack give an imperceptible nod. It was time to go.

Sylvia walked them to the front door. 'I don't want Dad to think that Polly did anything stupid,' she said, as they turned to say goodbye. 'The police suggested it, I know, but it's best that no one else does. It's why I keep telling him it was an accident.'

'But you don't think it was?' Flora asked sharply.

'Pol was very upset.' Sylvia fidgeted with the door handle. 'That man was frightening her.'

'But she was coming back to Abbeymead, to the family home.'

'So? He turned up at the funeral, didn't he, and he could just as easily turn up in the village again. Polly thought she'd be safer here, but I wasn't sure. She didn't want to worry Mr Barnes by keeping on about it and, though Dad would do what he could, he was no match for that Foster.'

They walked slowly back to the centre of Abbeymead, both of them deep in thought. Eventually, Jack said, 'I don't want you putting yourself in danger again, Flora. I hope you won't get any ideas.'

'You must have had them or you wouldn't be warning me,' she retorted. 'My goodness, if Polly's death isn't a tragic accident or a dreadful suicide, there are enough people to charge with murder to make Alan Ridley a happy man. Frank Foster, the creepy follower, Evelyn Barnes, the wronged wife, and did you see Raymond's face? There was something going on there, too.'

Jack stopped and looked searchingly at her, his grey eyes darkening. 'Polly seems to have been walking a tightrope, I agree. But it doesn't mean you have to walk it, too. Let's leave the investigation to Ridley.'

'And let him pronounce Polly a reckless young woman or a suicide? Which would you prefer? Either is unfair. Even more unfair if someone pushed her and their guilt is never discovered.'

'There's no evidence whatsoever to suggest any such thing. You heard what Ridley said – the few people who were on the pier at the time saw nothing. There was no one around to push Polly.'

'Really? Then how do you account for this?' Flora delved into her pocket and, with the air of a conjuror who at last has his chance to show his best trick, brought out the red wool bobble.

'What the hell is that?'

'It's a bobble.'

'I can see it's a bobble, but what, why?'

'It must have fallen off an article of clothing, a woollen hat maybe or a pair of novelty gloves, but worn by someone who was on the pier. And it wasn't Polly – she'd never have worn anything so lacking in style. Someone nobody saw, but who dropped this right by the gap in the pier railings. And don't say it could have been dropped at any time. It couldn't. The bad weather we've had recently would have degraded it badly, but as you can see, it's undamaged. The bobble fell off the morning that Polly died.'

She had stunned Jack into silence and, pursuing her advantage, adopted her most coaxing voice. 'We've time to spare at the moment. We could poke around a little, ask a few questions, maybe come up with a solution.' She tried not to sound too eager, though from the moment she'd seen Polly's poor, defenceless body, she'd been determined to find the truth. 'And then we'd hand over to the inspector,' she finished swiftly. 'What do you say?'

SIX

Jack didn't answer. He was being pulled two ways at once. The memory of those heart-thudding moments when Flora had been in danger during their last investigation still had the power to make him feel ill. He never wanted to venture into such dark territory again. Yet, at the same time, the lure of another intrigue was considerable. Especially now he wasn't writing. The book he'd just finished wasn't the best thing he'd ever done, not remotely. It was a workmanlike job, a way of fulfilling a contract, of keeping his agent happy, but there was a lingering disappointment with himself that he hadn't done better. Pursuing a puzzle outside the covers of a book might restore the inspiration he seemed to have recently lost.

He wasn't sure why he'd struggled with this last novel, other than having Flora constantly disrupt his attention. But if he were honest, he'd been struggling before she ever came into his life.

Six years ago, Jack's heart had been well and truly broken but, in fleeing back to England, he'd hoped he might leave the past behind. He'd settled in Sussex, buried himself deep in the countryside and erected a fence around a period of his life he'd no wish to remember. That had been the theory. The practice had turned out rather differently. He'd found forgetting impossible, the memories an itch he'd continually had to scratch, desperately wanting but never quite able to lose them. And, every so often, that itch, that desperation, grew harder, wilder, and writing became almost impossible.

Flora's crazy pursuit of a real-life murderer had in some ways been a welcome distraction. Flora herself had been a welcome distraction, though he'd been careful always to keep her at friend's length. It was fortunate she appeared to want nothing more – Jack sensed that disillusion with an old love had made her happy to settle for friendship, though one that at times could be strained. Before he'd left her today, he'd warned her to allow the police to do their job, but knew her well enough to doubt she'd listen. He smiled to himself. She would have decided already how Polly had died and who was to blame. Her next move would be to convince him. Would a new investigation help him to shake off the memories that plagued him? Or lead them both into danger once more?

He was still making up his mind when, early the next morning, a bang on the front door reverberated through the house. The only one who knocked in that fashion was Flora and he knew why she'd come. Still bleary-eyed from sleep, he stumbled down the stairs.

'I'm going to see Kate,' she announced, following him into the kitchen. 'I want to ask her about Frank Foster.'

He scratched an unshaven chin and glowered at her. 'Good morning, Jack. How are you?'

Flora was unabashed. 'Good morning, Jack. How are you? So, what do you think?' She studied him for a moment. 'Would you like to know the buttons on your shirt need doing up?'

'No, I wouldn't,' he said acidly. 'I had the vain hope I might get shaved and dressed before I had to entertain visitors.' Annoyingly, Flora looked wide awake. She was wearing her bright red coat again, and this time with black leather boots that shone.

'I'm not a visitor. I'm your partner in crime.'

He'd lost the chance to protest before she went on, 'Foster is our number one suspect and an intimidating man. He looks as though he could be a bouncer at his own nightclub, and he's clearly been stalking Polly. She was so scared of him that she was prepared to give up a luxury flat in Brighton to return to a village she disliked.'

Jack lit the gas and filled the kettle. 'Let me get this straight,' he said. 'You don't believe Polly fell by accident and you don't believe she jumped?'

'Of course I don't. It's obvious she was pushed.'

'Not so obvious to me, but if she was pushed, Frank Foster is your number one suspect?'

'Well, isn't he?'

'And you're here this morning because you've decided I should be part of this new investigation?'

'Well, shouldn't you? All these questions are making me hungry, Jack. Do you have any toast? And some coffee would be nice.'

He sighed and delved into the bread bin.

'I was wondering if you'd offer me breakfast.' She took a seat at the kitchen table. 'It's very early and I haven't eaten.'

'I'm well aware how early it is,' he said heavily. 'But why?'

'I need to speak to Kate before she has too many customers. And I can't be late opening the All's Well either.'

Several slices of toast and marmalade later, Flora wiped the crumbs from her hands and took a long drink of coffee.

'That was good, thank you. Now, are you coming?'

'I'm going nowhere until I've shaved, and why question Kate Mitchell about a man she barely knows – how useful is that?'

'Kate might know more than she realises. Even if she doesn't, she can tell us something about the club Foster owns. Also whether he actually caught the train back to London after the wake. I've a feeling he may have stayed on secretly, in order to harass Polly.'

It seemed to Jack the decision had been made for him, and the trip to Katie's Nook sounded reasonable enough. Or was it just that he wanted it to be reasonable? Stacking the empty dishes in the sink, he sped to the bathroom and whisked a razor around his chin. Then fetching the tweed ulster from its peg in the hall – the winter snow might have disappeared but it was still very cold – he joined Flora at the front door.

'You've forgotten your hat,' she said.

He grimaced. 'What would I do without you?'

'I really don't know.' There was a laugh in her voice. 'But think how lucky it was that Charlie caught mumps last year and you were forced from your cave. Otherwise, you would never have met me. How is he, by the way?'

Jack locked the front door and followed her down the path to the lane that ran to the village. 'He seems OK, more or less. He came round yesterday to do an hour's gardening – we're clearing the area behind the greenhouse, or trying to – it's not easy with the ground so hard. He wanted to talk about Polly, so I let him. The more he talks, the less he'll brood, I reckon. Finding Polly like that – it was a difficult thing for a child to see.'

Flora nodded. 'It was a difficult thing for any of us to see.'

* * *

Kate was serving breakfast when they got to the Nook. A couple seated by one of the bow windows had ordered a full English and she'd just delivered plates of sausage, bacon, egg, mushroom and tomato to their table. Her face brightened as they walked in and Flora was pleased to see that some colour had returned to her cheeks.

Before they could say more than a brief hello, the clang of the doorbell interrupted them. Elsie Flowers puffed her way into the café, trundling a basket on wheels.

'I just popped in for a couple of scones, Kate,' she said, breathing hard. 'Don't suppose they're ready yet?'

'They are. I baked them first thing this morning.'

'That's a relief. I've a friend coming to tea and Ivy does love your scones. I don't mind waiting, though,' she added, looking across at Flora.

'Please, go ahead,' Flora said. 'We're not in any hurry.' Elsie was the last person she wanted to overhear their conversation. Next to Dilys, the old lady was Abbeymead's most fertile gossip.

'Has the new Agatha Christie come in yet?' she asked Flora, as Kate bagged up the scones.

'Not out until autumn, I'm afraid. *Dead Man's Folly*, that's the title. I'm sure it will be worth waiting for.' Elsie was quite possibly the most bloodthirsty of all Flora's customers. 'I'll order a copy for you as soon as I can.'

'That's a promise?' The old lady delved into her purse and brought out a sixpence. 'Will that be enough?' she asked Kate.

'That will be fine.'

When the pensioner had closed the door behind her, Flora scolded, 'You're too kind, Kate. How will you ever make a profit?'

'If I can't do a good turn...'

Flora shook her head at her friend. 'Still, I suppose we're after a favour, too. We were wondering if you could talk to us about Polly.'

Kate's face clouded. 'That poor girl. But come and sit down.'

An uncovered table, bare of the Nook's customary blue gingham tablecloth, stood at the rear of the café and made for a quiet spot to talk. Flora couldn't ever remember seeing it occupied by customers.

When they'd settled themselves, Kate said quietly, 'That was a terrible thing to happen, and just when Polly's future was looking so bright.'

Flora was starting to say that she wasn't sure how bright that future had looked when Jack intervened. 'At the wake, Frank Foster seemed to like her a lot. Does he know about Polly's "accident"?'

Flora heard the emphasis on 'accident' and knew he was warning her to be cautious.

The lines on Kate's forehead deepened. 'Someone must have told him because he telephoned last night to ask me when the funeral was. He'd be down, he said, but would book in at the Cross Keys. I must say I was glad to hear it. I didn't fancy him staying at the cottage again, even though he was Bernie's friend.'

'What do you know about him?' Flora asked gently.

Kate spread her hands. 'Not much. Bernie talked about him from time to time. They were in the army together, he said, called up at the same time. Bernie was a bit in awe, I think. Frank had got this posh club in the West End whereas Bernie was still delivering cakes for the Nook.'

'Did your husband ever go to the posh club?'

'He went once. He had to go to London for some reason – I can't remember why now – and Frank invited him to the Blue Peacock for the evening. Bernie thought it was wonderful. Couldn't stop talking about it for days.'

'The club must be very profitable if Frank has enough money to think about buying the Priory as well,' Flora pursued.

'Yes.' Her friend sounded doubtful. 'I'm not sure where the money is coming from. Maybe he plans to sell the Blue Peacock before buying the hotel, although he didn't say so.'

'He could borrow,' Flora suggested, wondering just how financially secure the man really was.

'To do that, he'd have to have a very good relationship with his bank,' Jack put in.

Kate looked bemused. 'I don't know a thing about his business. I'd never met him until... until...'

'No,' Flora said hastily. 'Of course you don't. It's only that if he was tremendously wealthy, it might be why Polly was keen on him.' She hoped that might provoke a response and it did.

'She wasn't keen!' Kate looked shocked. 'Not at all. She called in here a few weeks ago. She'd moved out of her uncle's house, though she didn't say where she was living, but she'd come back to the village to see a friend. She popped in here for a cup of tea and I asked her about the club.'

Flora looked puzzled.

'I knew she'd met Frank there,' Kate explained. 'But Polly wasn't happy about it. She'd only been to the Blue Peacock once, she said, and Frank was a lovely host, really made a fuss of her which she obviously enjoyed, but then he wouldn't leave her alone.

Polly was insistent he kept following her. Apparently, he'd been down to Sussex several times, though I never saw him.'

'He might have stayed in Brighton those times. It's where Polly moved to.'

'Really? Brighton would have been good for her. But when I saw her, she was upset and I felt so bad.' Kate's fingers did a nervous tap on the table top. 'It was me who told her about the club. I never would have, if I'd known, but she asked me for a name. This was back in November. Said she was going up to London for a few days, she was after a photographer for her modelling pictures, but that she'd like to go to a club while she was there. Do some dancing, meet some young people. I knew about Mr Barnes helping her with the modelling, but I wasn't sure what their... their arrangement was. It all seemed a bit odd and I didn't like to ask, but I could understand she wanted younger company. Well, the only club I knew was the one Bernie told me about, so I passed on the name. Now, I wish I hadn't.'

'It's not your fault. You couldn't have guessed that Foster would behave in that way.'

'I couldn't,' she agreed. 'At the time, I hadn't even met him, but when he came down for Bernie's... for the funeral... and stayed at the cottage, it made me even more uneasy.'

'You didn't like him?' Jack look at her intently.

She shook her head. 'Not at all. And like I said, I don't want him staying again.'

'I suppose he did go back to London, after the wake?'

'As far as I know, although...'

'Although what?' Flora's ears pricked up and she saw Jack shift forward in his chair.

'Dilys said something strange to me in the post office yesterday. She asked me how long my guest was staying and I said she must mean Mr Foster and that he'd left straight after the wake. Then she asked me if I was sure and I said I was. She was going to say something else, but the postman came in with a sack of mail and she had to unlock the barrier to let him through, and by the time she'd done that, I was out of the shop.'

The Nook's two customers had cleared their plates, emptied the teapot, and were putting on hats and coats. The man made his way over to the till.

'I'll have to—' Kate began.

'We must be off anyway,' Flora said. 'Come round for supper tomorrow if you're free.'

'I'm always free,' her friend said a little sadly.

SEVEN

'Poor Kate,' Flora said, as they walked along to the All's Well. 'Her life must feel so empty now. Her father dying in that awful way and then Bernie Mitchell drowning – though he brought that on himself.'

It was clear to Flora that Bernie, coward that he was, had tried to escape his misdeeds by faking his death. He'd planned to swim to a neighbouring beach, she was sure, and emerge from the sea, an unknown man, free to adopt a new identity. But the sea had had other ideas and Mitchell had misjudged the strength of the Channel currents. Flora couldn't feel sorry for him, but she did feel sadness for Kate.

'Kate really didn't like Frank Foster, did she?' Jack asked, as they approached the bookshop.

'No one seems to have liked him, and it's the same story as we heard from Sylvia and her father. Polly was scared of Foster.'

Turning the large brass knob, she pushed the front door open. 'I'll need to get this painted again.' She pointed to the stains left on the door by the recent snow. 'And probably the window frames as well. It will cost a fortune, with all the fiddly lattice to do.'

'You've the money to pay for it,' Jack reminded her.

He meant the unexpected prize that last autumn had landed in Flora's lap as a result of their first adventure together. At the back of her mind, she still toyed with ideas of using the money to travel – to Europe and beyond. Maybe she still would, after the trip to Cornwall that Jack had suggested she make with him. Now, though, her most pressing concern was to recoup at least some of the sales she'd lost at the bookshop last year. The unexpected discovery one morning of a dead body sprawled on its floor had led to frenzied gossip in Abbeymead and a pointed reluctance on the part of villagers to walk through the door of the All's Well.

'It was useful talking to Kate,' she said, opening the till and tipping in the float. 'It's made me more certain than ever that Polly was pushed and that Foster is our chief suspect.'

Jack picked up one of the books she had put on display the previous day and began leafing through it. 'So what's the next move? I imagine there'll be a next move.'

'I might be in need of some postage stamps,' she said, her hazel eyes dancing.

'A visit to Dilys, then?'

Flora came to stand beside him. 'If that man has been hanging around the village, Dilys will be the one to know.'

He pulled a face. 'You should be safe at the post office.' She could hear from his voice that he wasn't entirely joking. 'I'd better go home, get stuck into those two-foot weeds. I foolishly bet young Charlie that I'd clear one area before he got back from school today.'

'He'll be pleased to win the bet, think of it that way. The boy has a head for money.'

After Jack left, Flora pulled a cloth from her desk drawer and a feather duster from the cupboard that passed for a kitchen, and set to work on the shelves. A wall of shelves a day, that was her task, *properly done, mind*, she could hear Aunt Violet saying. No flicking a cloth in the air, but every book taken down and dusted.

She had finished the second shelf when the shop bell clanged. Flora scrambled to her feet, surprised. It was early for an Abbeymead resident to be buying books. Ten o'clock had normally struck before anyone walked through the All's Well door, though

Violet had always insisted they were open and ready well before nine.

There was a second surprise waiting. It was Raymond Parsons, standing awkwardly just inside the door. It was the first time Flora had ever seen him in the bookshop and she had an uneasy feeling that it didn't bode well.

'Miss Steele? I dunno if you remember me,' he began nervously.

'Yes, of course, I do. Raymond, isn't it? You worked at the Priory.'

'That's right,' he confirmed. There was a long silence before he cleared his throat and said in a strangled voice, 'I was wondering, Miss Steele, if you knew anything about the Priory? About it reopening?'

Flora was taken aback. 'No, nothing.' She paused. 'I'm sorry, but why do you think I would?'

'You're a friend of Mrs Mitchell.' Raymond had begun to lose some of his nervousness. 'And the bloke she's had staying with her... well, I heard he could be buying the hotel.'

Goodness, she thought, the village grapevine had excelled itself.

'I heard that, too,' she said, and saw his face relax. 'It seems, though, that at the moment it's only a rumour. Nothing firm has been agreed.'

When his face tightened again, she asked, 'Do you miss your old job?'

'I miss the money,' he said honestly.

'Are you saving to get married?' She said it half-teasingly. 'Or is that a secret? I won't tell a soul, honestly!'

'It's nothing like that.'

'I'm sorry, that was rude of me. I thought... Sylvia... I thought, maybe...' She was digging herself into an ever bigger hole.

'It's nothing like that,' he repeated. 'I just need a bit more money. I help out at the Nook – Mrs Jenner does the kitchen and I serve the customers. And I've got a part-time job at the golf club, behind the bar, but it's only for a few hours a week.'

'The local golf club? The Lexington?'

'That's the one.'

'Couldn't you ask them for extra hours?' It seemed the most obvious solution if the young man needed more money.

Raymond twirled the cap he'd been wearing, circling it round and round on his finger until Flora felt quite dizzy. She would rather he put it back on his head. Rather, if she was being truthful, he left the shop and let her get on with her daily chores, since he'd evidently not come to buy.

'I could ask,' he admitted, 'but the thing is... the thing is, I'm not that keen on working there.'

'Still, if it pays,' she said, surreptitiously guiding him towards the door.

He made no response, hanging his head and looking at the floor. Flora thought it a strange reaction. If you were so much in need of money that you were counting on a vague rumour to be true, surely working in a place you didn't like was preferable to not working at all.

'You could always ask Mrs Mitchell if she's heard anything more,' Flora suggested, shuffling Raymond a little nearer the door. If Kate knew the boy was desperate to hear news of the Priory, her kind heart would ensure she'd pass on anything she heard.

'I don't want to be a bother,' he said uncomfortably. 'Not after Mr Mitchell. It's a difficult time for her, isn't it?'

'It is and I'm glad you came to me instead. If I hear anything, I'll make sure to tell you.'

'That's kind, Miss Steele.' At last, she noticed, he had his hand on the brass door knob. 'I wouldn't have bothered you, only...'

He left the rest of the sentence unfinished, and bolted out of the door.

Flora resumed her dusting, uncertain what to make of Raymond's visit. Everything about it seemed odd. Firstly, coming to the bookshop, a place he'd never thought to visit before. Then there was his dependence on what was the thinnest rumour. And, finally, his refusal to ask for more hours in a place where he already had a job.

Putting the questions to one side, she finished her cleaning routine well before her first customer arrived. Trade was slow this morning. A farmer's wife she knew by sight left with a single book, and the couple Flora had seen having breakfast at the Nook browsed the shop for a good half hour without buying.

By the time the clock showed twelve thirty, she was ready to lock up and disappear for lunch. It meant closing half an hour earlier than usual, but it also meant she would find the post office open and, hopefully, Dilys behind the counter.

The post office was at the top of the main street, almost at the point that the village straggled to an end, and rather than take the time to walk – she was desperate to catch the postmistress before she closed for lunch and the woman was well known for bringing the shutters down early if she was feeling peckish – Flora wheeled her bike, affectionately named Betty, from out of its shelter in the yard.

Betty had enjoyed a prolonged rest these last few months. She would not have liked the snow and Flora hadn't subjected her to the indignity. Instead, customers had been advised that their books had arrived and, if they wanted them, Flora was sorry but they would have to walk to the shop. A few of her favourite customers, elderly ladies who lived close but from frailty were scared of venturing out, were accorded a hand delivery. But now it was February and time for Betty to get back to work.

Pedalling at top speed, Flora skidded the bike to a halt as Alice Jenner came out of the post office.

'Hello, my love,' Alice greeted her. 'I've been meaning to call by, but I've been laid up these last few days. That dratted lumbago again.'

Flora immediately felt guilty that she hadn't thought to call on Alice herself – Polly's death had overshadowed her usual concerns. She'd not even spoken to her friend of their day in Brighton.

Alice did it for her, shaking her head dolefully. 'That was some dreadful thing,' she said. 'And you in the middle of it. How are you?' Without waiting for an answer, she went on, 'You do seem unlucky. First that man in the bookshop, now poor Polly.'

'I'm fine. No need to worry over me,' she said briskly, aware that Dilys would be shutting shop at any moment. 'Are you on your way to the Nook?'

'I am that. First time back for a few days. It'll allow Katie to get some lunch for herself. Poor lass needs feedin' up. I'll do a bit of bakin' later as well, stuff for her to sell tomorrow.' She moved closer to Flora. 'I did hear that the Priory might be sold. Katie told me.'

'I think it's very much up in the air. But would you work there again, if it were?'

'I might if they paid me enough.' Her friend thought about it for a moment, while Flora tried not to fidget. 'But I mustn't stop you.'

'I need some stamps,' Flora said, relieved. 'Several urgent letters to post, but come to supper tomorrow. Kate is coming.'

'Lovely. Want me to cook somethin'?'

Flora laughed. 'As long as you can put up with my cottage pie, you can have the evening off.'

Dilys had the shutter halfway down the iron grille when Flora almost ran into the post office, the familiar smell of dusty vanilla overlaid by wet wool and mothballs hitting her hard.

'You're cutting it fine,' the postmistress observed, her hand temporarily arrested.

Flora blinked – Dilys was a frenetic knitter and this morning's Fair Isle cardigan was startlingly bright. But then she tore into an apology.

'I'm so sorry, Dilys, I got held up. It's really important I catch the second post, but I need stamps.'

Reluctantly, the postmistress rolled up the shutter. While she tore off the requisite number from her sheet of stamps, Flora said casually, 'I saw Kate this morning. She's looking a lot better, but it's sad there'll be another funeral so soon. She's upset, like all of us, and not at all happy that her visitor wants to come back to Abbeymead – for Polly this time.'

Dilys fixed her gaze at the large black and white photograph of the new Queen that hung on the opposite wall. 'Stupid girl, that Polly. I'm sorry for her and all, but stupid.' She shook her head, tight little curls bouncing with energy. Leaning so far over the counter that her ample chest came to a peaceful rest on the gleaming wood shelf, she asked conspiratorially, 'What did you think of him?'

'Kate's visitor? I don't really have an opinion,' Flora lied. 'I didn't spot him in the church and barely spoke to him at the wake.'

'It was a shame I couldn't go. It was Dad, you see. Took a turn and I had to stay with him. But I saw that man – what was his name?'

'Foster. Frank Foster.'

'Looked a smarmy so-and-so. Kate Mitchell needs to look out. He's the kind who gets his foot in the door and never leaves.'

This was Flora's opportunity. 'Kate will be fine. The chap went back to London after the funeral.'

Dilys locked the counter and walked round into the shop. The patterned linoleum was brown and worn and still bore the ravages of the recent snow.

'Really? What if I told you that I saw him bold as brass the next day?'

'The day after the funeral? He was supposed to catch the train back to London. That's what he said.'

The postmistress pursed her lips. 'Lurking he was. Lurking.'

'Why on earth would he do that?'

'Why does anyone lurk?' Dilys responded sharply. 'They're up to no good, mind my words.'

EIGHT

The telephone was ringing when Flora arrived back in the bookshop.

'Miss Steele? Good afternoon. My name's Jim Hargreaves,' a voice announced. 'I'm a journalist with the *Worthing Echo.*'

'Good afternoon,' she said uncertainly. If he was after a particular title – for research most probably – why not try a Worthing bookshop? There were plenty of them.

'I don't know if you read the *Echo*, Miss Steele, but these past few weeks, we've been running a feature on local businesses. Unusual ones – in what they offer or where they're situated. I'd like to do a write-up of the End's Well, if you're interested.'

'The All's Well,' she corrected, wondering how accurate this write-up would be. 'You think my bookshop is unusual?'

'I've seen a photograph,' Jim Hargreaves went on cheerfully. 'It looks a fascinating building, and I know there's quite a story attached to events last autumn. I wonder if we could talk.'

'Not if it's about what happened last year,' she said firmly. 'The All's Well has turned a corner and that's where it's staying.'

'Oh.' He sounded disappointed. 'My photographer was looking forward to taking some great pictures.'

'He can take the pictures, but I don't want to dredge up old news.'

There was a pause while Flora thought rapidly. She was sharply aware of the need for publicity, and yet...

'I do have a new window display that might interest you.'

'Yes?' He didn't sound too interested.

'It traces the development of the Priory, first as a monastery and then as the family home of the Templetons.' There was silence at the other end of the phone. 'It also touches on the legend of the buried treasure,' she tempted.

'Right.' There was a little more enthusiasm now. 'It sounds the kind of thing our readers would enjoy.'

'I'm sure they would, but why don't you come and see for yourself?'

'I'm free the rest of today, if that's OK. What time would be most convenient?'

'Later this afternoon, perhaps. I'll be leaving around five. Could you get here an hour or so before?'

'I certainly could. Thank you.' The journalist was sounding a good deal keener now. 'I'll see you very soon, Miss Steele.'

The next few hours passed calmly enough, except for qualms on Flora's part that it might not have been such a brilliant idea after all to agree to the interview. She was determined that she wouldn't speak about last autumn, not allow Mr Hargreaves to exhume an event she thought of as closed. Wanted closed. But he was bound to try, to slip in a sly question when she wasn't expecting it and catch her off guard. She needed the publicity, though, she told herself severely. The meeting with Jim Hargreaves would help put the bookshop back on its feet, and if it involved a few uncomfortable moments, so be it.

She glanced at the clock. He would be here very soon, along with his photographer. Shoulders back, chin lifted, Flora braced herself for what lay ahead... then caught a glimpse of her face in the mirror. Making a dive for her handbag, she rummaged for the powder compact she was always losing. If she was to be photographed this afternoon, a shiny face was the last thing she wanted. A quick press of Crème Puff and a swipe of pink lipstick and she was ready to face the camera.

But by four o'clock there was still no sign of the journalist or his photographer. Should she telephone the *Worthing Echo* to check if he was still coming? It might, though, make her look too eager and she decided against. Half an hour later, as she was unpacking orders that had arrived in the second post, the shop door opened and a man she didn't recognise walked in, followed closely by his companion. All Flora could see of the latter was a huge bag, two large tripods and a cluster of cables.

'Jim Hargreaves,' the man said, walking up to her desk and offering his hand.

'How do you do, Mr Hargreaves?'

He stood back and looked around. 'This is an amazing building.' There was a crash from the doorway. 'Don't mind, Sam. He's just setting up. He'll take some photographs of the exterior first.'

'It will be too dark, surely.'

'He's got all the equipment, special lights and stuff. The prints can sometimes come out looking better when they're artificially lit. I can see them working really well alongside the interview.'

Flora suspected that the Priory legend would be featuring rather heavily in Mr Hargreaves' article, along no doubt with whatever ghosts he could uncover.

'May I wander?'

When she nodded, he began a stroll around the shop floor, zigzagging between shelving, and occasionally finding himself at a dead end. Every so often he stopped to direct Sam, who had finally emerged from the tangle in the doorway, where to point his camera.

'Quite a place you've got here,' he said ruefully, having found himself lost for the third time. 'Quirky.'

The window display was the last to be photographed, and it was only then that Jim took out his pad and pencil and began the interview.

'Sorry about the delay, but I always like to get a feel for the business before I speak to the owner.' He settled himself on a stool. 'And the All's Well strikes me as unique. So tell me, has this building always been a bookshop, do you know?'

'I believe it was a private home before my aunt bought it.'

'When was that?'

'Just before the war. It must have been...' she did a quick calculation, '...1938?'

'And your aunt bought it with the view of turning it into a bookshop?'

'I can't honestly say. She may have thought to live here but then decided it would make a great shop.'

Flora had been too young for her aunt to share with her what she intended, if indeed Violet had known herself. The impression Flora had always carried with her was of an aunt desperate to escape London who, when the opportunity came, grabbed it with both hands and worked out the details later.

'You don't live on the premises?'

'No, I have a cottage in the village.'

He scribbled several lines on his pad. 'And your aunt?'

'She died last year. Her name was Violet Steele.'

'I'm sorry to hear that.' He sounded genuine. 'She obviously established a very successful business. She left you the bookshop, perhaps?' he asked delicately.

And so it went on, Flora relaying the history of the shop and the way in which Violet Steele had worked incredibly hard to make it a success, so that now most of Abbeymead couldn't imagine the village without it.

Jim Hargreaves seemed sincerely interested and his questions intelligent – despite her earlier fears, Flora began to enjoy the interview. It went on far longer than she'd expected, but any chance to talk of her aunt was welcome.

It was gone six o'clock before she left the shop. These days with darkness falling so early, she preferred to leave Betty in her shelter behind the bookshop and use her for daytime errands only. Walking back and forth to the cottage, knowing the lanes inside out, Flora needed no torch.

She'd turned off the main road into a twitten, and from there into the wider lane that led to home, and had been walking for about five minutes, when she heard them. The footsteps. She walked on, listening hard. Who would be walking the lane at this time of the evening, and without a torch to guide them?

The footsteps were growing louder, she was certain. Or, at least, in the darkness, more distinct. The sounds of a rural night – the hoot of an owl, the wind rattling bare branches, the rustle of small creatures in the grass – fell away, and all she was conscious of was the man's step. She was in no doubt that it was a man. He had a heavy tread, an uneven tread, as though he were limping. No, not limping, she thought, but walking uncertainly, hoping, it seemed, not to give himself away.

Swallowing down panic, she quickened her pace, and heard the footsteps grow faster. If he was an innocent walker, why was he trying to catch her up? Her shoulders tightened, her heartbeat drumming in her ears and her breathing uneven. She was near to breaking into a run – a dangerous choice in unrelieved darkness and on a lane that bordered a deep ditch. It was then she sensed, rather than heard, something ahead.

'Flora, is that you?' It was Jack and he'd appeared out of nowhere. At times, he could move like a cat.

'I'm here,' she said, unable to prevent a croak in her voice. The piercing shaft of a torch beam forced her eyes shut.

Immediately, the footsteps behind her slowed, and when she came to a halt, they did, too.

Jack was at her side now. 'Why are you so late?' he asked, lowering the torch but studying her face in the muted light. 'Is something the matter?'

She half turned and Jack flashed the torch up and over her head, the light catching another face in its beam, pale and fleshy.

'Mr Barnes?' Jack asked, sounding mystified.

'Hello there.' The voice was overly jolly. 'Nice to see you both. Just out for my evening stroll.'

Flora was unsure whether she should be glad or worried that her pursuer had been Harry Barnes. She felt foolish at the panic she'd experienced. But why was he walking in the village at this hour? He lived at least three miles distant. And why had he been following her? She gave herself an inner shake – that was only her interpretation and he might not have been. Perhaps he'd driven into Abbeymead to take his walk. How strange, though.

'I was about to turn round,' Harry Barnes said. 'Got to get home. Time for supper, you know. I'll bid you both a good evening.'

'Why are you so late?' Jack asked her again, when Harry had disappeared, back the way he had come.

'A journalist from the *Worthing Echo* came to interview me about the All's Well. He stayed rather a long time.'

'Too long. I called at the cottage and was worried when you weren't home. I was walking to the shop to find you.'

'We only met this morning – were you so keen to see me?' She fell in step with him, glad of the comfort of torchlight and of Jack walking beside her.

'For once, yes.' He touched her arm lightly. 'I've a job for you. Nothing too onerous, but I'll tell you when I've walked you home.'

NINE

'That was a funny business, Barnes miles from home and walking the lane in the dark.'

Jack had taken off his trusty ulster and was sitting at Flora's kitchen table while she surveyed her larder for something to eat. The journalist's visit had put all else out of her mind and she'd forgotten to buy the pork chop she'd meant to collect from Mr Preece.

'Very odd,' she agreed, then decided on confession. 'I thought for a while he was following me.'

Jack frowned. 'Why would he do that?'

Why indeed? Was Harry Barnes another man who lurked? she wondered, remembering Dilys's words. Remembering, too, Harry's face at the wake, his evident anger with Polly.

Aloud, she said, 'He could be suspicious.'

Jack's frown deepened. 'Suspicious of what?'

Giving up on the larder, Flora took a seat opposite. 'I've been thinking, and don't grumble, but Harry Barnes could have gone to Brighton that morning, the morning Polly died, arranged to meet her on the pier, then in an argument lost his temper and pushed her over.'

'That makes him a suspect, not suspicious. Why would you think he was following you?'

'He might believe *I'm* suspicious. Of him. That I've evidence against him.'

'There's no evidence against him or anyone else, that's the point.'

'There is one thing,' she said stoutly, and walked back into the hall, returning with an outstretched hand. The red woollen bobble sat in her palm.

'That's not evidence, Flora.'

'Who's to say whether it is or isn't, until we know who killed Polly?'

'Until we know how Polly died,' he amended. 'It's only you who's convinced it was foul play.'

Irritated by his caution, she said impatiently, 'What did you want with me anyway?'

'This.' He delved into the pocket of his overcoat draped across a chair, and brought out a sheaf of papers. 'They're the first chapters of the new book.'

'The Cornish book? But we haven't got there yet.'

'I realise that. I wanted to get ahead, then when I'm there, I'll have more time to enjoy the county, rather than being shut in a room with a typewriter.'

'Do you think that's a good idea? The point of your spending time in Cornwall was to get a sense of the place before you began writing, wasn't it?'

'I'd like to do it this way,' he said stubbornly. 'But if you don't want to read it, that's fine.' He began shuffling the sheets of paper together.

Flora put her hand on his, and he stopped shuffling. 'Why have you asked me?'

'You sell books,' he said simply, 'including mine. You'll have an idea of how good an opening it is.'

'You've never asked me to read before.'

'I didn't know you before.'

'True.' She looked at him pensively. 'Does this mean you trust me?'

'Could be.' There was a small pause. 'Although not always,' he said, a smile in his eyes.

* * *

The Friday evening supper with Kate and Alice passed off well, Kate bringing a lavish trifle and Flora taking particular care with the ingredients for her cottage pie, even tramping to the bottom of the frost-ridden garden to dig fresh carrots. They had done well this winter, along with the potatoes and onions, and Violet's vegetable patch was looking a great deal better than Flora's first attempts at following in her aunt's footsteps. She hoped Violet would be pleased. The loss of her beloved aunt was still raw and whatever Flora did in the garden, in the cottage, in the bookshop, the spirit of that steadfast lady was always close.

She had stacked their supper dishes and brought a tray of tea into the sitting room when Alice turned the conversation to the sale of the Priory. Rumour was apparently rife.

'I hope people won't be disappointed,' Flora said, pouring tea for her guests. 'Mr Foster seems to have disappeared from view – unless you've heard anything, Kate?'

Kate shook her head. 'If you should,' Flora continued, 'let me know and I'll pass it on to Raymond.'

'Raymond Parsons? He's not mentioned anything to me.'

'He didn't want to bother you,' she said diplomatically, 'not at the moment.'

She saw Kate lower her head. Her friend still found it painful to speak of her husband's death, but each day she was looking better. This evening she'd worn a frock she hadn't put on for months, a pale blue woollen tea dress, the nicest one in her wardrobe. It was far from new, bought six or seven years ago, she'd told Flora, using her last coupons as clothes rationing finally dribbled to an end. But she'd been skilful, trimming the cuffs with blue velvet – rescued from a torn cushion cover, Flora guessed – and buying a dark blue belt to emphasise her slim waist.

'What's the boy's interest?' Alice asked, filling the silence.

'He seems very keen to get his old job back at the hotel. He called in at the All's Well yesterday to ask me if I knew anything.'

Alice slowly stirred her tea. 'The sale could still happen, I reckon. That man, Foster, has been hangin' round the village – after he left you, Kate. He must have been here for somethin'.'

'Where did you see him?' Flora asked sharply.

'Leavin' the Cross Keys, when would it be? A couple of days after Bernie's "do"? He was gettin' into a taxi.'

'What time was that?' It seemed suddenly vital to know exactly when Frank Foster had left Sussex.

Alice looked at her in surprise. 'Is it important? It was early, I know that. Tuesday mornin' I buy my veg off old man Richards – these days Houseman's too expensive – outside the pub with his barrow sevenish every Tuesday. I buy from the Saturday market, too, but by mid-week I've run out.'

'And you saw Frank Foster early on Tuesday morning?' Flora insisted.

Alice nodded, though she was plainly bemused by Flora's interest. 'Is something wrong, my love?' She was sounding worried now.

'Nothing.' Flora put on her best smile, at the same time calculating whether a visit to the Cross Keys might be a good idea.

Foster had still been in Abbeymead four days after the funeral and a day after Polly had been found dead. He'd lied to Kate when he said he was catching a train to London that Friday evening. Why had he lied, when he had a simple explanation for staying on in the village? Buying the Priory was a good enough reason. He could have made a virtue out of moving to the Cross Keys, saying he'd no wish to disturb Kate any longer than need be. And why stay holed up at the inn without anyone knowing, then leave at such an early hour? To avoid being seen – it was pretty obvious.

Flora became conscious that her friends were staring at her and was quick to excuse her silence. 'I was thinking of Polly, how sad it is.'

Kate and Alice sighed together, long and deep.

'The young'll always take risks,' Alice remarked.

'How is walking on the Palace Pier a risk?'

'Well, she fell in, didn't she? It must have been risky that morning. Ice, I'll be bound. The number of falls people have had this winter!'

'What if it wasn't an accident?'

Flora didn't know what had made her say that, other than an anger building inside. People were too willing to dismiss Polly's death as something inevitable. The girl had been young, foolish, sailed too close to the wind, so obviously she was going to come to grief sooner or later – that seemed the general opinion.

'The police say it's an accident, don't they?' Kate asked mildly.

'Yes.' Flora's agreement was unwilling. 'But the post-mortem is still to be done.'

'Mebbe,' Alice said, 'but I reckon the verdict's sure to be an accident. Why don't you believe it?'

Alice was clearly upset. Flora could see she wanted to tidy the death away as unfortunate and nothing that should mar their own lives.

'Polly was young and fit,' she said as gently as she could, 'and when I walked to the end of the pier – where there's a gap in the railings – there was very little ice. Even if she'd died some hours before, and I don't know the time of death, I doubt it would have been much icier. So a puddle of water, a gap in the railings? I can't see her slipping. And I'm sure, too, that she didn't deliberately throw herself from the pier.'

'You're just keen to find another murderer,' Alice accused, only half joking. 'And I'm not sure you're right – about Polly not doing it deliberately. I wouldn't have mentioned it, but now we're talkin', I met Ted Russell in the grocer's a week or so back and he told me that Polly was gettin' really fed up. She wasn't gettin' anywhere with the modellin', hadn't got any of those photographs done. No portfolio, I think he called it. He said she was really down in the dumps.'

'You think she killed herself for the lack of photos?' Flora's eyebrows shot upwards.

'I'm not saying that, Flora.' Alice sounded as cross as she ever could. 'I'm simply sayin' that there are things we don't know about Polly and we shouldn't jump to conclusions.'

Flora felt suitably admonished. 'Polly was adamant that Harry Barnes had promised photographs,' she murmured, 'and I'm sure in time he'd have come up with the funds for a portfolio.'

In truth, she wasn't sure. Not any longer. She still felt shaken by Barnes' appearance on the lane and didn't know what to think of him. His footsteps had haunted her sleep last night, but she wasn't about to share the panic she'd felt, not even with friends.

'Mebbe it wasn't so certain that Polly would get those photographs,' Alice said. 'If Harry's wife got a whiff of what was goin' on, or what everyone reckoned was goin' on, mebbe he wouldn't or couldn't do what he'd promised.'

'Do you know Evelyn Barnes?' Flora asked. She'd never met the woman herself, but the thought struck her that her guests might well have.

'We cooked for Evelyn, didn't we, Kate?' Alice appealed. 'A couple of years ago. She was havin' this posh dinner at their home with a large number of guests. It was Evelyn's retirement party.'

'She was a very successful businesswoman,' Kate put in, 'and knew lots of people.'

'And made lots of money,' Alice added succinctly. 'The house – like a palace it is, with huge grounds. Pelham Lodge, that's the name. Not much of a lodge, if you ask me.'

'There's dogs,' Kate offered. 'Roaming around, patrolling the grounds. Hulking great things. They terrified us, didn't they, Alice?'

'If you've got money, you have to protect it, I suppose,' Alice said philosophically. 'And Evelyn has money, all right, and she's very much in charge. It's common knowledge that it's her cash Harry Barnes lives on.'

Flora turned the information over in her mind, trying to fit it to what she already knew about them.

'It's a strange set-up altogether,' she said. 'Ted Russell seems happy to have ignored Harry's misdemeanours. Jack and I went to see Ted to say how sorry we were about Polly. He talked about Harry, excusing the man's liking for the girls, as he called it, so he was well aware of his friend's behaviour. Yet he was quite happy for Harry to fund his niece and was adamant his friend had only good intentions towards her.'

'I dunno how he could think that! Just kiddin' himself, I reckon. If there's nothin' goin' on, what was Harry Barnes gettin' out of it?'

'Ted seemed to be suggesting it was enough for him to have a beautiful young girl on his arm.'

Alice snorted.

'I think Evelyn Barnes would turn a blind eye – up to a point,' Kate said unexpectedly. 'They don't seem much of a couple and it's clear she has her own life separate from his. She's on the village council and captain of the women's team at the golf club. Maybe she doesn't mind her husband's... dalliances?'

'A dalliance, mebbe, Kate, but would she ignore a luxury flat on Brighton seafront?' Alice countered. 'Leastways, that's where I've heard Polly was livin'. Evelyn Barnes is a fierce woman and I can't see her toleratin' that. Especially if she's payin'.'

Evelyn Barnes hadn't turned a blind eye. She'd known about the apartment Harry was renting and, according to Sylvia Russell, had called at Rose Court to berate Polly in a furious row. If Evelyn held the purse strings in the family and was as formidable as Alice painted, it could mean only one thing – there was another suspect to add to the mix.

TEN

Just how luxurious Polly's flat had been, Flora was to see for herself the following afternoon. On their visit to the Russells, Jack had suggested Saturday as the best time to collect the girls' suitcases. Flora could close the bookshop at lunchtime and he'd abandon garden duties until Michael, the local odd-job man, could help with repairs to the greenhouse.

'Has the garage done its job?' she asked, slipping into the car's passenger seat. 'Are we likely to arrive in Brighton?'

'The mechanic seemed pretty confident, but think of it as an afternoon of adventure.' Jack gave a sly smile, then, seeing her expression, he said reassuringly, 'The head man swears the car is as good as new.'

Flora was still dubious and more than pleased when they arrived without incident, parking in the same spot as previously. From the address Ted Russell had given them, Polly's flat appeared to be only a stone's throw away.

The weather wasn't kind today, the sky overcast and an east wind blowing. Waves thundered to shore, churning sand from the seabed and flinging shingle high up on the beach. The smell of brine was unpleasantly strong. It was a very different day from the one they'd chosen for Charlie's treat, a treat that had turned out to be anything but.

The boy was still badly upset. According to Jack, he had ransacked the shelves at Overlay House, looking for any books that mentioned death by drowning. It was concerning that a twelve-year-old boy should be taken up with such thoughts, but there was a vague hope in Flora that if they could clear up the mystery of Polly's last moments, offer some kind of explanation to Charlie, it might help close the chapter for him.

'Jack...'

He gave a barely audible grunt, as he brought the car to a halt.

'What?' she demanded.

'When you say Jack in that voice, I know you're about to suggest something bad.'

'Nothing bad,' she insisted. 'Really. But before we go to the flat, I'd like to go back to the pier. Actually, I'd like to go to the hair salon first, the one that Sylvia Russell mentioned. You could always go ahead and I'd meet you on the pier.'

'What precisely am I supposed to be doing there?'

'Go into the theatre, talk to the cast. Ask them what they remember about last Monday. Who they remember.'

'Ridley and his team will already have done that.'

'They might not have, or not in detail. And even if they have, they're not going to be terribly interested in the response. The inspector has already made up his mind, but we should dig deeper.'

'If we must. It's one way of spending the afternoon, I guess.' Clambering out of the car, he crammed the fedora onto his head. 'Where's this hairdresser of yours?'

'Somewhere in North Street. I'll walk with you for a block or two, then cut up the hill.'

They reached the corner of West Street in record time, the biting wind hastening them on. Saying a temporary goodbye, Flora walked rapidly to the top of the road, before taking a right-hand turn towards the Pavilion, her gaze roving from one side of the street to the other, on the lookout for Annabel's. The salon didn't take long to locate. The hairdresser was halfway down the hill, on the opposite side of the road.

As soon as the traffic eased, she crossed over and pushed open the shop door.

'No appointments this afternoon,' the girl at the reception desk sang out before Flora had opened her mouth. 'Sorry, we're fully booked until the week after next,' she said, looking through Flora at the street beyond.

'I'm not after an appointment today or any day,' Flora said shortly. This was a place she would never patronise. If she hadn't taken the receptionist in dislike, the price list on the desk would have decided her.

'So what can we do for you?' the receptionist asked in a bored voice, studying her long fingernails.

'I have a friend who comes here.' It was only partly an untruth. 'Sylvia Russell. She asked me to call and check the date of her next appointment. She forgot to write it down, and as I was going to be in town this afternoon...'

The girl shook a head of bleached curls and opened a thick ledger ruled into columns. Twisting her body, Flora could see that each was headed with a name, a hairdresser, she presumed. The girl ran her finger down each column. 'Can't see her here. Which stylist does she have?'

'I think it might be Carol.'

'It is.' One of the women in the middle of adjusting the helmet of a hairdryer had overheard the conversation. 'Carol's not in today.'

'Sorry,' the girl said, beginning to shut the appointments ledger.

'Perhaps if you looked at when Miss Russell was last in and then counted forward, that might help?'

The girl gave a small huff. 'Do you know when that was?'

'I do. It was Monday this week. Monday morning.'

Reluctantly, the girl flicked back the pages. 'Ah, yes, here she is. She had the appointment after Mrs Barnes.'

'Evelyn Barnes is a client, too?'

The girl nodded, but her face held suspicion. 'You know Mrs Barnes as well?'

'Abbeymead is a small village,' Flora said. 'Everyone knows everyone.'

There was another small huff. 'If Miss Russell was here Monday, two months on would make her next appointment—'

'She didn't come in.' A young girl, carrying a tray of lethal-looking curlers, arrived beside Flora.

'She was down to come in,' the receptionist insisted.

'I know, but she didn't. Carol wasn't half mad when she didn't turn up. Didn't even let her know there was a problem.'

Flora had what she'd come for. 'In the circumstances, I think it's best if I leave Miss Russell to contact you,' she said grandly. Without waiting for a response, she whisked herself out of the shop.

She had hated the salon but had gathered two crucial pieces of information. Evelyn Barnes had been in Brighton the morning Polly died and, by the look of the appointment time, it had been early. And Sylvia Russell had lied. She had never visited the salon that morning, so where had she been?

Storing away these nuggets, Flora made her way to the pier, eager to discover what progress Jack had made, but when she arrived at the theatre, it was to find him standing outside, hands in his pockets, his fedora pulled low over his forehead.

'They're conducting a full-scale rehearsal inside,' he said in greeting. 'I thought I'd better wait. How did you get on?'

'Horrid hairdresser's but a useful visit.' A loud burst of chatter barrelled through the theatre's open doorway. 'I think they must be finishing – I'll tell you later.'

Jack craned his neck around the door. 'Looks like it. Who shall I tackle first, d'you think?'

'The theatre manager would be a good bet. While you talk to him, I'll try someone else.' Feeling the red wool bobble sitting in her pocket, she had a clear idea of who that would be.

Jack frowned. She had sounded vague and Flora knew he didn't like vague, but after checking again that the rehearsal had well and truly finished, he walked into the theatre and asked for the manager. In a few minutes, he was knocking on the door a stagehand had shown him. Flora caught the man on his way back.

'Is there a wardrobe mistress?'

'Sounds a bit posh.' The boy grinned. 'We've got a few racks of costumes and it's Tilly who looks after them.'

'Could I speak to Tilly?'

The boy gestured to her to follow him round to the back of the stage. Empty boxes, discarded props and costumes, spilt tea and the odd half-eaten sandwich cluttered what small space there was. Tilly, herself, appeared unfazed. She was a comfortably round woman, probably no more than thirty, Flora reckoned, but looking older.

'Thank you for taking the time to talk to me,' she began. 'I won't hold you up for long.'

'Don't worry, darlin'. Rehearsal's over and the performance doesn't start for a couple of hours. Plenty of time to sort this lot out.'

'Have you been here for the whole run?'

'If you can call it that.' She gave a deep chuckle that suggested a twenty-a-day habit.

'Business hasn't been good?' Flora ventured.

'Up and down,' the woman admitted. 'Mostly down. But then, what do you expect if you do a rubbish play like *Harlequinade*?'

'Someone must have thought it a good idea.'

'Him.' She jerked her thumb in the general direction of the closed office door. 'It's the manager who has the last say. We're only a small outfit, semi-professional, and he's the one who makes the decisions. Most times he gets it wrong.'

'That's sad when you put so much work into it – particularly into the costumes. We brought a young friend to see the show last Monday and I thought them wonderful. So colourful, so imaginative.'

'The costumes are OK,' Tilly admitted grudgingly. 'It's the play that's the problem.'

'I wonder...' This was the time for Flora to pull out her trophy.

'Do you recognise this? I picked it up on Monday and wondered if it might belong to the theatre?'

'It's part of Harlequin's get-up,' Tilly said immediately. 'But I don't think we're missing a bobble.'

'Would you mind looking? I'd like to think I've found a home for it.'

Tilly shrugged her shoulders. 'Come and look for yourself.'

She led the way over to the rear wall of the theatre where two hanging rails had dust sheets covering them. 'These are the spares,' Tilly said, pulling the covers free. The array of colour was dazzling.

She pointed to two Harlequin costumes at the end of the rail. 'There's four of these. All different sizes. The bloke who's taking the Harlequin part this evening has his costume on already – for the rehearsal – and so does his understudy.'

Flora took a hanger from the rail and held it up for inspection. The bodice was made of two different materials, half in black, fastened by white buttons, and the other half in a red check sporting black buttons. The same colour divide was present in each sleeve, and in each leg of the accompanying leggings.

'Where would the bobble go?' She was puzzled, despite her rising excitement.

'They're not on the costume itself. They're an accessory, if you know what I mean.'

Tilly pulled out a large cardboard box from under the hanging clothes. 'Here's all the extra stuff. Two of everything. Harlequin has one of these.' She picked up a red and black rattle and jangled its small bells at Flora. 'And a hat,' she went on. The hat had horn-shaped ears and was again red and black with a small bell at the end of each horn. 'And slippers. That's where your bobble goes.' The two pairs she indicated were entirely black and each of the four slippers had a large red wool bobble atop.

'As you can see, nothing missing, my darlin'. I checked at the rehearsal for any problem with the costumes being worn tonight, and they were both fine.'

Flora felt a crunching disappointment, but pasted on a smile. 'I can see everything is just as it should be, but thank you for showing me. I've never been backstage in a theatre before – it's quite an experience.'

'Always happy to please. I'm off for a cuppa. Fancy one?'

'Thank you, Tilly, but I'd better get going.'

Flora needed to think. Over the last day or so, she'd convinced herself that the bobble was an important clue and that it must have come from a theatrical costume – she couldn't imagine anyone wearing such a thing in everyday life. The link to the pier theatre and its show was clear. At least, she'd thought so, though she hadn't worked out how it related to Frank Foster or Harry Barnes or his wife. Now she never would. It turned out that it was a dead end. The theatre group owned four Harlequin costumes and every piece of every costume – suit, hat, rattle and slippers – was present and correct.

Feeling deflated, she walked out of the theatre door and stood by the white-painted railings to wait for Jack. She could only hope he'd have better luck. He seemed to have been talking to the manager for a long time and that might mean good news. Irritated with herself and restless, she wandered to the end of the pier, and stood at the gap from where Polly had fallen. What had been the girl's thoughts as she stood here? Was it possible that she'd felt her life so blighted that she'd jumped? Harry Barnes may have proved a massive disappointment, but—

Caught up in her thoughts, she was aware for an instant of someone behind her. Jack, it had to be. She had half turned to greet him, when she felt a hefty push in her back and found herself toppling. Desperately, she reached out for a railing to steady herself, but there was no railing and she felt her feet slip. She was falling sideways. Dazed by the suddenness of the attack, she felt herself lose any grip she'd had and, almost in slow motion, begin the dangerous plunge downwards. Frantically, she tried to grab something, anything, to curtail her fall, and managed, at almost the last moment, to clutch hold of an iron joist just below the level of the pier. It was wet and covered in green slime.

She hung there, feet above the water, her stomach clenched and her mouth filled with a bitter taste. Sickeningly, she felt her hand slip against the slime, her grip loosening all the time. It was high tide and, below, the sea thudded against the ironwork, a swirling grey mass, the waves whipped into teeth of white foam.

Flora couldn't swim. Polly hadn't been able to either. Were they both destined to drown?

ELEVEN

Jack's interview with the manager was lengthy but ultimately futile. The man was garrulous, constantly wandering from the point and repeating himself time and time again. What his information amounted to was that several of the actors had gone in and out of the theatre door on Monday morning while they were waiting for the dress rehearsal to begin, but had seen nothing unusual. Which got Jack precisely nowhere. He was beginning to think that Flora should forget this investigation. Polly had been the kind of girl, lived the kind of life, that left an explanation of her death wide open. She could well have been fooling around and slipped. She might even have jumped. Her nature tended towards the overenthusiastic, so why not the lows that came with that? The presence of someone else, someone no one had seen, who'd deliberately pushed her to her death, looked increasingly far-fetched.

Outside the theatre, he breathed in the tangy air. The sky had cleared a little and a weak sun was doing its best to shine. Spring was on its way and May would soon be here. He was looking forward to Cornwall, looking forward, he had to admit, to having Flora's company for longer than a few hours.

Where was she? He glanced up and down the pier. It had been empty when they'd walked on and it was empty now. It was Saturday afternoon and none of the kiosks or small shops were open so she couldn't be browsing, not that Flora was in any way addicted to shopping. He turned back into the theatre, thinking he must have missed her, and came face to face with Tilly.

'Looking for your girlfriend?' she asked.

'She's not—' he began. 'Yes, yes I am.'

'She was rooting through my costumes until a few minutes ago. Then she left.'

Jack was perplexed. Had Flora strolled back to the promenade or walked even further to Polly's flat, expecting him to follow? It seemed unlikely, but it's what must have happened. Before he left, though, he'd better check. From where he was standing, the rounded wall of the final kiosk was blocking his view of the end of the pier. Walking swiftly past the shops, and navigating deep puddles that had formed across the wooden boards, he rounded the corner but could see no sign of Flora. He was turning to go when something drew him to the open space at the very edge of the pier. He stared downwards, thinking what it must have been like for Polly that morning.

My God! Not Polly, but Flora, clinging desperately to the iron-work beneath the pier. She was hanging suspended, hanging by a thread. He threw himself down on the wooden floor and, trying to calm his voice so that it didn't frighten her, he said softly, 'Flora, I'm here. Just above you.'

She didn't look up. But her hands moved compulsively along the joist and, for one heart-stopping moment, the fingers of her right hand slipped.

'Don't move.' His voice was louder and he couldn't control the way it cracked. 'Don't move. I'm going to reach down and touch you. When you feel my hand, loosen one of yours and grab. Only one hand, mind – keep the other holding on tightly.'

It was easier said than done. With his first attempt, he could see that he was inches away, and that she was getting weaker by the second. He pushed himself forward, leaning so far over that he was scared he might plummet into the water and take her with him. At least he could swim and, if they both fell, he could save her – possibly. He didn't like the look of the water, though. The wind was whipping the waves into choppy mountains, crashing them hard against the iron stanchions. How would they survive that?

He slithered a few inches further, stretching his arms down as far as he could. This time he grazed the top of her hand. It was icy, frozen. As much by fear maybe as by the February cold. A minute more and she would lose her grip entirely. With one huge effort he forced his arms out and down so strongly that it felt he was levering them from their sockets. But now his hand was covering hers.

'Grab now!' he encouraged.

When she didn't respond, his entreaty became more urgent. 'You need to be brave, Flora. Loosen your hand and grab mine. Then reach for my other hand.'

This time, his words hit home and, falteringly, she let go of the joist and grabbed. His warmth seemed to brace her and, in an instant, he was holding both her hands. Then he pulled, his fingers gradually moving down her arms to increase his grip. Somehow, Flora managed to fix her feet against a second joist, steadying herself, while all the time he levered her slowly upwards until her upper body hit the wooden deck. Then, wriggling himself backwards, he reclaimed his hold on her arms and pulled for the last time. She slid onto the boards, her knee hitting the wooden edge of the pier, and lay shivering and silent. Jack scrambled to his feet, tearing off his overcoat to cover her.

A sudden noise behind him had him whirling around ready to face a likely killer, his doubts about Polly's death extinguished. But it was a figure in a Harlequin costume, scooping Flora up in his arms, while his companion, the clown, put a hand beneath Jack's elbow and helped him back to the theatre.

An open-mouthed Tilly greeted the little party at the door.

'Hot, sweet tea, Tilly,' the Harlequin said.

'Coming up. My goodness. What on earth...?'

Tilly never received an answer. Jack had no wish to explain and Flora's teeth were chattering so badly she couldn't speak. The theatre manager must have heard the rattle of cups. Emerging from his retreat, he took in the situation and dived back into his office, returning with a bottle of brandy.

Flora choked on the alcohol but gradually drank from the glass offered her, the ghastly white of her cheeks slowly fading. Taking a tot of brandy himself, Jack felt immense relief, though he was shaken and exhausted. He had nearly lost her – again – the phrase drummed in his head. He should have been more watchful, should have believed her when she'd said Polly's death was murder. She'd been right from the start. Not a crazy leap of imagination, but Flora's deep instinct for the truth.

He felt a light touch on his hand and saw that she was smiling.

'Are you well enough to leave?' he asked quietly.

She nodded.

Jack glanced at the anxious circle gathered around them. 'Thank you for all your help,' he said, 'but I think it's time we left you in peace.'

He held out his hand to Flora, knowing how weak she must feel.

'Yes, thank you so much,' she echoed. 'You've been amazingly kind.'

'Are you sure you're OK?' Tilly asked. 'That was an awful thing to happen. Would you like us to telephone for a taxi?'

'I've a car nearby,' Jack said. 'We can totter to that. But thank you again.'

Hand-in-hand, they walked along the pier and reached the promenade before he said, 'Can you tell me how you fell?'

'I wish I could. I simply don't know. I was waiting for you to come out of the manager's office, and Tilly wanted to get on, I could see – she had a lot of mess to clear before the performance. So I walked to the end of the pier, really to settle in my mind what happened to Polly.'

'And then it happened to you?'

Flora turned a relieved face to him. 'I was worried you might think it absurd if I told you someone really did push me.'

'Not absurd. Frightening. And when, once again, there was no one around,' he said thoughtfully.

'Except there must have been. This person, whoever they are, can make themselves invisible. How do they do that?'

Flora sounded tense. A change of subject might be good. 'Did you talk to anyone in the theatre?' he asked.

'I did. Tilly. She's the one in charge of the wardrobe. I had a hunch about the bobble,' she confessed.

He pulled a face. 'And were you right?'

'Only sort of. Tilly showed me the costumes for the panto and I know now where the bobble comes from – it's a decoration on Harlequin's slippers.'

'So why only sort of?'

'I was hoping it would fit one of the theatre's Harlequin costumes, but none of them has anything missing.'

Jack could see it was an effort for her to talk, but she wasn't giving up.

'How about your chat with the manager? How did that go?'

'The monologue, you mean? His monologue. I learnt absolutely nothing. The company was engaged in a rehearsal for the play and, while they waited for everyone to get into costume, one or two of the actors drifted in and out, but saw nothing and nobody.'

'All in all, we're not getting too far, are we?'

'My feelings exactly. Maybe it's time we talked to Ridley. I know he seemed convinced that Polly's death was an accident or worse, but how will he explain what happened to you today?'

She didn't respond and he wasn't surprised. Flora wouldn't like the idea of involving Ridley – he wasn't her favourite policeman.

He looked at his watch and sighed. 'We've lost time and it's already getting dark.' What sun there had been had disappeared and the clouds rolled themselves back into place, this time dark and rain-bearing.

'Time isn't important,' she said. 'We have a key to the flat.'

'Do you still want to go? You should probably be home, tucked up in bed. We could drive back to Abbeymead and come another day.'

She smiled faintly and shook her head at him. 'You should know me better than that, Jack.'

* * *

Rose Court proved to be a Regency building that must once have belonged to a wealthy family, but was now divided into luxury flats, each with its own balcony overlooking the sea.

'Quite a place,' he said, looking up at the curves of cream stucco.

'An expensive place,' Flora agreed. 'But it wasn't Harry's money that paid for it.'

'Intriguing. Tell me more.'

Despite the sweet tea and the tot of brandy, Flora felt a shadow of herself and was finding it hard to talk. Walking along the promenade, her legs had been so weak they'd hardly seemed part of her.

With an effort, she said, 'Alice and Kate came to supper last night and the conversation took an interesting turn. Apparently, they both know Evelyn Barnes a little, and they reckon the woman was well aware of what Alice called her husband's dalliances. In the past, she's refused to take notice, but they both made the point that if Evelyn discovered her husband was paying for an expensive flat for one of his "girls", she would be up in arms. I didn't mention what Sylvia told us about Mrs Barnes storming round to Rose Court, but it all made sense.'

'I remember now – the woman had a blazing row with Polly.'

'Somehow Evelyn must have found out about the flat and charged round here to confront the girl.'

'Why do you think this place so enraged her, when she hasn't been unduly bothered about other women?'

'I'm not certain, though I can make a guess. According to Kate, Evelyn was an excellent businesswoman and made a lot of money when she sold up. It's her fortune that Harry lives on, and it could have been the thought of him squandering the money she'd worked so hard for, that made her react in that way.'

'Sounds likely. Shall we go in?'

She nodded, though dreading the staircase she'd have to climb. Three staircases, in fact, since Polly's flat was at the top of the building. In retrospect, Flora wondered how she'd ever got to the top, but at the time there was no space to think because Jack was turning the key in the lock.

As the door swung open, a figure appeared. A solid column of flesh in the doorway. It was Frank Foster and he looked as shocked as Flora felt.

'I needed to collect something.' His voice jarred.

It was a kind of explanation, she supposed, but it hardly went far enough. How had the man got in? Was there another key? And what was he doing here rather than back in London? What had he come to collect that was so important that...

He had broken in. Flora's gaze fixed on the broken latch and she saw that Jack's eyes were riveted there, too. Foster must have realised he'd been rumbled and pushed roughly past them, running down the stairs to the entrance before they could stop him.

'Well,' Flora breathed out. 'Breaking and entering.'

And possibly attempted murder. Foster had been in Brighton this afternoon, but had he also been on the pier? Following her? He'd not think twice about pushing her to her death if it suited him. But if he had, how had he managed it without being seen?

'Whatever he'd come to collect must have been important,' Jack said over his shoulder, leading the way into the flat. 'Or he'd never have risked a break-in.'

The apartment was beautiful. Chandeliers hung from high ceilings and wide windows allowed what light there was to flood each room. They walked into the sitting room and Flora slumped down on the ivory leather sofa, one of the few items of furniture that wasn't antique.

Jack took one look at her. 'Stay there,' he said. 'I'll fetch the luggage from the bedrooms.'

For once, Flora did as she was told. She ran a finger along the soft leather cushions of the sofa and felt soothed. Curtains of cream velvet draped the windows and a stunning Axminster carpet, woven to a blue and cream pattern, spread itself wide across the floor. Polly had certainly been living the high life.

Jack was back in a minute, a suitcase in each hand. 'There's one other small bag,' he said apologetically. 'Do you think you could take it? If not, I can carry these to the car and then drive back and collect you.'

'Of course I can take it. It's been a punishing afternoon, but I'm not an invalid. Let's take the luggage and scoot. I don't like the fact that Foster broke in here and can come and go at will – he and whoever he hangs around with. I've a feeling that none of them would be very nice.'

'Or very law-abiding,' Jack added.

Flora heaved herself from the sofa and walked into the main bedroom to collect the last item. It was another beautiful room – space, air, light. A large bed, long curtains, a carpet inches thick. The bag was box-shaped, made of black leather, with two long handles. It looked the kind of small case you kept make-up in if you had enough to fill it, and no doubt Polly had.

Flora bent to pick it up but, still uncertain on her legs, she stumbled on the Turkish rug and caught hold of the bag so awkwardly that it swung outwards and knocked hard against the iron bed frame. A small padlock flew off and landed on the floor. The lock must have been attacked to a zip that Flora hadn't noticed at the rear of the bag. Why would you lock a handbag?

Curiosity got the better of her, and she eased back the zip. A narrow compartment was revealed and there was something inside that she fumbled to pull out. Paper, it was paper. Two thin slips. Grasping them between her fingers, she slowly withdrew them and held them up to the light.

'Jack,' she called. 'You've got to come here.'

TWELVE

'Airline tickets!'

'Airline coupons,' she amended. 'Two of them, made out to Toronto. And for a one-way journey.'

Jack picked up the coupons where she'd laid them on the bed and fingered the slips of paper. 'No names mentioned, but it's a fair guess it was Polly who was leaving – and for good.'

Flora nodded. 'The suicide theory is hereby consigned to the dustbin! Sorry, Inspector Ridley, and Alice, too, but you don't buy tickets to Canada if you're intending to end it all.'

'Why the locked compartment, do you think?'

'She must have wanted to keep the journey secret, didn't want anyone knowing she was leaving.'

'I suppose that's it, or she wouldn't have taken such elaborate precautions.'

Flora plumped down on the bed, needing to rest. 'Even more interesting – who was the other ticket for? Who was Polly planning to leave with?'

Jack was silent for a moment, pushing back the flop of hair that would never lie flat. 'Frank Foster maybe? It would explain why he was here. He was looking for the tickets before anyone else found them, wanting to keep it quiet that he was about to leave the country.'

'Frank!' she said in disgust. 'That makes absolutely no sense. Polly hated him.'

'So everyone says, but how do we really know? It could have been a smokescreen to distract from what was really going on.'

'*I* know,' Flora said with certainty. 'I saw her face when he walked up to her at the funeral breakfast. She couldn't fake that. She hated him all right.'

A fleeting impatience showed on Jack's face. 'If the extra ticket wasn't for him, then who? I can't think she'd be going away with our friend Harry.'

Flora rocked back on the bed. 'I wonder... it's a long shot.'

'Isn't it always?'

'I'll ignore that. Raymond Parsons has been looking woebegone ever since Polly died. I'm wondering, was there was anything special between them?'

'If he was a good friend of Polly's, he's bound to look sad. It doesn't mean he was preparing to leave the life he had here to be with her.'

'He looks more than a little sad. He looks... shrunken. Before it happened, I never saw him when he wasn't smiling. What if Raymond really was more than a friend to Polly? What if one of those tickets was for him?'

'He's already got a girlfriend, hasn't he?'

Getting to her feet, Flora picked up the make-up case and made for the doorway. 'I'm not sure how much of a girlfriend Sylvia Russell is. When I mentioned her the other day, he didn't seem too enthusiastic.'

'Then again,' Jack said, following her down the stairs, 'he wasn't too happy with Polly either. We saw them quarrelling badly.'

'It could have been a lovers' tiff – one they regretted straight away.'

'You've made up your mind, haven't you?' Jack closed the front door of Rose Court behind them. 'The trouble with you, Flora, is that you're stubborn. Once you get hold of an idea, nothing will make you think differently. Raymond is the latest.'

'I'm not stubborn,' she protested. 'Just realistic. It makes more sense than anything else. Think, who was Polly most likely to go away with? Frank Foster, a man who thoroughly scared her, her cousin Sylvia who doesn't seem to have liked Polly a lot – or Harry Barnes? He's the only person left. Would you plump for Harry?'

Jack fell into step beside her, his face breaking into a grin. 'Personally, no.'

'Imagine you're a beautiful young woman—'

'That's going to take some imagination.'

'Try. Imagine you're Polly, who would you choose to leave England with? Raymond is a good-looking young man, he's near her own age and, when he's not moping, a lot of fun. I still remember how good they looked dancing together.'

'You're forgetting, conveniently, that there could always be someone else. A person we don't know about.'

'There could,' she admitted. 'There's so much we don't know. So much guesswork. Perhaps it's time I had a serious talk with Raymond. If he was involved with Polly, I'm sure I could persuade him to admit it. But first, I think I should track down Evelyn Barnes. I want to know how she really felt about Polly. Did the row at the flat satisfy her, or did she want to punish the girl further? What did she do after the hairdresser's appointment the morning Polly died? Was she in Brighton today, and decided it was time for me to have a dip, too?'

'You need to row back, Flora,' he said earnestly. 'Take a break from the sleuthing and let me talk to Ridley. This afternoon was horrific.'

'It was, but thanks to you, I'm still in one piece. And while there's a mystery to solve, we need to keep going or the trail will go cold. By the time Inspector Ridley picks it up, it will be frozen.'

'At least step back for a day or two. It's Sunday tomorrow and you can relax. I'll come by later to see how you're doing.'

'I'll be fine. I am fine. There's absolutely no need for you to fuss.'

* * *

Though she would never admit it, Flora felt far from fine. Once Jack had dropped her at the cottage, her only thought was to sleep. She was utterly exhausted, as much from tension, she suspected, than from any physical exertion, although her arms felt as though they'd passed through a particularly cruel form of torture. Medieval torture. But it was those moments, when she'd hung suspended between life and death, that continued to play on her mind. Even now, she could feel the slime on her hands, hear the harsh squawk of seagulls overhead, taste the salt-laden wind as it harried her defenceless body, and feel the splash and crash of broiling water below.

Fatigued though she was, it was too early to go to bed. Darkness had only just fallen and she forced herself to close the curtains, light the fire, and make tea and toast which she took into the sitting room to eat. Aunt Violet smiled out from her photograph on the sideboard. What would she have made of this afternoon's adventure? Would she have approved of Flora's quest for justice, or would she have thought her niece foolish, too ready to involve herself in business that wasn't hers?

She hoped her aunt would understand the compulsion she felt to get to the bottom of Polly's death. It was an oddity, she admitted. There could not have been a girl more different from herself. A glamorous, beautiful young woman, obsessed by the fashion world, with only one idea in her head. Polly had been unwise, sometimes silly, but she had not deserved to have her young life cut short in such a brutal fashion.

And to be fair to her, she hadn't only the one idea, had she? Those tickets to Toronto proved that she had another life in mind, one it seemed that no one knew about – not Frank, not Harry, not Evelyn Barnes. But just possibly Raymond Parsons. He was someone she must speak to as soon as possible.

With that promise in mind, she gave the cottage a quick tidy and took herself to bed. Her last thought was not of Raymond, but of Frank Foster. She hadn't properly considered his appearance at Rose Court. He was a physically intimidating man, but he'd seemed as scared to see them as they had been to see him. Scared of what, though? And if he hadn't been looking for airline tickets, why had he been there? What had he been looking for?

THIRTEEN

Jack parked the car outside Overlay House and sat staring through the windscreen at the dark lane ahead. He wasn't happy. Flora had brushed off this afternoon's events but he couldn't. She had nearly died, would have died if a casual impulse of his hadn't led him to the end of the pier. The thought sent his heart racing again. There was someone in Abbeymead who was immensely dangerous and, if Flora continued her questioning, she was laying herself open to further attack. An attack that next time might be successful.

He started up the engine again and turned the car in the lane. He'd made up his mind. He would telephone Alan Ridley whether Flora liked it or not. Whether Ridley liked it or not. It was Saturday evening and the chap might well be off duty, but Jack knew he must act fast before Flora could resume the crusade she was set on. He drove to the telephone box on the corner opposite the Nook, hoping that this evening no one else in the village felt the need to make a call.

Alan Ridley was at home, Jack's first piece of good luck. His second, he hoped, would be to convince the man to reopen Polly's case.

'Jack, how are you?' The inspector sounded in a good mood. 'I didn't know you had a telephone. When did that happen?'

'It didn't. I'm phoning from a telephone box.'

'Desperate to speak to me, eh?' the inspector joked.

He wasn't far wrong, Jack thought, striving to keep his voice casual.

'I was wondering if you fancied a drink, Alan? At the Cross Keys.' It was a favourite pub of Ridley's and he held his breath to see if the inspector would take the bait.

'That's quite an invitation coming from you. Yes, old chap, love to have a drink some time. When were you thinking?'

'This evening perhaps.'

There was a silence at the other end of the telephone. Had that been a step too far?

'This evening—'

'Not, of course, if you've got plans,' he said quickly. 'It's only that I've finished the last novel I've been working on – just this minute, in fact – and I felt like celebrating.'

It was a white lie and Jack crossed his fingers that he hadn't mentioned the book the last time they'd spoken.

'Got it!' Was there relief in Ridley's voice at this innocent explanation? 'Big thing, writing a book,' the inspector continued. 'Of course you want to celebrate. How about I meet you there in an hour?'

'Splendid! I'll go ahead – get the drinks in.' He put the phone down, hoping he hadn't sounded too eager.

An hour later, they sat opposite each other, squeezed into a table below a window of the saloon bar. The small table lamps were an innovation, casting the old building in a soft light, but the smell of beer still made Jack's head ache and the fug of cigarette smoke floating below the ceiling timbers still made his eyes water. He disliked the pub, not just the Cross Keys but all public houses, and didn't particularly enjoy beer, but this was in a good cause.

'So, finished the latest novel?' Alan Riley began. 'How many does that make?'

'Half a dozen,' Jack said. 'Churning them out, as my father has it.'

'You didn't come to me for help this time, though.'

'The plot was set in Turkey and I wasn't sure you had much of a handle on Turkish policing.'

'Too right. Do they have police there?' he asked, then broke into a loud laugh. 'Well, cheers, here's to novel number seven.'

'Thank you, Alan.' Jack clinked his glass against the inspector's. 'And how's policing in Sussex?'

'Much the same as usual. A small-scale riot in Lewes at the cinema, when tickets for the extra showing of *Guys and Dolls* ran out. Other than that, all quiet on the Western Front, as they say.'

'Nothing came of the Polly Dakers death then?'

'Dakers?' The inspector made a play of ransacking his memory. 'That's right, it was you who found the poor girl. No, nothing. The post-mortem results came back with what we'd expected. Nothing more sinister than the cuts and bruises you'd get drifting in and out of that ironwork. The coroner's yet to rule, but I can't see the verdict as anything but accidental death.'

Ridley stopped drinking and put down his glass. He fixed Jack with a severe look. 'Is that what this is all about?' He waved his hand at the crowded bar.

Jack's spirits sank. Ridley wasn't a policeman for nothing, he supposed. 'No,' he protested, but knew he sounded half-hearted. 'I fancied coming out for a drink and I know you like this particular pub.'

'But—'

'I just wondered if you'd heard anything more, that's all. Call it natural curiosity. We were the ones to find the girl, and Flora – Flora Steele – knew Polly.'

'Flora Steele? That young lady of yours?'

'She's not my young lady...' he started to say.

'I'll spare your blushes, Jack, but you tell Miss Steele from me that she needs to accept her friend Polly had a bad accident. A better verdict than suicide, don't you think? Better for her folks.'

It was now or never, Jack thought, and plunged in. 'Someone tried to push Flora off the edge of the same pier,' he said. 'This afternoon.'

Ridley stared at him, astonished. 'What were you doing on the Palace Pier?'

The policeman's methodical approach, it seemed. First things first. 'We'd gone to return a scarf that someone dropped in the theatre.' Inevitably, more white lies. 'The day we found Polly we'd been to see the pantomime, but you know that. Flora picked up the scarf as we were leaving. Someone from the audience must have left it behind and there was no theatre staff to take it. I've been wanting to run into Brighton and hand it in ever since, but today was the first chance I'd had.'

The excuse rolled smoothly off his tongue – he'd had it worked out in advance. Ridley continued to stare at him, half believing and half suspicious.

'So, why did Miss Steele go to the end of the pier?'

'I got caught up talking to the theatre manager' – that was true – 'and Flora became bored and wandered to the end of the pier. The scene was a replica of the day that Polly died. There was no one around, yet when Flora turned to walk back, someone pushed her hard in the back and she fell.'

Ridley's eyes opened wide. 'She's not...'

'Dead? No. Just very shaken. She managed to grab hold of a joist and cling to it. I went looking for her and found her fighting for her life. I managed to pull her back up and onto the pier.'

'Jack, the hero, eh?'

'I'm serious, Alan. Someone tried to harm her today, if not kill her.'

'I hear what you're saying, old chap, but you must admit it's a lot to swallow. Why would anyone want to do that?'

'You could say the same of Polly Dakers. Why would anyone want her dead? But I'm convinced that someone did. And this afternoon that same someone felt sufficiently threatened by Flora's presence on the pier to do the same to her. Don't ask me why, I don't know. All I'm certain of is that Flora is in danger.'

'Sounds a hotchpotch to me.' Alan took up his beer again. 'Too many "don't knows" in that speech.'

'It's possible that if you looked,' Jack said tentatively, 'you might find some "do knows". You said things are fairly quiet at the moment.'

The inspector gave a long, deep sigh. 'My mistake. OK, if it's that important to you, I'll have a look at the case again. Any suspects for the crime writer?'

'Plenty. Do you want a list?'

Alan Ridley smacked his lips. 'If I'm going to get a list, I'll have a pork pie first. How about you?'

FOURTEEN

Sunday gave Flora the chance to take the step back that Jack had advised, but it didn't stop her thinking and planning. She would see Evelyn Barnes tomorrow, she decided. After shutting up shop, she'd fetch Betty from her shelter and ride to the Lexington Golf Club. She might be lucky to find Raymond, as well, serving behind the bar.

When Monday evening came, though, she held back. On Tuesday evening it was the same. A deep reluctance had her in its grip and she struggled to understand. She told herself it was because in her heart she knew she should concentrate on the shop, and that anything else was a distraction. The All's Well was still feeling its way back into profit after the catastrophic decline in sales last autumn and she couldn't afford to let up on the hard work of attracting more customers. That was all true, but she suspected her diffidence was more deeply founded – the terror she'd experienced on the pier had dented her confidence badly and she needed time to recover.

Now the snow had well and truly retreated, trade was brisk and the week was busy. People from outside the village were emboldened to travel again, taking a bus into Abbeymead or, more rarely, rescuing their car from the garage where it had sat for most of the winter. Wednesday was half-day closing and the high street hummed with shoppers scurrying between grocer and greengrocer, butcher and baker, before the village shops shut their doors until the next day.

As Flora was turning her own sign to Closed, Kate walked through the door. Her face was plumper these days, Flora noticed, her bob of brown hair shining, and she had on a new coat. A swingy wool velour in a deep blue. Flora made no comment, but it seemed to her a sign that Kate had taken one more step away from the years of wretchedness with her husband. While Bernard Mitchell had been alive, there had been no money for new coats. Too much of it had gone on gambling.

'Have you shut up shop already?' Flora asked.

'I've been naughty,' Kate confessed. 'You know I do a cheap lunch on Wednesdays for pensioners? I had the usual early birds in today, but after Elsie and her neighbour left, I decided to close before anyone else came in. I was hoping to catch you before you left. There was a book mentioned on the wireless the other day and it seemed just the thing for me. Here – I've brought you a couple of sausage rolls. Large ones.'

'What a treat!' Flora took the paper bag Kate offered and reached for her pen and pad.

'It's called the *Constance Spry Cookery Book*. I'm thinking of introducing a few new dishes to the menu and the book should help. Trade has picked up a bit these last few weeks, but I want people to keep coming.'

Flora made a note of the title. 'I'll order it tomorrow,' she promised. 'I might even pinch some of the recipes myself.'

Kate lingered at the desk for a moment, seeming undecided. 'You know you mentioned Evelyn Barnes the other evening?' she said finally. 'It's a strange thing, but the very next day she came into the Nook. She's never been to the café before, not that I can remember. The last time she wanted me to cater, she telephoned.'

'She wants you to cater again?' Flora was surprised, but interested.

'Yes, at her house next week. It's a party of some kind. She mentioned twenty people, so not a large gathering. She wanted a special cake made and said something about celebrating a fresh start.' Kate sounded puzzled.

'A fresh start from what?'

'That's what I wondered. The whole visit was strange. The café was empty when she came in – it was as if she'd been waiting for customers to leave – and she kept glancing out of the window, as though she didn't want anyone to come in and hear what she was arranging. I don't think it's a secret birthday party, though.'

'She would have been better to telephone,' Flora said, locking the cash register.

'Not if she's on a party line, and most of the village telephones are. Even if she's not, Dilys listens in, I'm convinced.'

'Will you do it? The party?' Flora fetched her coat from the peg in the cupboard that Violet had insisted on calling a kitchenette.

'Oh, yes. It's good business. Mrs Barnes will pay well and I've already booked Alice to help me. It just seemed an odd coincidence – after the conversation we'd had.'

Odd indeed, Flora thought, turning the key in the bookshop door. Why the secrecy behind the party? It made little sense. And a fresh start from what? From Polly's death, from getting rid of a girl who posed a greater challenge than the others who'd caught Harry's fancy? A girl who could have destroyed Evelyn's marriage?

Lunch was a brief affair, the sausage rolls from the Nook, a tomato and a helping of Branston pickle. Flora often used Wednesday afternoon to clean the cottage, but she very much wanted to talk to Jack and today the cleaning was a good deal brisker than usual. She hadn't seen him since their trip to Brighton and she missed him. She'd told him that she wanted no fuss, and he'd taken her at her word, so really there was no need for her to feel put out. Yet she did, just a little. They'd become friends over the months she'd known him, something she hadn't expected. But really, they were... she searched her mind for the right word... 'business partners,' she decided, and checking up on her well-being was not part of the arrangement.

She had a shrewd idea, though, that something else was at work, that Jack was deliberately keeping a low profile to ensure she took – what was it he said? – a break from her sleuthing. But she'd had her break, and now it was time for them both to get back to work. He might not welcome a visit, but she would walk to Overlay House this afternoon. There was still time before the light began to fade.

She took the path that Jack himself used when he walked to the village. It was a shortcut, turning down an alley off the main street, then a walk through the spinney to a gate that led to farm-land on one side and, on the other, to denser woodland. It was the path they'd taken when Jack had been shot. The memory sobered her, but made her more determined than ever to get to the bottom of this latest mystery.

The pathway wound its way round and about, dipping in and out of the now leafless trees, and emerging finally a few yards from Overlay House. There was no answer to her knock at the front door, though she was fairly sure Jack was at home, since the Austin was parked at the side of the lane. The garden, she thought, and walked around the house and through a side gate whose timbers were slowly rotting. The long expanse of garden appeared empty, but then she heard the unmistakable sound of breaking glass and a voice cursing. The greenhouse, it had to be.

Charlie Teague stood holding a large pane of glass while Jack furrowed both hands through his hair until it almost stood to atten-tion. He looked up then and, seeing her, tried to smile, but it was a weak effort.

'Trouble?' she enquired.

'As you see. It appears I'm better at breaking glass than mending it.'

'You're trying to mend the greenhouse?'

'We wuz gettin' on OK,' Charlie said, his voice blurred behind the pane of glass, 'but then Mr Carrington went and dropped his bit.'

Jack reached out for the boy's pane. 'If you'll trust me with this, Charlie, I think we'll call it a day. The light's going anyway.'

'Have you ever rebuilt a greenhouse before?' Flora looked around at the pieces of frame scattered across the grass.

'No,' he said shortly.

'Wouldn't it be more sensible to call someone in? I thought you were going to ask Michael.'

'I was, but now I can't afford it.' When her eyebrows rose, he added, 'The car, remember? That and the bill to put it right has more or less cleaned me out.'

The mention of the car reminded her that she wanted to ask Charlie a question she hadn't felt able to before. It had been too soon, too close to the discovery of Polly's body.

'Charlie, now we're a little way on, can you remember being on the pier that afternoon?' She didn't need to specify what afternoon.

'Yeah,' he said. 'The show wuz rubbish.'

'It was. But after the show, when we came out of the theatre, and you ran over to the railings?'

'That's when I saw—'

'I know, and I don't want you to think too much about it. Instead, can you focus on the pier itself? Did you notice anything that struck you as odd? I know the policeman asked you at the time, but can you think about it again? Did you see anyone nearby?'

'Just some actor blokes. They'd come out for a cigarette.'

'How did you know they were actors?'

'They wuz in costumes.' Charlie's tone suggested that grown-ups could really be quite stupid at times.

'The actors would have been the spares,' Jack put in. 'Understudies, who weren't needed for the curtain call.'

'I shouldn't think anyone would be needed after that performance.' Flora was disappointed. The boy was sharp, quick-witted. If there had been anything to notice, he would have noticed.

'You'd better get going,' Jack said to him. 'Your mum likes you home before dark. If you can, come again tomorrow after school, we could fit in an hour.'

After Charlie had banged his way through the side gate, they walked back to the house together, Flora keen to tell him what she knew of Evelyn Barnes.

'I can't see that planning a private party points to her guilt,' he said stolidly, after Flora had emphasised the woman's secrecy. 'It just means she doesn't want the whole village talking. She and her husband have had a rough time and maybe she's hoping to rescue the marriage, but do it without gossip.'

'If it is a rescue,' Flora muttered.

He fixed her with a stern look. 'You're not giving up?'

'No, I'm not.'

Opening the kitchen door, he stood back for her to pass through. 'I've a confession to make,' he said to her back. 'Let me wash my hands and I'll tell all.'

She wasn't too sure she wanted to hear it. A confession sounded ominous. When he came down from the bathroom, she was waiting for him, her arms crossed.

'I saw Alan Ridley...' he began.

'Saw, as noticed him in the street?' She knew that was nonsense, but it was vexing that Jack had involved the inspector.

'I telephoned him Saturday evening when we got back from Brighton and arranged to have a drink with him at the Cross Keys.'

'You hate the Cross Keys.'

He spread his hands in a gesture of resignation. 'Needs must. I wanted him to know what had happened that afternoon. How close to death you came.'

'I wish you hadn't.'

'Why not? It can only help. Another pair of eyes, another brain working on the mystery. I handed him our list of suspects.'

She gave a small snort. 'He'll interfere, you can be sure.'

'If he interferes for some purpose, that's all to the good. We're in dangerous territory, Flora. *You're* in dangerous territory, and I wanted him to know.' He looked at her closely. 'How are you feeling now?'

'Better. Rested. Just as you wanted.'

'Not quite as I wanted. It's obvious you're still determined to carry on and I wish you weren't.' He paused. 'I wish you'd leave it up to Ridley. You won't like me saying this, but you need to look after yourself. You need cosseting.'

'That sounds good. Cosset away! How about you cook me supper this evening? And I do mean cook – no ham sandwiches.'

'I'll do my best, but only if you promise to back-pedal.'

'I can't, Jack. You know that. And neither can you.'

FIFTEEN

Jack's regret was immediate. He shouldn't have issued an invitation. Not that he actually had, but he'd agreed blithely enough to her suggestion, without giving it much thought. Realisation came quickly. There was nothing in his larder that would make a decent supper for the two of them.

Feeling glum, he shooed her into the sitting room, while he retreated to the kitchen to investigate. Jack didn't cook. He didn't much care about food so why bother with cooking? Working in New York, he'd had enough fancy meals to last him a lifetime: business lunches with colleagues, raucous suppers with friends, intimate dinners with Helen. And look how that life had ended. He stood at the kitchen window and gazed out at the gathering gloom. What could he do? Ring Alice or Kate in a panic, the only two women he knew at all well in Abbeymead? No, he couldn't ring Kate. She would have left for home by now and the last time he'd seen her, she still looked fragile. Coping with the café was more than enough. But Alice – he'd ring her. Ask her to bring over one of her special casseroles.

In the meantime, there was cheese and biscuits to keep Flora from going hungry. Wednesday was a busy day for her, he knew, and he had no idea if she'd found time for lunch. His own stomach felt hollow – he'd had to share his sandwiches with Charlie. The boy appeared to eat ten meals a day.

When he opened the larder door, he was surprised. Surprised and joyful. Of course, the dairyman had called this morning while he was in the front garden, oiling the ancient mowing machine to be ready for better weather, and he'd asked the chap to leave whatever he had on his van. It varied. Some days it was just milk, other times butter and cheese. Occasionally eggs. And yes, he had eggs. And today Mr Sweetman had excelled himself and brought bacon, storing the entire delivery in the larder. There was a new loaf in the bread bin, and maybe the tomatoes he'd bought a few days ago would still be fresh. Perfect.

Flora had her feet up on the lumpy sofa, the cause of many of her complaints. Her head was lolling slightly and she seemed to be dozing. He tried not to disturb her, but when he brought in two glasses of elderflower wine – donated by Charlie's mother – she opened her eyes. Making a second trip to the kitchen, he returned with a plate of cheese and biscuits.

'Balthazar's feast!' Flora said, swinging her legs off the sofa.

'Do you know who he was?' Jack plumped himself down in the chair opposite.

'Not a clue. We need Aunt Violet here. She'd have the answer.'

'She was a keen churchgoer then?'

'Every Sunday at St Saviour's, no matter the weather – rain, wind, snow or sun.'

'A devout woman,' he remarked, taking a chunk of cheese and balancing it on a dry biscuit. 'This is good, by the way. Cheddar straight from Somerset.'

Flora took a chunk. 'You're right. Delicious. Violet wasn't devout, not at all. In fact, I don't think she really believed. If she had any faith, she lost it when her fiancé was killed on the very last day of the war. That's the First War, of course. But going to church was a duty she inherited from Victorian parents and it stuck. Meeting in church every week was something that bound the community together, that's what she always said. And community was important to her. Abbeymead and its people were important.'

'Even though she wasn't born in the village?'

'*Because* she wasn't, I think. Her family, my father's family, came from London. That's where she was brought up and lived her younger years. She never liked the city, though. Said that life there felt anonymous, detached. Villages are very different. You can't be detached in a village and somehow she felt more at home here.'

'Do you remember where your family lived in London?'

Flora cracked a biscuit between her teeth. 'I don't. Not really. Except that we lived in my grandparents' house, that's what Violet told me. My father inherited it before I was born, but other than that I know almost nothing – I was only six when my parents died. The house was probably quite close to Violet's flat in Highgate. That's where I went to live after the accident.'

'What happened to your grandparents' house?'

'It was sold. Years later, Violet told me that my father had run up debts so the house had to go. I never knew the details. It was pure luck that her godfather left her enough money to buy the All's Well. She couldn't wait to leave London and, as soon as she had the money, we moved to Abbeymead. This village is really all I've ever known.'

'Where are they buried,' he asked, 'your parents?' The question sounded abrupt, even tactless, he realised, but Flora had confided so little of her past life that he wanted to know more.

'Highgate Cemetery,' she said briskly, and he sensed the topic was closed.

Pushing the cheese plate aside, he got to his feet. 'I'll be off to do my worst with the bacon,' he said.

Flora settled back onto the sofa. 'Call me if it looks like winning.'

He tried hard to make the supper as appetising as he could, browning the bacon to the right colour, frying the tomatoes until they were only just soft, managing to keep the yolks of the eggs intact and slicing and buttering the bread at the last moment, so that it was still soft and bouncy.

While he cooked, he thought about Flora's childhood. She'd been very young when her parents died in that car accident. She'd claimed before that she had no memory of her young life with them, but he wondered if that was strictly true. After they'd died, she'd gone to friends for a while, but it had been a temporary arrangement and the threat of ending in an orphanage had been constant. Not until Violet, a single working woman, who knew nothing of children, had offered her a home, could she have felt safe.

Such uncertainty for a small child was bound to have its effect. It seemed to have made Flora cautious, on a personal level. 'Contained' was how he'd put it. She was fun, and great company, but there was always a part of her that, during the months they'd known each other, he'd never fathomed. Other life events, too, must have strengthened her reserve. Being deceived by the boy she loved and her plans for travelling destroyed. Losing her aunt after several years of illness. It was nearly twelve months ago that Violet Steele had died and he could see the coming weeks would be painful for Flora.

'Ready,' he called out, flipping the last egg from the frying pan. 'Come and get it.'

Her eyes widened as she came into the kitchen.

'Surprised? Didn't expect a supper this evening?' he taunted.

'I was wondering... but it looks very good.'

He hoped it tasted as good and looked across at her as she took the first bite.

'You've cooked it beautifully, Jack, so... there's no excuse for you now. You have to give up the sandwiches.'

'I can't. They're my lifeline.'

'That's nonsense. You're not writing at the moment which means you've plenty of time to cook decent meals.'

'I may not be writing,' he protested, 'but I am researching.'

'No, you're not,' she contradicted. 'Don't tell porkies.'

'No, I'm not,' he admitted.

'*And* you have time to continue with the investigation.'

It wasn't worth even a groan.

'I know you've spoken to Ridley,' she went on, 'but we shouldn't give up what we're doing. Agreed?'

'If we must, but quietly. I can talk to Evelyn Barnes, if you like. See if I can discover what else she was doing in Brighton the day Polly died, apart from having her hair cut.'

'I should have spoken to her this week,' Flora confessed, 'but maybe we should tackle her together. By all accounts, Evelyn is a fearsome woman and her dogs even more so. They're free to patrol the Pelham Lodge grounds and they don't like visitors!'

She paused. 'I should talk to Raymond Parsons, too.' Seeing Jack's frown, she said quickly, 'I'll do it subtly. Buttonhole him when he's on his own.'

'You think he's more likely to confess to an undying love if it's a woman asking?'

Flora was undaunted. 'Something like that. This bread is too nice. I could eat the whole loaf. Now that's something you could do – learn to bake. Not that I'm very good, though Violet was always trying to teach me.'

He got up quickly from the table and started to clear the dishes. 'No more suggestions, thanks.'

She put out a hand to stop him. 'My turn. You cooked and I'll do the washing up. Go and laze and I'll bring in the tea.'

'Are you sure?'

'I'm not that feeble. I may nearly have died in Brighton, but so did you. Just think, I could have pulled you down at any moment – into the frenzied waves.' She was laughing, making undulating movements with her hands and whooshing noises to mimic the wind.

'I'll wait for the tea,' he said, smiling. It was good to see the sparkle back.

He'd stepped into the hall ready to cross to the sitting room, when the door knocker sounded.

Flora poked her head out of the kitchen. 'It's late for a visitor. Were you expecting someone?'

He shook his head, mystified. 'Probably somebody trying to sell me something.'

'At this time of the evening?'

He walked to the door and pulled it open. For seconds, he stood staring at the figure on the doorstep.

'Aren't you going to invite me in, Jack?' the woman asked softly.

His brain jerked into gear and, without saying a word, he waved his visitor across the threshold.

Flora had come out of the kitchen and was standing in the hall, a tea towel in her hand, her expression confused.

He turned to her, finding his voice at last. 'Flora, this is...'

'Helen,' the woman said, coming forward to shake Flora's hand. 'Helen Milsom. I knew Jack in America.'

Jack carried Helen's suitcase up to one of the spare rooms, finding fresh sheets in the airing cupboard and leaving her to use the bathroom.

Downstairs again, he poured himself a large tot of whisky. He rarely drank spirits but tonight the occasion called for it. He felt stunned. Shocked. Mortified, even. Helen Milsom appearing out of nowhere was something he couldn't have conjured in his worst nightmare. She'd contacted his father, she told him, as soon as she'd decided to come to England, and Ralph Carrington had given her Jack's address. She'd travelled down from the airport today to see a Canadian friend in Brighton, with the idea that she'd come on to Abbeymead later. Drop in and say a brief hello. Somehow, though, the time had gone on and she hadn't got away as early as she'd expected and now it was getting late and she hadn't a bed for the night. Jack didn't believe a word of it.

They'd speak again tomorrow, she'd promised, when she was feeling and looking fresher. But why was she here, for God's sake?

His last sight of her had been a guilty smile as she left him to travel to the Hamptons with his best friend, three weeks before she was supposed to marry in an English church. Whenever he'd thought about her, and in the early days it had been often, he'd assumed that she'd married Mark, if not on that holiday to the Hamptons, then later. Married him and moved into his New York apartment – it was big enough.

Yet he hadn't seen a wedding ring on Helen's finger tonight, so perhaps the marriage had never happened. Perhaps she'd split up with Mark and found someone new, someone she considered a better bet. Just as she had with him. It didn't explain why she'd come to England, though, and travelling alone. And why she'd dashed down to Sussex directly from the airport.

What she hoped to achieve by coming to Abbeymead, he had no idea. Surely, not some kind of grim reconciliation. The more he thought about her gatecrashing his life in the way she had, the angrier he became. It had been a happy evening, he and Flora comfortable with each other. Until Helen had walked in. Flora had shaken hands with the woman, said an automatic *Nice to meet you*, then launched the tea towel at him and walked out of the door, her face frozen. She'd been gone in seconds, leaving him no chance to talk to her. Though what could he say?

He wanted to know she was all right. He couldn't telephone – he was still on that interminable waiting list – and he couldn't drive round to her cottage, leaving his unwelcome visitor alone in the house. He would go to the bookshop first thing in the morning, he decided. By then, he might be able to offer Flora some kind of explanation.

SIXTEEN

It was to be another two days, in fact, before Jack saw Flora again, and not at her bookshop as he'd planned. The day following Helen's arrival, his visitor stayed late in bed, drifting into the kitchen halfway through the morning, her face woebegone. She was wearing a flimsy wrapper, which left little to the imagination and which at Overlay House in February was hardly a sensible choice.

'I'm awfully sorry, Jack. I think I must have caught something horrid on the plane. I feel like death. Would you mind if I went back to bed?'

He didn't have much choice, he thought sourly. She didn't look particularly well, it was true, but that could simply be fatigue from a long flight. Other than marching her to the local doctor, there was nothing he could do. He was stuck until Helen chose to feel better.

She stayed in bed most of the day, only appearing when Charlie Teague arrived after school for greenhouse duties, and still wearing the inappropriate wrapper. The boy stared at her and Jack felt the stirrings of unease. Charlie was on the cusp of young manhood and this was not a situation Mrs Teague would appreciate.

'Why don't you get some clothes on, Helen?' he suggested. 'You might feel brighter when you're washed and dressed. I'll see you later – I'll be working in the garden until supper.' It would have to be eggs and bacon again – the only items in the larder – but he'd get Helen to cook while he slipped out for half an hour to call on Flora at her cottage.

Charlie was set to work, washing down paintwork on the greenhouse frames, but stayed only an hour or so – Jack made sure of it – and thankfully by the time he was ready to leave, Helen was fully dressed. The boy was bound to take the tale back to his mother and, from his limited experience of the village, Jack guessed it would soon be all around Abbeymead that the writer chap had this fancy woman staying, not a wedding ring in sight, and her walking around half-naked, too.

'It's a simple supper, I'm afraid,' he said, when Helen followed him into the kitchen. 'I wonder, would you mind cooking? I have to slip out for a few minutes.'

'Sounds interesting. Where to?'

'I need to speak to someone.' His tone did not invite questions, but Helen seemed oblivious.

'Who are you going to see?' she asked in an over-sweet voice.

'No one you know.'

She gave a small shrug. 'Don't be long then or you'll get burnt bacon.'

Grabbing the torch from a kitchen drawer, he was out of the house in minutes and walking at full speed in the direction of Flora's cottage. Tonight, he chose to go by the lane. It was a longer journey than walking through the spinney, but at dusk infinitely safer.

Approaching the house, he was surprised not to see a light. There was no answer when he knocked at the front door, and no answer when he walked to the back of the house and banged on the kitchen door. He wondered if he should continue on to Alice's cottage, or even Kate's. Flora was bound to be with one of them, but then he thought of the bacon burning and the fact that he had yet to tackle Helen on exactly why she'd arrived on his doorstep. Disappointed, he made his way back to Overlay House.

'Just in time,' Helen greeted him. 'Did you find who you were looking for?'

'No,' he said shortly.

'Oh, dear. I hope that wasn't too upsetting.'

'Shall we eat?'

Sitting opposite her at the kitchen table, he could feel her gaze and was conscious of her measuring him, working out how best to use the evening to her benefit. Jack was sure of one thing. Helen Milsom would never again take advantage of him. He settled to eat his bacon and eggs in dogged silence.

'I'll clear,' he said, when they'd finished.

He had the plates and pans washed in record time and joined her in the sitting room, where she was idly flicking through one of his books that she'd picked off the shelf.

'You're a published author, Jack. I had no idea.'

'Why would you?'

She smiled warmly at him. 'I'm impressed. I know you dabbled with short stories and you were always insisting that one day you'd write a novel, but I never thought you would. But there, what do I know?'

'Why are you here, Helen?' he asked bluntly.

'I told you. My friend in Brighton—'

'The truth, please.'

She started to protest, then her voice faltered and there was a sag to her body. She looked fixedly down at her lap.

'Mark,' she began. 'We're finished.'

'Right.' He wasn't going to help her out.

'Look, Jack, I know how you must feel.'

'No, you don't.' He remained standing, staring at her from the opposite side of the room. 'You have no idea how I feel. You haven't seen me for six years and you had no idea how I felt then.'

'I know I did something bad.' Her fingers, he noticed, were curled inwards.

'You think so?'

'I was stupid. Mark can be very persuasive. I was young and I had my head turned.'

'Not so young you didn't know what you were doing.'

'It was the whole living in England thing. Mark persuaded me to think again. He said it wouldn't work for me. The wedding and then setting up home in some small out-of-the-way place.'

'Like Abbeymead,' he put in.

'No, not like Abbeymead. I'm sure the village is delightful.' She was gushing now, he thought. 'I just didn't want that kind of life.'

'I can see that two weeks in the Hamptons would have it beat,' he said bitingly.

'But after the Hamptons, there was New York and being with Mark. He was fun, full of life, going places.'

'And I wasn't?'

Why was he bothering? Why trawl over painful ground? Except that it no longer felt anywhere near as painful.

Helen leaned forward in her chair. 'You've always been a bit of a closed book, Jack. There was a part of you I could never reach. It wasn't like that with Mark. I knew exactly where I was with him.'

'And where are you right now?'

'I told you. We don't see each other any longer.' She shuffled back into her chair.

'So there was no wedding ring?'

'There never would be. Mark's not the marrying type. Not like you.'

'You couldn't be more wrong, Helen. I'm no more the marrying type than Mark, but unlike him I'm happy with my own company. I don't need someone else to prop me up.'

'Not that happy,' she said slyly. 'Who was that girl last night? The one with the tea towel. Laura or something.'

'Flora,' he said shortly. 'She owns the local bookshop.'

Helen pinned an arch smile on her face. 'Something in common then. But not your girlfriend?'

'I don't have a girlfriend and, strangely enough, I don't want one.'

Helen drew herself up to sit ramrod straight and stared him

out. 'If you think I'm here to seduce you all over again, you're mistaken.'

'That's as well, since there's not a chance in hell of your doing so. But you still haven't explained just why you bothered to contact my father to find me, why you bothered to take a taxi directly from the airport to this "out-of-the-way place".'

He saw immediately that he'd hit the nail on the head. That was just what she'd done.

The pride had gone. Her chin dipped and she stared down at the floor. 'To be honest, I don't know. It was just something I felt I had to do. A kind of unfinished story, after Mark and I finally parted – that was last summer. It was good with him while it lasted, at least most of the time, but I knew it was never going to be permanent.'

Jack couldn't stop his face crumpling slightly. 'Five years is quite some time,' he remarked quietly. It was far longer than she'd gifted him.

'It was always a bit on and off with Mark,' she admitted, 'and when I lost my job just before Christmas, the world kind of caved in. I decided I couldn't bear to look for another post or spend another year in New York, so I made plans to go back to Canada. But then my mother wrote to say my grandmother was poorly. She's in a residential home on the south coast. In Bournemouth. I thought I should see her before, well you know... but call in on you first. You were a friend once, Jack.'

'Once being the operative word.'

He didn't care if he hurt her, then felt cross with himself. He didn't need to hurt her. He was over Helen. And looking at her now, sitting on his bulging sofa, long legs elegantly crossed, blonde tresses immaculately styled, he wondered how he'd ever thought she was what he wanted.

'I'm going to bed,' he said. 'I've some reading I need to get done. If you're OK with it, I'll drive you to Brighton station tomorrow. There'll be a train from there to Bournemouth.'

She nodded, seeming to accept his decree. 'I'll clean up in the kitchen,' she said, picking up their empty cups, her voice subdued.

It was when she picked up the tray that Jack saw the newspaper. 'Is this yours?'

'I bought it at the airport, waiting for the taxi. It's two days old now. You can bin it if you like.'

Jack rarely bought a paper – it was too reminiscent of his old life and he had all the news he needed from the wireless – but out of curiosity, he flicked through its pages. Then stopped, his hand hovering, his attention arrested. The sounds from the kitchen, drawers opening and closing, china clinking, faded into the background. He brought the paper closer, peering at the photograph splashed across half a page. The accompanying article gave details of a crime syndicate caught laundering their ill-gotten gains through various legitimate businesses. The police had arrested the main suspects and were holding them until they appeared in court. The photograph was from happier times, the journalist wrote. Happier times, maybe, but at the rear of the group of men, barely visible, was a face Jack knew. Frank Foster.

That Frank knew criminals, that he socialised with them, was unwelcome confirmation that he was a man with whom it was best not to tangle. A man who, from their last sight of him, had appeared desperate. The photograph bore out Flora's suspicions and blew wide open the question of what Foster had been searching for at Rose Court. Not air tickets – they'd already dismissed that idea – but possibly something incriminating, something that might lead to his joining his companions in a police cell. What might it be? In his pursuit of Polly, had he left papers with her, perhaps? Papers that were dangerous. Or given her some kind of keepsake that he now wanted back, very badly?

If Frank Foster were mixed up with the kind of people he appeared to be, he was a man to avoid. Jack didn't want Flora rushing in, acting rashly. He needed to speak to her. On his way back from taking Helen to Brighton station tomorrow, he would call at the bookshop.

SEVENTEEN

Flora had walked out of Overlay House within seconds, unable to trust herself to be polite. That woman – Helen Milsom! The woman who had broken Jack's heart so completely. How dare she suddenly walk through his door six years later as though nothing untoward had happened? Flora seethed. And Jack, standing back, inviting her into his home! How could he after the pain she'd caused him? Flora stormed along the lane leading back into the village, unnoticing of the gloom, arriving at her own front door before she realised she'd walked at least a mile in the dark along a stretch of road she used infrequently, and without a torch.

The anger didn't subside. Tossing and turning in bed that night, she couldn't stop herself from speculating on what might happen next. Constructing a future that infuriated her, and one she feared could leave Jack devastated. Would Helen ingratiate herself all over again and Jack forgive her? It was perfectly possible. Men could be so stupid, and the woman was very attractive, she thought viciously. No wonder he'd fallen for her. Except that now Flora had seen her in person, the two of them didn't quite seem to fit. Jack was crumpled, his face handsome but lived-in, his hair flopping every which way, whereas Miss Milsom was box-fresh: a carefully styled blonde, slim legs encased in silk stockings and clothes far too fashionable for a Sussex village.

She was still fuming the next morning when she wheeled her bicycle out of the garden shed – improved weather meant she was using Betty again – and rode to the All's Well. Once through the shop door, the familiar woody smell and the bright splash of book jackets steadied her. It wasn't her affair, she told herself. If Jack wanted to make the same mistake, that was up to him. Their partnership, though, or whatever she chose to call it, was at an end. From now on, his focus would be Helen and his life divided between her and his writing. He'd have no time to play detective and no wish, in all probability. Feeling an unaccustomed emptiness, Flora took the feather duster from the cupboard and began her daily routine.

The hours dragged. She supposed she must have served the usual number of customers, but her mind was elsewhere and her interest half-hearted. Locking up for the day came as a relief. She was pocketing her keys when she saw Alice walking down the street towards her.

'Have you heard?' her friend asked.

Was Helen Milsom's arrival common knowledge already? That would beat all village records.

'About poor Ted,' Alice went on.

'Ted? Ted Russell?'

'Sylvia's just come by the Nook. She got home from work this evening to find her dad in a terrible state. They've had a break-in.'

Flora's pulse quickened. 'What was taken?'

'Looks like nothin' was. Least, that's what Sylvia said, but her father is in such a state that he's not makin' much sense. It was him who came back from work first, found the kitchen window broken and the place in turmoil.'

'Turmoil as in someone searching for something?'

'I suppose so. Mebbe they couldn't find anythin' worth takin', but Sylvia said every drawer in the house had been opened and the contents strewn everywhere. Books thrown on the floor, cupboard doors left hangin' off their hinges. The place has suffered a real goin' over.'

Flora stood irresolute, unsure of what to make of this new development, her uncertainty prompting Alice to say, 'Kate's just finishin' up at the café, then comin' round for supper. Why don't you come, too? We can have a chat.'

'I'd love to.' She was glad to accept, faced with a lonely evening at home and plagued by thoughts she'd rather not have. 'See you in about an hour?'

Flora rode slowly home, turning over in her mind what Alice had told her. A burglary in which nothing had been taken suggested it was not a random break-in. A casual thief would have found something he could sell. The fact that the house had been reduced to one enormous mess suggested a search for something that hadn't been found. Might it have a connection to Polly's untimely death? It seemed unlikely, but Kate had been the one to speak to Sylvia and it might be that she'd have more to add, something that would make that connection.

In truth, Kate had little more to say. Both Sylvia and her father were shocked, bewildered by the wrecking of their home. They weren't exactly poor, but they owned nothing likely to attract a burglar.

'If they'd had one of them new television sets,' Kate said, bringing a tureen of vegetables to the table, 'Sylvia could have understood it. Polly was going to buy one for them, but then... well, you know.'

'And nothing was taken?' Flora asked again.

'Not that they could see. They might come up with something later, I suppose, when they're looking for an item and can't find it.'

'Sounds to me like it was one of them vandals. Someone who'd nothin' better to do but hurt other folks,' Alice declared. 'Can you eat two chops, my love?'

'One is fine, thanks,' Flora said.

'There's one or two boys, I've noticed,' Alice went on. 'Old enough to know better, hangin' around the village at night. Idlin', you know.'

'This was in daylight,' Flora countered, helping herself from the dish of carrots. 'That's taking quite a risk.'

A risk, she thought, that made plain the importance of whatever the burglar had been seeking. And, since it would be clear from one glance at Ted Russell's modest home that there was little to steal, it had to be something the burglar knew was there, or thought he knew. Frank Foster was the obvious suspect. She had discounted him searching Rose Court for airline tickets, but had never worked out exactly what he'd been after.

When they'd cleared the dinner plates and Alice retrieved an apple pie from the oven, Flora realised that no one had mentioned Raymond Parsons.

'Does Raymond know about the break-in?' she asked casually.

Kate was the first to respond. 'I don't think so. He was the reason Sylvia called at the Nook. She was looking for him, but I told her he hadn't worked at the café today.'

'For two people who are supposed to be a couple, they don't seem very close,' Flora threw in, just in case she could learn more. She was on her own now in this investigation, and every small clue must be hoarded.

'I did hear talk of a wedding,' Alice hazarded. 'But now with Polly gone, it don't seem appropriate. A funeral will have to come first, and there's no news of that.'

'Poor Mr Russell. He has that to face as well.' Flora wondered how well he was coping – a much-loved niece dead and now his home destroyed.

Her two friends nodded in unison, their faces grave.

'Have some custard,' Alice offered, trying to lighten the mood. 'Kate's made it to a special recipe.'

* * *

Two days on from Helen's arrival, there had been no word from Jack, but that was hardly surprising. She hadn't expected to hear from him, Flora told herself crossly. He would be tucked away at Overlay House with his newly discovered love. There would be gossip once the village got wind of it, mutterings about young people, though neither of them were particularly young, and possibly a visit from the vicar of St Saviour's to stress the importance of matrimony. But for Flora, it had only one meaning. She was now on her own, her fingers very tightly crossed that she wouldn't meet trouble. From this moment, there would be no Jack to rescue her.

Questioning Raymond was at the top of her list, though without any idea of where to find him, she settled for the moment on a visit to Evelyn Barnes. She and Jack were to have confronted the woman together, but she determined now to brave Mrs Barnes alone, no matter how intimidating she turned out to be. The roaming dogs gave Flora pause, but she had to hope that during the day, at least, they were kept kennelled.

She'd go at lunchtime, she decided, and nibble something when she got back to the shop. It was a fair distance to Pelham Lodge, according to Alice's directions, and would take her most of the hour – up Fern Hill, past Miss Lancaster's Gothic monstrosity and then just before the Priory, she'd need to take a minor road that branched left. If she was to be back at the shop in time to reopen at two o'clock, Betty would need to work hard.

She ought to squeeze in a visit to Ted Russell, too, if only for a few minutes. Mulberry Crescent was on her way out of the village and she felt she owed it to the poor man to say how sorry she was to hear of this latest trouble.

The small estate had never taken on an air of permanence and, steering her bicycle into the Crescent this lunchtime, it felt again to Flora as though a giant hand had inadvertently dropped a clutch of buildings on its way elsewhere. Like one of those games at the fairground where, for a penny, if you were lucky, a steel claw would rummage through a pile of sweets and drop you a winning handful.

Sylvia was standing outside number twenty-four when Flora arrived.

'Good afternoon,' she called out to her, wheeling Betty towards the garden gate.

'Is it?' The girl's expression was sour.

'I heard what happened, Sylvia. I'm so sorry.'

The girl gave a brief nod and carried on looking down the road.

'I can see you're waiting for someone, so I won't stay, but could you tell your father I called? Tell him please to ring the bookshop if he thinks of anything I can do to help.'

'I don't think I'll be telling my father anything much for a while,' Sylvia said tonelessly. 'I'm waiting for an ambulance.'

'Mr Russell is ill?'

'You could say that. The doctor's with him now.' She jerked her head towards the house. 'He thinks Dad has had a heart attack, and wants him in hospital for monitoring.'

Flora's face fell. Things for the Russell family were going from bad to worse. 'I'm so sorry,' she said again, struggling to know what best to say. 'I'll leave you to wait, but let me know how your father does in hospital, won't you?'

Sylvia made no response and, feeling awkward, Flora wheeled the bicycle back onto the road. It was evidently the wrong day to call. 'Do let me know how Mr Russell gets on,' she said again.

Taking hold of the bike's handlebars, she was about to ride away when a thought struck. Had Jack delivered the suitcases stored in his boot or had Helen Milsom been too much of a distraction?

'Did you get your cases, by the way?'

'Oh, yeah. Thanks. I haven't had time to unpack them.'

Flora wondered what her reaction would be when she did. With the padlock broken and the secret compartment no longer a secret, the girl was bound to find the airline coupons.

'I'm glad the luggage got to you. I should get moving now or I'll be late opening the shop.'

'Better not to go too far then.' It was the first interest the girl had shown in her visitor.

'I'm hoping the bike will get me up Fern Hill,' Flora said, not wanting to mention the visit to Evelyn Barnes.

Sylvia's response was brief. 'Tough climb,' she said.

EIGHTEEN

It was a tough climb, made tougher by recent heavy winds. Flora found herself forced to zigzag in and out of a mass of twigs, even small branches, scattered across a road that was lined for several miles by woodland. By the time she turned off into the lane that ran past Evelyn's expensive home, she was puffing heavily. Thankfully, the new road was relatively flat, and she reached the gates of Pelham Lodge, as a palatial dwelling as Alice described it, feeling a good deal better.

Mrs Barnes would not be an easy woman to talk to and Flora doubted she would get very much out of her, but she knew she had to try. Evelyn had been in Brighton the day Polly had died. She had quarrelled fiercely with the girl the previous week, and both Kate and Alice reckoned that Harry's renting of the Brighton flat had been the final straw for his discarded wife. A woman pushed too far would be quite capable of murder.

But despite Evelyn as a possible suspect, the figure of Frank Foster continued to dominate Flora's thinking. He fitted the bill in so many ways. A man obsessed with an unwilling girl was classic territory for murder, but did his frantic searching at Rose Court and then at Ted's house – Flora reckoned it had to have been him – make it more or less likely that he was the killer? It was possible the break-ins were unconnected to Polly's death. It might simply be that she'd rejected Foster once too often and his infatuation had led him to push her off the Palace Pier in anger. That could have proved a costly mistake – if Polly had in her possession something important. The man's desperate search suggested as much. Had he thrust her to her death before realising too late that he needed her alive?

What *was* certain was that the person who had pushed Polly had also pushed Flora, and Frank had been the one they'd seen in Brighton that day. There would have been time for Foster to attempt murder and then gone on to Rose Court where they'd met him at the door of Polly's apartment. She and Jack had been drinking tea with the theatre cast for at least twenty minutes after the incident. It might explain, too, why Frank had looked so agitated when they'd found him coming out of the flat. The obvious explanation was that they'd caught him red-handed, rifling the apartment. Not so obviously, it could be that minutes previously he'd tried to kill her... it would hardly be surprising then if he looked disturbed, meeting her face-to-face, after believing she had plunged to her death.

Flora wheeled her bicycle up the long paved drive, seeing the outline of Pelham Lodge come into view. Alice was right – there was nothing remotely lodge-like about the sprawling building ahead. It was three storeys high, sporting incongruous Dutch gables, and on one side had seemingly been extended to include another entire wing. More than enough space for Evelyn and Harry to avoid each other for a year. It was an architectural mess, though evidently a very expensive mess, and one that was well-kept. The lawns on either side of the driveway were pristine, heavily manicured even during these winter months and, though the planted areas were empty of flowers, they were also empty of weeds.

Flora was approaching the massive front door, porticoed and painted a dark green, when there was a rush of wind, a tremble underfoot, and two large black dogs came hurtling towards her, barking ferociously, their mouths dripping saliva and hanging open to reveal two sets of sharpened teeth. Unsure whether to retreat back along the drive or run ahead to the front door, she stood completely still. She'd read somewhere that this was what you should do if you were unlucky enough to meet a wild animal making ready to attack. These dogs looked wild enough.

Before she could retreat, they'd hurled themselves at Betty, scratching her already battered paintwork and tearing at the wicker of her basket. Flora reached out, trying to protect the tray – an essential for delivering books – and two sharp claws furrowed deep into her hand, producing a spurt of blood. The dog who'd injured her emitted a throaty growl and, with his companion, fixed her in an unwavering stare. Maybe the smell of blood had made her even more interesting. She tried thrusting the bike at them in an attempt to frighten them away, but this only incensed them more and they began to pad around her, their growling becoming deeper and more intense.

Flora felt her skin tighten and panic begin its crawl. She needed Jack. Needed him to be here. She had no idea how to save herself from the mauling she felt sure was imminent. If she tried to run, the dogs would attack – she saw their muscled hind legs and knew they were easily strong enough to knock her down. But if she stayed motionless, they would continue to circle her until they got bored or had destroyed Betty entirely. Then what?

'Badger, Rocco, come!' An older woman dressed in black and wearing a white pinafore had opened the front door.

The dogs' ears shifted slightly and when the maid called again – my goodness, a maid, Flora's confused mind registered – Badger and Rocco reluctantly slunk away in the direction they'd come.

Flora took a deep breath and wheeled the bicycle up the remainder of the drive. The woman stood waiting.

'Can I help you?' she asked.

She had a snaggle-tooth and a worn pair of hands. It felt to Flora as though she had stepped back years, to a time before the war when servants were the norm for such a wealthy family.

'Those dogs should be locked up,' she said, her hand throbbing. 'You do know they attacked me?'

The maid said nothing, her face immobile, waiting, it seemed, for the uninvited visitor to state her business.

Stating her business was the only thing she could usefully do, Flora decided. 'I'm here to speak to Mrs Barnes,' she said, averting her eyes from the tooth.

'Mrs Barnes is not at home.'

There was a hollowness in Flora's chest. She had foregone lunch, exhausted herself on Fern Hill, then risked being mauled to a pulp, all for nothing.

'Can you tell me where I might find her?'

She was too daunted to face cycling further today and, in any case, it was too late, but it would be as well to know something of Evelyn's movements.

'Mrs Barnes plays golf,' the maid said unhelpfully.

'So I've heard. Is that where she is today? At the golf club?'

'I imagine so. That's where she usually is.' The woman had begun to close the door before Flora could thank her, though what for was difficult to say.

Tomorrow was another day, she told herself, wheeling a badly scratched Betty to the gates. And tomorrow happened to be Saturday and half-day closing, which meant she could visit the Lexington Golf Club in the afternoon. There'd be no dogs there with fangs ready to strike, and it was almost guaranteed that she'd find Evelyn.

Meanwhile, the journey down Fern Hill awaited, and that was always a treat – today, a consolation prize for the fear she'd endured. The carefree swoop down the long, snaking hill was pure pleasure, grassy banks rushing past, trees a hazy blur, until she arrived breathless at the bottom, swinging back into the village and onto the high street.

She was hurtling downwards at full speed, hair flying free, its long strands streaming behind her, when a sudden roar brought a speeding car into view. Flora barely had time to absorb the fact that the vehicle was being driven uphill far too fast and way to the right of the centre line, before the wheel arch caught her handlebars and drove the bicycle into the deep ditch that ran alongside the road. She was flung from the saddle and thrown into the gully beside poor Betty.

She struggled to her knees, in time to see the car disappearing around the bend at the top of the hill. Had the vehicle been deliberately driven at her? Was this another attempt to stop her investigating? It had been the shape of a woman in the driver's seat and for a moment she'd thought it looked like Sylvia. The girl had known where she was headed – Flora had mentioned it when she'd called at Mulberry Crescent. Did Sylvia Russell also want her dead? Then common sense reasserted itself. That had to be a nonsense. And, as far as she knew, Sylvia had no driving licence and, if she did, where would she have found a car?

Holding on to clumps of long grass that grew at the side of the ditch, she stumbled to her feet and tried to heave Betty upright and drag her back onto the road. But the bicycle's front wheel was stuck in thick mud and had been badly bent. She tugged on the handlebars, the saddle, even the basket, but without success. She couldn't leave the bike here to be stolen or suffer worse damage – Betty was her lifeline. But her attempts to dislodge the machine were feeble and she was making no headway. She was too shaken, too weak, she realised. Her ribs hurt and when she looked down at her torn skirt, she saw her legs were bruised and cut in several places.

She paused for a moment, trying to regain her breath, trying to recover a strength that was lacking, when the thrum of a car engine sounded in her ears. Flora froze. Was this the driver returning to finish her off?

NINETEEN

Flora knew that engine, though, knew it before she even saw the car. The Austin owned a very distinctive sound. In seconds, Jack had pulled in at the side of the road and was flinging open the car door, almost falling out of the vehicle.

'Flora! What happened?'

She peered over the top of the ditch and into the car. The beautiful Helen was absent – he must have left her behind at Overlay House. He was by the side of the ditch now and reaching down to her.

'Take my hand,' he said, 'and we'll have you out in seconds.'

'I can't,' she said. 'I've got to get Betty onto the road.' To her annoyance, her voice shook.

'I can see that, but let's get you out first. Come on, take my hand.'

Reluctantly, she did as he said and, with his help, climbed up the steep bank and onto the roadway. Jack kept her hand in his, holding her at arm's length and fixing her with a stern gaze.

'What the hell!' He looked her up and down.

'I was run off the road – again. Just my luck,' she said, trying to sound unconcerned, but not succeeding. It had happened to her last autumn as well, but nowhere near as dangerously.

'Your legs, your hands. And why are you clutching yourself like that?'

'My ribs hurt,' she admitted.

'I need to get you to a doctor. Then we'll report it to the police. They've a road hog to find.'

'Don't do that!' She put what strength she still had into the command. 'I don't want the police involved and I don't want a doctor. All I need is to sit down. But Betty...'

'I'm taking you home and we'll telephone Michael from there. He can pick Betty up in his van, and maybe put her to rights.' Jack peered into the ditch. 'She looks as if she'll need it.'

Flora couldn't argue. She felt near to collapse, and allowed herself to be eased into the passenger seat and driven back to her cottage. Much to her chagrin, Jack took charge, finding her front door key, telephoning Michael, dabbing her cuts with disinfectant and then making a large pot of strong tea.

After two cups of the heavily sweetened liquid, Flora recovered her spirits a little – enough to be in no mood for Jack's questioning. When he asked what she'd been doing on Fern Hill, her response was abrupt.

'Cycling,' she said.

'Out for the exercise?'

'Something like that.'

For a moment at Pelham Lodge, she'd wanted him with her, but it had been fleeting. Now she'd no wish to disclose what she'd been doing. She was on her own in this investigation, and that was the way it was staying.

She took a last sip of tea and struggled to her feet. 'I'm late. I should have opened the shop an hour ago. I must go.'

Jack pushed back his cuff and looked at his watch. 'It is late, but you're never going back to the shop, surely?'

'I have a business to run, remember,' she said tautly, stopping herself from saying *unlike Miss Milsom*.

She wondered what the woman was doing at Overlay House. Had she ventured into the village yet and, if so, what was she making of Abbeymead? She'd need to brace herself for a very different life to the one she'd known in New York. The house she'd have to live in was hardly comfortable – it was a happy thought.

Flora shrugged herself back into her coat while Jack watched, a deep frown on his face.

'Thank you for your help,' she said with a formality intended to dismiss him.

'At least let me give you a lift back to the shop.' She was about to refuse, when he added coaxingly, 'Come on, Flora. You can barely walk. And I want to talk to you.'

She didn't want to talk. She would much rather forget Jack Carrington and his complicated love life, but neither did she want to seem churlish, to seem to care too much.

He was going to tell her of his plans for the future, she was certain, and she didn't want to know them. But, on second thoughts, it was probably better to get it over with. She could go her own way then and forget she'd ever had a 'business partner'.

He parked immediately outside the All's Well and went to help her out of the car, but somehow she managed to crawl from the front seat and stand upright. Her legs felt wooden, her cuts stung and her ribs hurt badly. She was being stupid, but pride was involved and she wouldn't let him see how badly shaken she was.

He followed her into the shop, taking off his hat and standing awkwardly by the display table.

'Well? You wanted to talk to me?' Her tone was uncompromising.

'Just to get things straight.' He started to feed the fedora through his hands.

'Yes?'

'I was on my way back from Brighton when I saw you,' he began. 'Brighton station, to be precise. I gave Helen a lift there.'

'Yes?'

'She was catching a train to Bournemouth this morning. Her grandmother is in an old people's home there and she needs to visit.'

'Naturally. And when is she coming back?' Flora didn't want to know, but the remark helped to mask the anger she still felt.

He propped himself against the table. 'She's not.'

Flora took a deep breath. 'She's not coming back to Abbeymead?' she asked, unsure if she'd heard rightly. Then she realised. 'So you're leaving?'

He shook his head. 'I'm staying right here.'

There was a moment's silence before she said, 'You didn't make it up with her?'

'What makes you think I would? There was nothing to make up. I knew that the minute I saw her.'

'But *she* didn't know?' Flora ventured, wishing she didn't feel so glad.

He gave a crooked smile. 'Let's say it took her a few days to realise that life has moved on and me with it.'

Flora had a hundred questions buzzing through her brain, but she let them go. Time enough to find out how he really felt.

'Do you fancy a sandwich?' she asked prosaically. 'I've drunk two cups of tea but no lunch.'

'I've not eaten either. Shall I nip over to the Nook?'

'Good idea.' For the first time in several days, her smile felt as though it was real.

He returned within minutes and, pulling out the stool that Flora kept beneath the table, settled himself down to eat. With few customers at that time of day, they munched their way through a plate of cheese and pickle sandwiches without interruption.

'Where *had* you been?' Jack asked, wiping the last of the crumbs from his hands.

They were partners again. She would tell him.

'I went to Ted Russell's house first. You won't know, but poor Ted has been taken to hospital. Sylvia was waiting for the ambulance to arrive when I got there. The doctor suspects he's had a heart attack.'

Jack gave a subdued tut. 'The trouble over Polly, I imagine?'

'That, certainly, but there's something else. The Russells have suffered a break-in. You won't have heard that either.'

He shook his head. 'News doesn't travel that fast to Overlay. A burglary? What was stolen?'

'Nothing, but the entire house was wrecked. Everything thrown everywhere.'

His eyebrows rose and she said, 'I know – someone was looking for something.'

'Frank Foster,' he said immediately.

'I think so, too. He's been searching – at Rose Court and now Ted's house. But for what?'

'I might be able to enlighten you there – at least a little.' He shifted on the stool. It wasn't the most comfortable seat, Flora acknowledged. 'You know I never bother with a newspaper? Well, Helen brought one with her and guess what I found, right in the middle?'

'An advert for shampoo,' she said acidly.

Jack ignored the remark. 'A photograph of several men, taken a few years ago. They're currently awaiting trial for money laundering, and who do you think was in the background of the picture?'

'Frank!'

'Frank, indeed. He may own a West End club but he mixes with strange company.'

'It's probably *because* he owns a West End club. So what could he be looking for?'

'That's a mystery still. It has to be something that Polly had in her possession, and I would guess it's something that links Foster to these men.'

'Would it be a reason for him to kill her, though?'

'Who knows? To answer that, we'd need to discover what he's hunting for.'

She unlocked the till, thinking over what Jack had said. 'The photograph is an interesting find, but perhaps we shouldn't get too fixated on Foster. His obsession with Polly, the break-ins, his contact with criminals – none of it need point to murder. There are others who could have killed her just as easily.'

'You haven't given up on Evelyn Barnes?'

'She was in Brighton that Monday. And where was Harry? He could have driven Evelyn into town that morning, arranged to meet Polly on the pier while his wife was at the hairdresser's.'

'Why would he kill Polly? I can't see he'd have a reason,' Jack objected.

'He could have. What if he'd told Polly she had to get out of the flat?'

'She was getting out of the flat. Moving back to Abbeymead to escape Frank Foster.'

'But once Frank faded from view, and he would eventually, she'd want to go back to Brighton. What if Harry told her that she couldn't? Even, that he couldn't see her any more, couldn't pay for her modelling as he'd promised or his wife would throw him out? Polly's dream was to be a model. It burnt so brightly in her, Jack, and she'd see her chance fading from sight. What if she clung to Harry, threatened that she'd tell the world what they'd been up to?'

'The world already knows.'

'They're guessing. Polly could threaten to spread the word wherever she went, and she'd be believed. If it was widely known that Harry Barnes had kept a permanent mistress on his wife's money, Evelyn wouldn't hesitate. Harry would be out of the door at Pelham Lodge in an instant. It could have been high stakes for him, as high as murder.'

'OK, I'll allow you Harry.'

'Allow me Raymond Parsons, too. There was something going on between those two and they fell out spectacularly. We witnessed it for ourselves.'

He sat looking at her for a moment, then reached out and touched her arm. 'I've said this before, and I still mean it – more than ever. You have to be careful. *We* have to be careful. Any one of these people could be dangerous. An hour ago, you ended up in a ditch, badly hurt. You're still badly hurt. You say you were run off the road, but what if it wasn't a case of dangerous driving but someone deliberately driving at you? The same someone who pushed you off the pier.'

The same thought had been in Flora's mind since the accident, but gradually she'd come to dismiss it. 'Now whose imagination is going crazy?' she asked lightly.

He spread his hands. 'Have it as you will, but I'd lay a bet with you that if I'd been a few minutes earlier, that's what I'd have seen. Did you know the car? Did you see the driver?'

'It happened too fast. Everything was a blur, although... I did catch sight of a woman driving,' she admitted.

'A woman?' He seemed taken aback.

'Does that change your mind? A woman would never deliberately drive at anyone? You could be very wrong. But why don't we stop the guesswork and find this person – man or woman? A person who feels the need to murder. Someone who's living right here amongst us.'

TWENTY

The following day, Flora closed the door of the All's Well at twelve o'clock, and walked outside to find Jack parked a little way up the main street.

'We'll have to miss lunch,' she warned, climbing cautiously into the passenger seat. A good part of her body still hurt, but she was determined to ignore the discomfort. Jack seemed to take the hint, careful not to ask how she was feeling.

'The golf club is sure to have a bar. They may even do a ham sandwich,' he said teasingly.

He was looking younger today, she noticed, the furrows on his face less deep and the ever-changeful grey eyes animated. It was as though for a long time he'd shouldered a burden he hadn't realised he'd been carrying.

'I'm not certain the bar serves food.' She thought about it for a while. 'In fact, I'm not certain they allow non-members into the club at all. Guests probably have to be invited.'

'I'll get ready to be thrown out then.'

'If we walk in confidently enough, I'm sure we won't be challenged. We'll go straight to the bar, find Evelyn, and pretend we're her guests.'

'If she's in the bar.' Jack sounded gloomy. 'More than likely, she'll be miles away in some bunker or other.'

'You obviously know a lot about golf.'

'About as much as you,' he retorted.

Leaving him to park the car, Flora began to make her way to the club entrance, but just before the flight of steps up to the glass doors, she stopped at a car parked awkwardly across two bays. Looking more closely, she saw it had a deep dent on one of the wheel arches and scratched paintwork along the driver's door.

'Jack,' she called to him. 'See what I've found.'

'A car,' he said, walking towards her, 'and in a car park. Something to think about.'

'I'm serious! It's a car with a large dent and bad scratch marks down one side.'

He bent down to get a better view. 'You think this might be—'

'It has to be. It was a member of the golf club who nearly killed me!'

'It could be coincidence. There are accidents all the time.'

She shook her head. 'The car was dark green and so is this. That would be too much of a coincidence.'

Jack pushed back a strand of hair from his forehead and grimaced. 'Even if it is, we can't discover the owner. We'd have to ask whoever's in charge of this place for their list of registrations and, if we do that, we'll be shown up as intruders. It looks like we're scuppered.'

'We'll just have to keep our eyes open.'

The bar was easy to find, a large space that opened out to the right of the entrance, and though a quick scan told Flora that Evelyn wasn't there, Raymond Parsons was. He was serving drinks and Flora went straight over to him.

'Hello, Raymond.' She saw a scared expression pass across his face. Now why was that? 'I'm looking for Mrs Barnes. Do you know if she's at the club today?'

If anything, Raymond's expression became more furtive. 'I don't think so—' he started to say, when a club member drinking his beer close by intervened.

'Evelyn's definitely here. Saw her go off an hour ago. She's with that gaggle of women.'

'On the course?'

'Where else?' the man asked, giving Flora a pitying look.

She thanked him, though she'd rather not have, and turned to bid Raymond goodbye, but he'd disappeared from sight.

Jack caught up with her at the players' entrance and before he could speak, she broke the bad news. 'You're right about the bunker. We have some walking to do – let's go now, before we're spotted.'

Ramming his hat on his head, Jack followed her. 'It would make sense to start at the end of the course and work towards the beginning.'

Flora, two steps ahead, nodded agreement. 'A man at the bar said Evelyn had been out on the course for an hour.'

'How long does it take to get round one of these things?' he demanded.

'I've no idea. I've never picked up a golf club in my life.'

'One of the few sensible things I know about you, Flora Steele. OK, sleuth, let's get walking.'

Luckily, the weather for early February was clement. A little grey, a little depressing, but the rain had held off and the strong winds that had recently swept the Sussex coast seemed to have abated. Flora was happy to be out in the fresh air and, she admitted to herself, happy to have Jack as a companion again.

'It makes for an agreeable walk,' she said, 'as long as you don't have clubs to carry.'

A svelte expanse of green stretched as far as she could see, broken only by several tight clumps of trees and the odd patch of yellowish sand. In the distance, she spied a small lake.

'Or if you don't mind getting hit on the head by a golf ball,' Jack muttered. 'Oh, no!' He stopped walking.

'What's the matter?'

'That's Alan Ridley coming towards us. He'll want to talk and he'll want to know why I'm here.'

'Be creative,' she advised. 'Otherwise known as lying.'

'I didn't know you were a member, Jack,' Ridley said, striding up to them. 'And Miss... Steele, isn't it? You here as his guest? Good idea. You might want to sign up, too. It's a great game. But you're not playing today?' he finished in a puzzled voice, his eyes roving over them, looking, it seemed, for where they might be hiding their clubs.

If they weren't playing, why were they here? Flora tried to think fast in case Jack's imagination failed him. He'd given the inspector a list of their suspects, and the Barnes name would be on it. Confessing they were here to see Evelyn would alert Ridley to the fact they were continuing an investigation he'd warned them against.

'I'm thinking of joining,' Jack said quickly. Flora gave him a silent pat on the back. 'It seemed sensible to have a look around and Flora was keen to see the club, too.'

'And you, Inspector,' she joined in, 'are you here on business?' She looked pointedly at his golf trolley, hoping to unnerve him. 'Have you found a body in the sand pit?'

Ridley gave a forced laugh. 'Nothing like that. Playing truant, I'm afraid. It's the weekend, after all. Sets me up for the week to come.'

'Does your week include the Polly Dakers enquiry?'

Jack gave her a sharp nudge, but she was unrepentant.

'I looked at what you gave me, Jack,' the inspector said, 'but nothing doing. Only one name on your list was of any interest and I can't bag him. He belongs to the London police. As for Miss Dakers, I'm sorry for the poor young woman, but her death was a tragic accident, pure and simple. And your little contretemps,' he beamed down at Flora, 'take my advice and avoid the pier in future. It needs renovating – badly – but local councils,' he shook his head, 'always dragging their feet.'

Alan Ridley's partner was getting impatient and had begun to pace up and down, occasionally stamping his feet as though to keep warm, and swinging his club backwards and forwards.

'Better go,' the inspector said, becoming aware of his friend's growing irritation. 'But it would be great if you joined the Lexington. We could have a game, Jack – once you're up to speed.'

'How long is that going to take?' Flora asked crossly, as they said goodbye and walked on.

'Getting up to speed or joining the club? Both might take a very long time.'

'Good. You mustn't join any club that man's a member of. Did you hear what he said? My little contretemps!'

'Ignore it. More to the point, will you recognise the Barnes woman when you see her?'

'I've never actually met her,' Flora admitted, 'but I've seen her in the village a few times and, by the look of it, there aren't that many women who play.'

'I wonder why that is.' Jack's face spread into a wide grin.

It was when they had walked a third of the way back along the course that they came across their first and only group of women.

'That's her,' Flora said excitedly.

'And she's wielding a club, which is awkward. We can't barge in.'

'We can ask to talk to her when she's finished the game.'

'That's likely to be a long time.'

'You're thinking of lunch,' she accused.

'Naturally, I'm thinking of lunch. We should have called in at the Nook before we set off.'

'But we didn't, so forget food for a moment and think Evelyn,' Flora said, as they walked up to the group of women, who were preparing to move on to the next hole.

'Mrs Barnes?'

The sturdy figure who had played the last shot turned round quickly. She had capable hands and a strong face.

'Yes?' The strong face was not looking pleased at the interruption.

'I'm Flora Steele.'

'Yes, I know. The bookshop in the village.'

'That's right. And this is Jack Carrington – he's a writer.'

The information did not appear to interest Evelyn greatly.

'We wondered if we might talk to you when you've finished your game.'

'What on earth for?'

'It's a private matter. About Polly Dakers.'

The words had a volcanic effect. 'I've nothing whatever to say,' Evelyn spat out, and turned her back on them.

'We want to help you,' Flora pleaded.

The woman ignored her.

'The thing is,' she went on, now improvising wildly, 'Mr Carrington has a friend on the local newspaper – he used to be a journalist, Mr Carrington, that is – and he's been told the paper will be doing a feature on Polly. Up and coming model, dead before her time, that sort of thing. A kind of commemoration. They intend to publish details... that you might not like. When we heard what they planned, we thought it terribly unfair – to you. If they had the true story, Jack could speak to his friend and make sure the facts were right.'

Jack had taken off his fedora and was fanning his face. In embarrassment, Flora presumed.

Evelyn's eyes narrowed. Flora's words must have appeared preposterous and yet if something detrimental was about to be splashed across a local newspaper, hadn't she better talk with these wretched people? Flora could see the wheels turning, the calculations whirring.

'Are we playing, Evie, or settling down for a tea party?' one of the group asked plaintively.

'I'll see you later,' Evelyn said. It was almost a hiss. 'In the car park.'

* * *

It was another hour before she appeared, by which time Jack had threatened several times to go in search of sandwiches, not to mention personally strangling Flora if she dared involve him any further in the lies she was about to tell.

'Well, what do you have to say?' Evelyn began, her face hard with suspicion.

Flora cleared her throat and breathed deeply. 'Apparently, the local journalist – he writes features – heard on the grapevine a while back that your husband intended to file for divorce... or he did, until Miss Dakers' death. The newspaper understood that Mr Barnes wished to remarry.'

'What!'

'It makes a good story, particularly now the girl Mr Barnes intended to make his wife has died in tragic circumstances. I said to Jack, though, that I thought it sounded unlikely.'

'Unlikely! Marry that little tart! She wouldn't have a hope in hell – if she wasn't already dead.'

'So your marriage isn't under threat?'

'My marriage is finished.'

Stunned at the bald announcement, Flora stammered, 'The rumour of a divorce wasn't false then? The paper wouldn't be wrong in publishing their story?'

'If they publish, I'll take them to court.'

'But—'

'Look, little girl, there'll be a divorce, sure, but there's a crucial difference. I'm the one doing the divorcing. Harry is a fool and always has been.' Evelyn gave a stifled snort. 'He believes that squiring young girls makes *him* look young. I've let him have his playtime, but when it comes to spending my money on renting an expensive flat for that little trollop... let's see how much the girls like him when he's flat broke.'

'Did you tell Polly that yourself? She mentioned your visit when the journalist called on her and he's likely to include it in his article.'

'Told her? I'll say I did. Gave it to her full in the face. It's why she jumped, isn't it? Couldn't stand to think she'd been landed with Harry, and not a penny between them.'

'You think Polly committed suicide?'

'Evident, isn't it? All her little plans smashed to pieces. My God, did she really think Harry would divorce me and marry her? He might be a fool, but he knows where his bread is buttered. Or knew. He'll have to find someone else to buy the butter now.'

'And Polly?'

'Good riddance,' she said harshly. 'She was a leech. I was in Brighton that very morning, you know! The morning she died. At the hairdresser's, then the beauty parlour, then on to Hanningtons for a new outfit. And all the time poor little Polly was floating around Palace Pier.'

If that were true, it ruled Evelyn Barnes out as a suspect, no matter how monstrous she was.

'Who told you about the Rose Court flat, Mrs Barnes?' The question had little to do with the story Flora had spun, but it was a question she wanted answered.

Evelyn seemed more relaxed, as though the ten-minute harangue at people she didn't know had cleansed her ill temper.

'The estate agent,' she said. 'Hard to believe, isn't it? He rang me to enquire whether I'd be renewing the lease! Harry had not only given him his real name but his home telephone number. Like I said, the man's a fool.'

She hiked the bag of clubs on to one shoulder. 'Make sure your journalist acquaintance puts the record right,' she said to Jack. '*I've* thrown my husband out. *He's* the one on the scrap heap.'

'A charming lady,' Jack remarked, 'and also… a dangerous one.'

Evelyn Barnes had climbed in to the badly dented car they'd spotted earlier.

'She was the one,' Flora said, wonderingly. 'She must have been driving back to Pelham Lodge at the time.'

'And decided to pulverise you on the way. Damn, I must have dropped my hat.'

'It was probably when you were fanning yourself.'

'To cover my blushes. I've never heard such a ridiculous story.'

Flora pulled a face. 'It worked, though, didn't it? She believed it.'

'I'm not sure she did. She's too sharp for that, but she strikes me as the kind of woman who has to tie everything up very tightly and trample underfoot any likely weakness.' He grinned at her. 'When we get back to the village, remind me to contact my mythical journalist friend and warn him not to publish! But before I do, I've a fedora to rescue. It's too precious to lose.'

'Not back to the golf course,' she moaned. Her shoes, bought on impulse during her and Violet's last visit to Hove, were barely worn but pinching badly.

'Afraid so.'

TWENTY-ONE

They found Jack's fedora at the fourteenth hole, looking a trifle sad. A golfer must have caught it with the wheels of his caddy and squashed the hat deep into the soft turf, so that when Jack fitted it gingerly back onto his head, the felt brim, now damp and muddy, drooped to one side.

'It's different,' Flora observed, looking up at him. 'More Sussex now than Mexico.'

'Mexico has nothing to do with the fedora. It got its name from a French play way back.'

'How do you know these things?'

'An innate brilliance. I'm surprised you haven't noticed. It's my innate hunger that's uppermost at the moment. Let's get back to the village and eat.'

Making for the entrance, they had once more to pass by the bar. 'Raymond's back,' Flora said, peering through the open doorway, 'and I need to speak to him. Just a few minutes,' she pleaded, hearing Jack's sigh.

'If you really must. But five maximum.'

Flora wasn't to get even five minutes. She was making her way to the counter when Harry Barnes suddenly materialised feet away, stopping her in her tracks.

'Have you seen her?' His face had contorted into a series of cracks and crevices, and he sounded frantic. 'Someone told me you were talking to her.'

'Your wife?' Flora made a guess.

'Yes, yes. Of course, my wife. Who else?'

'Mrs Barnes left a while ago. I imagine she'll be home by now,' she said quietly, hoping to lower the temperature.

It had the opposite effect. 'Home! What home?' His jowls shook, his mouth all but disappearing in a mound of surplus flesh.

It seemed that Evelyn had spoken nothing more than the truth when she'd said that she had thrown her husband out.

'I'm sorry you're upset, Mr Barnes, but I don't think I can help.'

There was compassion in her voice. He had behaved badly, behaved stupidly, but he looked so clumsy and distraught, so desperately unattractive, that she felt real sadness for him.

'No one can help me.' He lowered his eyes, staring down at his substantial stomach. Then jerking his head upwards, he said, 'Polly did it, you know.'

'Did what?' Was he saying that he, too, believed the girl had jumped to her death?

'Sent this.' He fumbled in the inside pocket of his jacket and brought out a single sheet of paper. 'This letter. Warning me that if I didn't pay up, she'd tell Evie.'

'Blackmail?' Flora was aghast and shot a glance at Jack, who'd walked up to them and was standing by her shoulder. 'You think Polly was blackmailing you?'

'It had to be her. She was always wanting more money. Grasping little bitch! She had no interest in me, not really. All she ever wanted was money.'

His figure crumpled, the letter dangling from his hand. 'I spent pounds on her, but it was never enough. Clothes, jewels, that bloody flat. Then this came.' He waved the letter at them again. 'Demanding money, more than I had. More than I could ever get. I tried to raise some of it, but I couldn't – not in time. Not before she wrote to Evie. Or maybe she telephoned. It was all lies, whatever story she told.'

'Do you have any proof that Polly did that?'

'Well, no, but she must have, otherwise Evie wouldn't have known about the flat. And I wouldn't be a fifty-year-old man without a home and sleeping on a friend's sofa.'

Flora wondered if she should mention the estate agent who had rung Evelyn Barnes, but then decided it might add fuel to a fire that was burning bright. Instead, she set out to exonerate Polly. 'Do you remember when the blackmail letter arrived?'

'I should do. It was the day after that wake Pol dragged me to. What does it matter when it arrived?' he asked angrily.

'Because, in that case, your wife already knew where Polly was living before you received the threatening letter. Sylvia Russell told us that Mrs Barnes spoke to Polly at the Rose Court flat the week before she died – that was days before the letter was sent. Polly didn't write to your wife or telephone her, or if she did, it was old news to Mrs Barnes.'

Harry looked as though his brain might explode from the intense effort he was making to understand.

'You're saying it's important this letter came when it did – two days before Polly died?'

'Even more importantly, a good week after your wife visited Polly in Brighton. Whoever sent that letter, it wasn't Polly. There would be little point in trying to blackmail you over something that was already out in the open.'

'If it wasn't Polly, then who was it?' he demanded, an angry red flush suffusing his face. 'I'll have them. I'll make them pay. They've ruined my life. Ruined, do you hear?'

'We hear, Mr Barnes,' Jack said quietly, 'and so, I imagine, does the entire bar. No matter how much you bellow, it won't alter things.'

The man's body seemed to lose any remaining strength, arching almost double. 'I came here to ask Evie to reconsider,' he said, his voice barely above a whisper.

'Why not drive to Pelham Lodge and talk to her?' Flora suggested. By now, her feet were on fire and she was eager to leave.

'You think she'll talk to me?'

'You can only try.'

Privately, she thought it a hopeless task – Evelyn's face had been rigid with fury. But what else was there to say? Pocketing the unhappy letter, Harry Barnes gave them a nod and turned towards the entrance.

'Mr Barnes,' Flora called after him on impulse, 'do you remember meeting us in Abbeymead one evening? It was the week before last, a Thursday, I think.' That was the day the journalist had interviewed her.

Harry looked flustered. 'I don't know. Yes, yes, I remember now. On Greenway Lane.'

'That's right. Had something happened that day, to take you miles from home?'

The man's face turned from a florid red to sickly white. 'It was when she told me.'

'Your wife? She told you she knew about the flat at Rose Court?'

'Told me to get out,' he said brokenly.

'And that's why you were walking along the lane in the dark that evening?'

'I didn't know what I was doing.' He paused, looking hopelessly over Flora's head. 'I still don't.'

He turned again and shambled towards the club entrance.

'We should wish him luck,' Jack remarked. 'He's going to need it.'

It had been an upsetting encounter and Flora stood for a while, thinking it over.

'Harry evidently wasn't following me that evening. It was silly of me to panic. He might still have done it, though. Pushed Polly. If he thought she was responsible for that letter. It arrived a couple of days before she died. By the Monday morning, he could have worked himself into a tempest, you can see how volatile he is. "Grasping little bitch" is what he called her. Evelyn spent the day in Brighton, too. What's to say he didn't drive her there, or didn't follow in his own car, and arrange to meet Polly on the pier?'

'You've suggested that before.'

'I was imagining a motive then, speculating that Harry might grow desperate to break with Polly, but that letter, the blackmail demand, gives him a far more powerful motive. He obviously didn't know his wife had visited Rose Court, didn't know the blackmail demand was pointless and that what he feared had actually already happened. Polly could have told him, but maybe he didn't give her the chance.'

She stood motionless, thinking of the possibilities their encounter with both Evelyn and Harry had opened up.

'Food, Flora,' Jack reminded her.

'One moment, and we'll go... oh, Raymond has disappeared again. Whatever's the matter with that boy?'

She went over to the bar and a harassed older man popped up from below the counter. His badge announced that he was the chief steward.

'What can I get you?' he asked.

'Nothing, thank you. I was hoping to have a quick word with Raymond.'

'You're not the only one, miss.'

'He was here a few minutes ago.'

'But now he's not, and nowhere else in the club. Disappeared without a word. I'll have something to say to that young man when I see him next.'

Disappointed, she walked back to Jack. 'We'd better go. This time, Raymond has disappeared completely.'

Walking down the steps to the car park, she was aware her mind fizzed with why that might be.

* * *

Jack drove as fast as the Austin could manage to the Cross Keys and was just in time to order a ploughman's lunch for them both.

'No orders after two o'clock – we've made it by the skin of our teeth,' he said, bringing their glasses to the table.

'Thank goodness. I don't think I could have walked another yard in these shoes.'

Jack looked down, seeming to notice her treasured footwear for the first time.

'Why on earth would you wear those to tramp across a golf club?'

'Perhaps because I'd no idea I would be tramping. Or not as far,' she added acidly. 'Most people manage to keep hold of their hats.'

'The shoes are very nice.' There was a conciliatory look on his face.

Flora stretched out her feet and gazed at the black and red court shoes. Block heels, delicate ankle straps. Despite the pain, she still loved them.

'They're nice,' she agreed, 'but they hurt. And don't ask me why I bought them if they weren't brilliantly comfortable. If all you'd had for years was a single pair of lace-ups, you'd have bought them, too.'

'All I had for years were army boots.'

'At least you had new ones when they wore out. Civilians didn't do as well. Twenty-four coupons at the end of the war to cover dresses, coats, stockings, everything, and a pair of shoes bagged five of them! Aunt Violet always made sure I had decent shoes for school, but it meant that for years she had to patch up her only pair. I remember, once, she mended them with Elastoplast.' Flora paused. 'Now I feel guilty complaining of painful feet!'

'Drink your lemonade. It will make you feel better.' Jack took a long, appreciative sip from his glass. 'I didn't think beer could taste this good.' Stretching his legs beneath the table, he lay back against the wooden settle.

'I thought you disliked pubs, but you don't seem that uncomfortable,' she remarked.

'It's strange but I'm not. I avoided pubs for a long time,

restaurants and shops, too. Any place where I'd have to meet people and talk to them. But these days I'm doing better – thanks to you.'

'You are,' she agreed. She leaned forward. 'You realise, I can't call you a recluse any longer? And I loved that word. I can still call you Jolyon, though. It's almost as much fun!'

'Don't!' he threatened, as two huge bread rolls arrived, along with chunks of cheese and a pot of pickle.

They said goodbye at the All's Well door. Jack had offered to drive her home to the cottage, but she made an excuse that there were several jobs she needed to finish in the shop to be ready for Monday. As soon as the Austin disappeared from sight, she relocked the bookshop door and walked across the road to the Nook. It was almost dark but Kate wouldn't yet have closed.

From the moment Raymond had disappeared from the golf club bar, Flora had thought he might surface at the café. The boy couldn't afford to abandon all his work. If he was there, it would be best that she was the one to talk to him. Jack wasn't insensitive, but she had the feeling that Raymond would say more if she met him alone.

As she went to cross the road, she sensed a movement close by and hesitated for an instant, stepping back onto the pavement. Was it a cyclist bearing down on her? Several of the locals were known for riding after dark without lights and Flora had had enough of ending in ditches, or in this case, a gutter. But the road, when she looked, was empty both ways. With the moon riding high, shadows could play tricks.

Her hunch had been right about finding Raymond at the Nook. There was no sign of Kate, but he was clearing tables as she walked through the door.

'Mrs Mitchell's just left,' he said, looking up as the café bell rang. 'You should catch her at home.'

'But you're still here.'

'Just finishing. I called in to check on my hours and she was looking pretty tired, so I offered to lock up.'

'That was kind of you. I didn't actually come to see Mrs Mitchell—'

'If you're here for food, you're too late, I'm afraid, Miss Steele. You should have stayed at the golf club.'

'So should you, apparently. The chief steward was most put out by your disappearing act.'

'I had to go,' he mumbled, piling an empty tray high with crockery and carrying it to the counter.

'Why was that, Raymond?'

He didn't answer, but took a miniature brush and pan and began to clear crumbs from the gingham tablecloths.

'Would it be because of Harry Barnes? When he walked in, you walked out?' It was a guess, but she saw immediately that she'd guessed right.

'I don't like the bloke,' he muttered.

'Is there any particular reason that you don't?' When he didn't answer, she asked gently, 'Because of Polly?'

He nodded.

'If he was the reason you left the club today, it must have been difficult for you to work at the Lexington with the Barnes family being members there. I imagine that's why you were so interested in the Priory reopening. But walking out today has put your job at risk. You must dislike Mr Barnes a great deal to do that.'

He shifted awkwardly from side to side, but finally broke his silence. 'I hated that Polly had anything to do with him. The flat he gave her and the clothes and the jewellery.'

'You were in love with her.' It wasn't a question but a simple statement of fact.

'Pol loved me, too,' he said a trifle belligerently.

'What about Sylvia? I thought she was your girlfriend. She seemed to think she was, too.'

He looked past Flora at the café wall. 'She was, kind of. I knew her from school and we started going to the cinema together. I'd pick her up from work in Shoreham and we'd take the train to

Lewes. Have tea and a bun in the Odeon café and then see the film. It was never more than that. Not for me, at least.'

'But for her?'

'Mebbe. But that wasn't my fault, was it? I tried to tell her about Polly, but she wouldn't listen. So I didn't bother any more.'

'You and Polly planned to go away together?' she hazarded, the mists clearing for an instant.

He pounced on her. 'How d'you know that?'

'I found airline coupons when Mr Carrington and I collected Polly's bags from the flat. It was clear she was leaving the country for good – the tickets were for a single journey – and as there were two of them, she must have been planning to travel with someone. Someone she wasn't talking about.'

'I'd have shouted it from the roof – we've been together since last October – but she said we had to keep it under wraps or all her plans would fall to bits.'

'You've been together since her farewell party at the Priory?'

He smiled reminiscently and the years fell away from his young face. 'That was a great party. I knew Polly before, of course. I was a waiter at the hotel and she was the receptionist. She was so beautiful and bright, I thought she was way above me. But then we danced at the party and spent the evening together. We had fun. It was like we were...'

'Kindred spirits,' Flora suggested.

'That's right,' he said gratefully.

'Such a shame you had to keep things a secret.'

'It was Polly that insisted. Because of him. He was going to set her up, get her going on the modelling and she didn't want him to know she had a boyfriend. As if that old... as if he could think he'd ever be her sweetheart.'

'I imagine that's what he did think. He spent a lot of money on Polly.'

'All for stuff she didn't need or want. What she wanted was photographs. A portfolio from a top photographer. But that didn't happen.'

'Why not, do you think?'

'I dunno. Polly reckoned it was because Barnes wanted to keep her tethered here. That's why he rented the flat in Brighton, so he could visit her when his wife wasn't looking. If she'd ever got the portfolio done, she'd be taken on by an agency. She was pretty sure of it, and I thought so, too. Then she'd be travelling and Barnes wouldn't see her.'

'But neither would you. If she had become a model, where would you have fitted in?' She wondered if Raymond had really thought this through.

'We talked about it a lot. I wasn't going to stop her making a success of her life. I told her I'd travel with her, go where she went and get work when I could. There's always waiting jobs to be had. Then when she'd made enough money, we'd buy a little place together. Maybe open a café.'

'You were thinking ahead.' It seemed that Raymond had been a good deal more sensible than Flora suspected. 'And the tickets to Toronto? Were they thinking ahead, too?'

'We bought them after Pol had given up on him. "He won't come up with the photos, Ray," she told me, "so we need to go. Find somewhere we can start over where no one knows us."'

'The quarrel you had with her at the wake – was that because you didn't want to go to Canada and start over?'

He gave a violent shake of his head. 'Of course I did. I'd have followed her to the ends of the world.'

'What was the quarrel about then?' she nudged gently.

Raymond flashed her a sullen look and clamped his mouth tight, but Flora was determined to get to the bottom of his involvement.

'When you walked out of the club today,' she said, 'it wasn't just because you'd seen Harry Barnes, was it? You must have seen him fairly frequently in the months you've worked there, so what had changed?'

He looked away, refusing to meet Flora's eyes. 'It was the letter,' he said at last. 'Polly had saved a bit from what Barnes gave her and I had some money from the work I'd been doing. It was just about enough to buy the tickets. But I knew we'd need money when we got to Toronto and by then we were both cleaned out.'

'That's when the two of you decided on blackmail.' It was an ugly word, but he needed to face the truth of what he'd done. 'You sent a letter trying to blackmail Harry Barnes into paying out more money.'

He hung his head low. 'It was me, not Pol. She didn't want to do it. She wanted to ask Barnes for the money, try persuading him to give her more. I knew that wouldn't work. He'd want to know what it was for and she couldn't tell him, unless she spilled the beans about us going away.'

'You went ahead anyway?'

'I was desperate, Miss Steele,' he pleaded. 'We'd spent every penny of our savings on those tickets and couldn't use them unless we had money to keep us when we got to Canada – just until we found jobs. Polly drove me mad, umming and ahhing. She just wouldn't accept that she'd never get enough money out of Harry Barnes to escape. In the end, I sent the letter,' he finished bleakly.

'I'm guessing that Polly didn't know you had.'

'I told her at the wake, and she went crazy. Said Harry was bound to suspect she was behind it and now she'd never get any money from him. She wouldn't have done anyway, but she just wouldn't see it.'

He gave a subdued sob and Flora saw tears gather in his eyes. 'After that quarrel, she wouldn't speak to me and I never saw her again.' He sank down on a chair and cushioned his head in his hands. 'I reckon I murdered her.'

'You what!'

'I pushed her off that pier – as good as. I said bad things to her. I broke her heart, Miss Steele, and she must have decided she couldn't go on. I'd never harm a tiny piece of Polly, but it's like I put my hand on her back and pushed her to her death.'

Flora walked over to him and took hold of his arm. 'Raymond.' He looked up, tears shining in his eyes. 'You did a truly wicked thing in sending that letter, but Polly didn't jump and she didn't slip. I'm convinced she *was* pushed, but a real push, not an imagined one. If you think of anything that might help find Polly's murderer, please tell me.'

That left the door open, she thought, walking home from the Nook. Raymond had a guilty conscience – certainly about the letter and the ensuing row with Polly, but did he have anything else to feel guilty about and, if so, would he seek her out to confess? The path ahead was still unclear, but Flora was satisfied with the afternoon's work. They were making progress, she was sure.

Digging her hand in her pocket for the door key, she touched the red wool bobble she always carried with her. Was it the vital clue she'd once believed it to be or simply a lost item of clothing its owner hadn't bothered to retrieve? It was a question she hadn't solved – not yet, but she would.

Unlocking the front door, her good mood diminished. The cottage had been unheated for hours and there was a disagreeable chill in the air. With no wish to spend the evening shivering, she ignored the demands of the kitchen, and instead did a round of the house, pulling curtains and lighting the fire before she'd even hung up her coat. Only when the lamps were glowing and the flames licking their way up the chimney, did she give any thought to what she might eat for supper.

TWENTY-TWO

After he left Flora, Jack drove straight back to Overlay House. Walking into the sitting room, he switched on the lights and slumped into an armchair. He needed to think. This afternoon was the first time he'd met Evelyn Barnes, and he wasn't sure what to make of her. On the surface, she appeared the tough business-woman she'd been for years, dismissive, even hostile. Not a woman given to excess emotion. Yet the way she'd spoken of Polly, her clear fury that her money had been used to provide luxury for a girl she considered nothing better than a... suggested a passion that lay deep but rarely showed itself. It could have shown itself the other day. Driving recklessly up Fern Hill, Evelyn Barnes could well have become a killer. Had that been an outburst, triggered by passion, or had the driver been the cold, contained version of the woman, a person who would deliberately drive at another human being?

Flora refused to accept she had been a target, maintaining her plunge into the ditch had been pure accident. She'd been excited rather than worried when they'd found the guilty car at the golf club, intrigued when she discovered it belonged to Evelyn Barnes. Jack wasn't at all sure she was right to be so unconcerned. It was true she'd not exempted Evelyn from the murder of Polly Dakers. He shouldn't either. The hairdresser's appointment was a fact,

Flora had checked it for herself, but it had been early on that Monday morning, leaving the woman ample time to meet Polly on the pier. Evelyn had seemed eager to tell them she'd spent the rest of the morning at the beauty parlour and then gone on to shop, but her alibi remained unchecked and would be difficult to verify – her visit to the department store, in particular.

Others were more likely suspects, he agreed with Flora on that. Frank Foster was first in line. Alice had seen him leave the Cross Keys three days after Polly died, when he was supposed to have returned to London immediately after Mitchell's wake. His continued presence in the village could be explained by his plan to buy the Priory, but then why make a mystery of it? It could equally be explained by his need to be close to Polly.

Where had he gone when he'd left the Cross Keys? He'd been in Brighton the day Flora was attacked, they'd seen him for themselves at Rose Court. But then what? The break-in at Ted Russell's house had taken place nearly a week later, but it had all the hallmarks of Foster's continuing search, so where had he been between their finding him in Brighton and the burglary in Mulberry Crescent? Had he gone back and forth between Sussex and his London club or had he found some kind of hideout locally? There were too many unknowns about the man and it was worrying.

He should get some food, Jack decided. The ploughman's lunch had not been exactly generous and eating might help him think more clearly. On the other hand, he could forget the food and go to his study and work. He wondered if Flora had read the chapters he'd given her. He wasn't sure why it was important to him that she approved, but it was. His confidence had been knocked by the struggle he'd had with the 'bad novel', as he'd begun to think of it. It didn't take much to destroy a writer's confidence and his had always been paper thin. He should just get on with this new book, he told himself, not wait for her judgement, but the investigation, the fear for Flora, the sudden entrance into his life of Helen, had crowded his mind and left little space to be creative.

He'd half risen from his chair, when a sound from outside had him pause. It seemed to come from the front garden, but before he'd had time to process the idea, there was a loud crash, glass spilling onto the tattered cotton rug, and he was hit on the side of the head with something very sharp. His head stinging, he turned towards the garden and peered through the window at the darkness beyond. A gaping hole met his gaze.

He turned back to the rug and, with some difficulty, bent to pick up what looked to be a stone. It had landed feet in front of him. Not a stone, he saw at closer range, but a slice of flint, sharpened to a lethal point. It came to him forcibly that if he hadn't decided to move at that moment, the weapon could easily have severed a vessel in his neck and he could even now be lying on the floor bleeding to death. Instead, it had grazed the side of his head and nicked his ear. It was then he realised that blood was oozing from the wound and dripping drop by drop onto his hand.

Stumbling up the stairs to the bathroom, he washed with soap, then, clenching his teeth, doused himself in disinfectant. His face in the mirror was pale and drawn. One more shock to add to the rest. A shock that someone had been in his front garden, had taken advantage of the open curtains and the circle of lamplight to take deliberate aim at him. Had they hoped to cut an artery?

It was easy to understand why he'd been targeted. He was frequently in Flora's company and she'd been attacked at least once, maybe twice, so why not him? They'd been together the whole of this afternoon. Who might have seen them at the golf club and thought them out of place, speculated on why they were talking to Evelyn, to Harry Barnes, to Raymond Parsons, and decided they were poking their noses into something that didn't concern them and needed to be warned off? Or worse.

Fear aimed a punch at his stomach. Had this person gone to Flora's cottage first? Crept into *her* front garden, watched *her* through the window and, when she was in range, launched a missile? But he had the weapon here, in his hands. It was surely unlikely that another sharpened piece of flint was out there. No, she must be safe, he had to believe it. Her cottage was draughty and she always pulled the curtains once light faded.

He walked slowly back downstairs, ticking off names in his mind's eye. Who could be his attacker? It had to be Frank Foster, didn't it? The man's whereabouts was a mystery and he could easily have been skulking at the Lexington this afternoon. Strength would be needed to launch that flint through the window, and an accurate eye to hit a target. In Jack's experience, that meant a man. A young man.

* * *

Flora's determination to continue the enquiry was undiminished, but the following day was not ideal. The village more or less closed down on a Sunday, the church being the sole source of interest. Jack had mentioned he intended to spend the day in the garden – with Charlie's help he had somehow managed to reassemble the greenhouse – and, before saying goodbye yesterday, had invited her to help him plant the large number of bulbs and seeds donated by the villagers.

There were potatoes from Mr Houseman, the greengrocer, which he'd told Jack to plant in buckets or flower pots and keep in the greenhouse, winter lettuce from Elsie, and numerous flower seeds – salvias and cosmos among them – along with herbs such as mint and parsley. Flora guessed Abbeymead had showered him with gifts in gratitude that, after nearly six years, he was making an attempt at last to control the wilderness he'd allowed to rampage.

She had been tempted by the invitation to Overlay House, but waking to the sound of church bells early this morning, she decided to stay at home. She had the opening chapters of Jack's new book to read, a good programme on the wireless, and a tasty joint of beef in the larder. She would roast it for lunch with potatoes, cauliflower and carrots, dug fresh from the vegetable patch. Keeping her distance from Overlay House was sensible.

Her reaction to Helen Milsom had shocked Flora. She'd been

unprepared for the strength of feeling the woman evoked. Some of her upset had been for Jack – she hated the thought that he could be walking into unhappiness again – but some of it, she had to admit, had been for herself. She'd felt jealousy and that was something she hadn't expected. She wanted Jack as a friend. Wanted him as a partner in the detective work she'd come to enjoy. But the fact that she felt almost too happy in his company, that they talked together, joked and teased as though they'd known each other for years, was a danger signal.

It was absurd to think of Jack Carrington as any kind of threat, but instinct was warning her to hold back or she could be laying herself open to hurt. The kind of hurt she'd suffered at Richard's hands when she'd walked blithely into disillusionment and months of unhappiness.

She'd been a girl then, but now she was a woman and someone who knew better. When Violet was alive, it hadn't seemed to matter that neither of them had a man in their lives. Neither had wanted one, but now her aunt was gone and she'd lost the person she'd loved most dearly, there was a hole, a void, and she was scared that Jack was beginning to fill it. It would be better to stay at home today.

By the time she had peeled the vegetables, washed the kitchen floor, and half listened to the wireless programme, most of the day still stretched ahead. Empty, a little lacking. She opened the larder door and gazed at the beef. She had bought the joint yesterday morning, slipping out of the All's Well for five minutes and asking Mr Preece to deliver after he'd closed. The butcher was relatively new to the village and, unlike his fellow tradesmen, had not watched Flora grow from a girl in pigtails and Clark's sandals to the young woman she was now. It made for a subtly different relationship and, in the past, when Flora's livelihood at the shop had been threatened, she'd had sharp words with him. Now, though, they seemed to have come to an accommodation, neither the earlier prickliness nor the casual affection of Mr Houseman, who'd given the small girl an apple each time she'd passed his shop. Mr

Preece had taken to keeping back anything he thought Flora might like: a few freshly made sausages, pork chops from the local farm, even a chicken last Christmas. Jack had shared that, too, she remembered.

She wondered how his gardening was progressing. Would he even know how to plant seeds? Shutting the larder door, she put on her outdoor shoes. She would call at Overlay for a few minutes only, just to make sure he was on the right road. The beef could wait. She would cook it this evening instead.

The walk from her cottage to Overlay House took less than a quarter of an hour along a relatively straight lane, and from a long way off she spied Charlie Teague's bicycle propped against the front gate. Charlie would know about seeds and which way up to plant bulbs, so perhaps she need not have bothered.

Nevertheless, she walked through the gate and up the front path. There was little point in knocking at the door – there'd be no one to hear. Slipping around the side of the house, she found them both in the greenhouse at the end of a path that bisected the large back garden. Jack was wielding a shovel, filling several buckets with earth from a hessian sack while Charlie, beside him, picked over the seed potatoes.

Jack looked up at that moment and straightened his back.

'Flora, you've come!' He sounded very happy to see her. Probably hoping her arrival would grant him a break from his young taskmaster.

He met her at the greenhouse door. 'Are you here to help?'

'That was the general idea, but you've enough already by the look of it.'

'Mr Carrington don't know nothin',' Charlie said with disgust.

'I'm sure you're teaching him well.'

'I never met anyone who knowed nothin about plantin'.'

'That's because you've never met anyone who has led such an exciting life as Mr Carrington. He hasn't had time to learn how to plant seeds.'

She kept her expression bland, but Jack's smile told her he

knew she'd spoken tongue-in-cheek. He turned back to his shovelling and she caught sight of the side of his head.

'What's happened to your ear?' she asked, peering at him closely. 'And your neck. They look really nasty cuts.'

'Shaving – I can be careless at times. But if you've come to help,' he said quickly, 'we've still flowers to do. You can amuse yourself with those if you like, while Charlie and I finish the men's work.'

'Pff,' she said, stepping into the greenhouse and shuffling through the several packets of seeds. She was curious about those cuts. If he'd done it shaving, she would eat these seeds, so why wasn't he being honest? It was something she'd ask when Charlie wasn't around.

'Did these all come from your neighbours?'

'Most of them, and I found a few in the garden shed. I've no idea how old they are or if they'll even grow. And there are several brown envelopes from Diggory, down the lane. A great name for a gardener, don't you think?'

Flora picked up an envelope. 'Sweet peas,' she read aloud. 'My favourite. I'll make a start with these.'

For the next hour or so, they worked side by side, until Flora wiped a muddy hand across her forehead and stood back to view her handiwork.

'That is a satisfying sight,' she said with pride. Two long shelves were filled with seed trays, planted and watered.

'Do you really think they'll grow?' He'd come to stand beside her.

'Why shouldn't they?'

'For one thing, I don't have any heating in this place. When Elsie came by with the lettuce seeds, she said I needed to heat the greenhouse. Hers, apparently, has all the latest equipment.'

'It would have. She's a keen gardener when she's not solving half a dozen murders a week.'

Jack's eyebrows gave a slight waggle.

'In fiction,' Flora said, laughing. 'Elsie likes to pit her wits against the writer, unmasking the villain before she's supposed to. But don't worry about these.' She waved her hand at the neat rows of trays. 'Unless we have a really severe frost, they'll be fine. They'll just grow more slowly than Elsie's, and that will give you more time to prick them out.'

His eyebrows did another waggle.

'It will be OK,' she reassured him. 'Charlie will know what to do when the time comes.'

'I'm hungry,' the boy announced. 'I gotta go. Mum's cooking lunch and she'll skin me if I'm late.'

'You must leave straight away,' Jack said. 'A skinned Charlie would not be a pretty sight.'

They watched as he galloped down the path and disappeared around the side of the house to collect his bike.

'I don't have any lunch to offer, I'm afraid,' Jack said. 'Only—'

'No, don't tell me. I am not eating ham sandwiches on a Sunday. I've beef in the larder. We could do another hour and then I'll go home and cook an early supper.'

'I'm invited?'

'Why not? There'll be too much for me to eat.'

It was a bad idea to spend too much time alone with Jack, she knew that well enough, but the desire to share the remainder of the day with him was annoyingly strong.

'That sounds like one of your better ideas. I need bolstering after this morning's hard labour.'

Flora's glance took in his tall, slim figure. He could eat half a dozen roast dinners, she thought, and still not look an inch fatter.

They worked on, tackling the vegetable seeds that remained, and slotting the planted trays into the last few spaces on the rack. Pulling herself upright, she rubbed the soil from her hands. 'That's it, I think. I'd better rinse this off before I leave.'

'Use the bathroom, you know where it is – I'll wash in the kitchen. Then we'll lock up and go.'

But when she walked back down the stairs, hands scrubbed

clean, it was to find Charlie returned and heaving a basket onto the kitchen table.

'No need to cook that beef,' Jack said, grabbing a towel from the rail. 'Mrs Teague has provided.'

'Really?'

'Mum says as you won't want to be cookin' after all the work and she cooked extra cos my uncle was comin' for lunch and then he didn't.'

'What a kind thought.' She reached up to the kitchen's one shelf. 'I'll put these to warm,' she said, and slid two dinner plates into the oven. 'Thank goodness you don't have an Aga, Jack. We'd be here till midnight.'

'I wouldn't have a clue how to get it going. Not that I know much more about the oven that's here.'

'The food shouldn't have lost too much heat on your ride over,' she said to Charlie. 'Your mum has wrapped it very well.' Mrs Teague had decanted the meal into lidded glass containers and covered them with several layers of newspaper.

'It wuz difficult,' he said. 'I had to ride one-handed.'

'I'm sure you were up to it.'

The boy grinned. 'I'm not allowed us'lly, but Mum said it wuz OK, just this time.'

'Your mother is a very kind woman.'

Generous, too, Flora thought, when the plates were warmed through and she unwrapped the dishes. Her spirits lifted. Yes, beef and Yorkshire pudding in this one, and in the other, roast potatoes and several green vegetables. There was even a closed jug of gravy!

'It smells scrumptious,' she said, crumpling the newspaper into a ball. She was about to throw it in the rubbish bin, when a black headline halfway down a page made her stop and smooth out the creases. She bent over the table to look more closely.

'Look what I've found. Our friend, Mr Foster. It seems he can't keep out of the papers.'

Jack walked round the table and bent over the flattened newsprint. This time, there was no photograph, but a small paragraph headed *Club Owner Charged*. The article went on to say that a Mr Frank Foster had been arrested the previous evening at the premises of a nightclub he owned in the West End, the Blue Peacock in George Yard.

'Is that the bloke Polly didn't like?' Charlie asked.

Flora turned to him in surprise. 'You knew about Frank Foster?'

Charlie nodded. 'I didn't know his name, but I saw him followin' Polly one day when she came back to the village for somethin'. She said for him to leave her alone, but he wouldn't. Then he was at the party.'

'The party?'

'The one for Mr Mitchell.'

'The wake? Yes, he was,' Jack said. He bent his head again. 'What's he been arrested for, I wonder? Money laundering, like his chums?'

Flora's finger followed the paragraph down, line by line. 'Receiving stolen goods, it says. Perhaps he'll be charged with money laundering, too. They're both serious crimes.'

'Is he in prison?' Charlie sounded pleased.

'He'll be in a police cell waiting to go to court,' Jack told him. 'That's where the judge will decide whether he goes to prison or not.'

'I hope he does. I hope he stays there for the rest of his life. He scared Polly.'

Flora looked over Charlie's head at Jack. 'I think it's time we ate,' he said swiftly.

'Do you want to wait for the dishes, Charlie,' Flora asked him, 'or shall I bring them round to your mum tomorrow?'

'Nah, I won't stay. I've got mates waitin' for me at the rec. We're playin' football.'

'Let's hope his thirst for blood will be satisfied at the rec,' Jack said, as the front door closed behind Charlie. 'There's bound to be fisticuffs.'

'He's an odd mixture.'

'He has a good heart.' Jack delved into the top drawer of the kitchen cabinet looking for knives and forks. 'Which reminds me there was something I wanted to say.'

He sat down at the table, taking one of the plates. 'This looks good.'

'Doesn't it! What were you going to say?'

'I've been feeling a bit guilty about Charlie.'

'You mean you haven't paid him for all the work he's done,' she joked.

'He's had more than enough money but, to be fair, he's worked really hard. It's the treat we promised him. His day in Brighton came to an abrupt end.'

'He loved the waxworks and there was the aquarium and the roller skating, and don't forget the fish and chips.'

'The aquarium wasn't a hit, was it, and the pantomime we took him to was dire. And after he found Polly, the day collapsed.'

'Are you saying you want to do another Brighton trip?'

'Not necessarily, but I think we should take him out again. Not for a whole day this time, but an afternoon. I was thinking... if you've not planned anything this Wednesday, and the weather is good, we could invite him for a picnic. You'll be closing the All's Well at lunchtime and Charlie is on school holidays this coming week.'

'A picnic mid-February? Is that a sensible idea? These carrots are really sweet. Mrs Teague must grow them herself.'

'I did say if the weather was good. We could take a basket – Charlie loves food – and I'll try to think of something to pack other than ham sandwiches. If we drove to the Adur, we could have a picnic on the river bank, then take a boat out for an hour.'

'You have a boat?' This was news to Flora.

'I don't, but one of my neighbours – Diggory, the one who gave me the sweet pea seeds – was talking about the rowing boat he keeps near Small Dole. Apparently, he's not managed to take it out all winter. He's getting on a bit and he's had a rotten few months.

One cold after another. He was saying what a shame the boat was going to waste and would I like a trip on it?'

'If it hasn't been taken out all winter, it won't be in very good shape.'

'He's been over to the river quite regularly, keeping the boat ticking over. He's just finished painting it, he told me. A bright red. We'll spot it a mile off, even before we see the name.'

'And what is the name?'

'*Mabel*.'

'It would have to be,' she said, laughing.

'So what do you think? A good suggestion?'

'As long as you can row because I definitely can't.'

'I've rowed before,' he said briefly.

'In America? I remember now... you mentioned the Hamptons.'

As soon as she said the words, Flora wanted to bite them back. Anything to do with America was a sensitive topic. Jack had been adamant his failed love affair would stay failed, but the need to tiptoe around the subject hadn't gone away.

'The Hamptons were far too exclusive for me,' he said a little sharply, pushing his empty plate to one side. 'The lake in Central Park was more my mark. So, the river on Wednesday?'

'If Charlie thinks it's a good idea. It's his treat,' she cautioned.

'He will.' Jack shuffled back his chair. 'That was very good. The beef particularly. You're excused duty, by the way. I'll do the clearing up.'

TWENTY-THREE

It took only a little time for Jack to reappear in the sitting room, carrying a tray of tea. He'd left the blind pulled down to mask the hole in the window, still unsure whether or not to mention last night's events.

'This sofa...' Flora began, as soon as he walked into the room.

'I know, it's lumpy. You've told me often enough.'

'Can't you get your landlord to change it?'

'Since he's never replaced a thing for the last five or so years, I doubt it.'

'Then *you* should,' she said decidedly.

'I've no money for sofas. I've just bought a car.' He sighed. 'Is it such a problem?'

'Yes. It's extremely uncomfortable. Think of your guests.'

'I don't have any guests,' he pointed out. 'Except you, and we could always stay in the kitchen.' When she continued to wear a pained expression, he was goaded into saying, 'I'll buy something new when I get a decent royalty cheque – a chair, though,' he warned. 'Not a sofa.'

He didn't mind Flora mocking his furniture. Not at all. He'd felt such immense relief when she'd walked unharmed into his back garden this morning that she could mock the entire contents of Overlay House if she felt inclined. Waking in the night, he'd felt his earlier fears return and, first thing this morning, had been on the verge of setting out for her cottage when he'd heard the sound of Charlie's bike being slammed across his front path. It had made him pause. If she was in trouble, he would have heard by now – she must be OK. And if he charged round to her house with tales of flints flying through windows, it might scare her unnecessarily.

'I'll keep you to that promise!' she said jubilantly. 'But why is the blind down? It feels odd in here.'

He would have to tell her, knowing from experience that she was unlikely to let the matter go. Reluctantly, Jack walked to the window and raised the blind. 'I thought you might not appreciate my repair.'

He'd taped a large square of cardboard over the offending hole late last night. It did nothing to enhance a house that already looked tired beyond its years.

Flora stared. 'Even odder. How do you have a hole in your window?'

'Because someone decided to throw this.' He walked over to the mantelpiece and picked up the shard of flint to show her.

'When? Was it last night, after you got back from the golf club?'

'It was.'

'And it hit you! That's where you got the cuts from, not shaving. Not that I believed that for a minute.' She paused for a moment, seeming sunk in thought. 'You know, I sensed someone last night, as I was crossing the road from the shop, but I put it down to the way shadows can seem to move. Do you think we were being followed? Did our villain see us yesterday asking questions at the club, and decide to warn us off?'

They were his thoughts precisely.

'A warning or worse,' she murmured, taking the flint from his hand and holding it up to the light that now filled the room. 'This edge is incredibly sharp. If it had hit your neck at a certain angle—'

'I realise that,' he said quickly. 'Fortunately, it didn't.'

She sank back on the sofa. 'Why you, Jack? Why not me, too?'

'I'm not sure, but I'd hazard a guess it was because the blind was up, the lights were on, and I made the perfect target.'

She was thoughtful. 'Whereas I pulled my curtains as soon as I got in, and the only light in the sitting room was a table lamp which was fairly dim.'

'Whoever it was had a good aim,' he remarked.

Flora seemed still to be thinking and, when she spoke, it was to say regretfully, 'I can't see many of our suspects being that good at throwing. Frank Foster remains our best option. And what about that snippet in Mrs Teague's newspaper?'

'It was an interesting find. What did you make of it?'

'That Foster is a criminal. I always had my suspicions and now they've been confirmed in black and white. He's not only a pest to women, not only friends with some unsavoury characters, but involved in serious crime himself.'

She took a sip of her tea, then sat bolt upright, the cup wavering dangerously in her hand. 'He was searching for something at Rose Court, wasn't he? And then at Ted Russell's house.'

'We *think* he was searching for something.' Jack looked hard at her. 'Does that have a connection?'

'It does. What if he was looking for some of the stuff that's been stolen? For jewellery?'

'The article made no mention of what the goods were.'

'It's as likely to be jewellery as anything else. Admit that, at least. And if he gave jewellery to Polly – a bracelet, a necklace, a ring – it would fit.'

He stretched his arms above his head, smiling faintly. 'Why did I know it would?'

Flora wriggled to the edge of the sofa, leaning so far forward that she almost touched his knees.

'It does fit, doesn't it?' she insisted. 'Foster is obsessed with Polly, but she doesn't want to know. So he tries to bribe her, not with flowers or chocolates, but with something far more precious. He knows Polly likes expensive things, he's seen her in the fur coat, so he reckons that a piece of valuable jewellery might do the trick and he has just the thing stashed away at the Blue Peacock from a recent robbery. He gives Polly the trinket hoping she'll look more kindly on him, but when the police start enquiring about stolen goods and begin to close in on him, Foster needs to get rid of the haul – including the gift he's given to Polly. But with the girl dead, where exactly is it?'

'I love the way you construct an entire story out of so little. You really should be a writer, Flora.'

'It's blindingly obvious to me. Why are you so sniffy?'

'First of all, why would Foster bother to look for one piece of jewellery? He's been charged for receiving stolen goods. The police will already have enough evidence against him from their raid on the club. They won't need an extra necklace, and he must know that.'

'He's only just been charged. I noticed the date on the newspaper. It was Friday's and he was arrested the evening before. That's only three days ago, which means he hadn't been charged at the time we found him at Rose Court or when the Russell house was burgled. And,' she continued inexorably, 'even if he was expecting to be arrested, even if he thought the police might find the stuff he was keeping at the nightclub, it's what he gave Polly that would seal his fate.'

Jack waited for the explanation. It was the easiest thing to do when Flora fell into the kind of fervid guesswork she was prone to.

'Foster could deny knowledge of whatever the police found at the club,' she went on. 'An awful lot of people must go in and out of the place every week. He could insist that he'd never seen the goods before, whatever they were. That someone else had hidden them on his premises, or left them behind accidentally.'

'That would make for a very poor defence,' he protested.

'I agree, but it is a defence, and unless the police can prove through fingerprinting, for example, that he handled those goods, there would be enough doubt for a court to acquit him. But... if he gave a bracelet or whatever to Polly, she couldn't have come by it other than by him. He had to have been the one who handled it, who knew about the stolen goods.'

Jack found himself reluctantly agreeing. 'I'm not as sure as you that he'd escape all punishment, but you're right in saying that any stolen piece of jewellery he gave to Polly would seal his fate. As long as he didn't wear gloves when he gave it to her! He'd have to come up with a fantastic story to account for it. I wonder where the jewellery is now, if it exists?'

'If Polly was wearing it that day—'

'The police would have it.'

'Except, it might have fallen off in the water. Or if she was still wearing it when the police found her, the salt could have blurred any fingerprints. The thing is that Frank can't be sure what happened to it, which is why he's been searching, hoping to find it before the police do.'

Jack could see the argument. 'He'd be nervous, certainly. He'd know his chums had been arrested and maybe he hoped to get shot of the rest of the haul, expecting the police would investigate him very soon.'

'Exactly, but he'd need the item he gave to Polly before he did, which is why he'd try his darndest to get it back from her. It might be why he approached her at Bernie Mitchell's wake. There was something creepily intense about the way he looked at her. At the time, I thought it was because he was a pest, which he was, but it could equally have been that he was desperate for her to hand back the goods.'

'And the day she died,' Jack said pensively, 'he could have tried again to persuade her to return the item. He was still in Sussex, according to Alice, in Abbeymead at the Cross Keys, but he could easily have travelled to Brighton.'

Flora nodded. 'Let's imagine he did. He turns up at Rose Court to ask for the jewellery back, and when Polly prevaricates, he takes her for a walk on the pier, with her wearing the pendant or bracelet. She refuses to take it off, they row, maybe he lunges for it, and pushes her over.'

'But if he knew that had happened, he'd also know the necklace had been lost with her and he wouldn't have bothered searching.'

'That's true. Then it's more likely he asked to meet her on the pier and she left the jewellery behind at the flat. When she told him she wasn't giving it back – that was a mistake, I think – it could have blown up into a row with Foster getting very angry. You can see he's a man who would be quick to fight, and he's a big man. Polly wouldn't have stood a chance. If he shoved her in a temper, she would have fallen like a stone.'

They fell silent for a moment until Flora said, 'It might have been an accident and not deliberate, but it was still murder.'

'Manslaughter,' he amended. 'So we're putting all our eggs in the Foster basket? What about Evelyn Barnes and her doleful husband? You thought that one or other of them could have been on the pier that morning, and neither of them had any love for Polly.'

Flora jumped up and walked to the French doors, looking out on what he hoped was a smarter garden. 'Evelyn and Harry are still a possibility,' she said, 'but I'm beginning to wonder. I'm sure Evelyn would feel it was below her dignity to confront Polly again. She'd already visited Rose Court and told the girl exactly what she thought of her. I think she'd feel that was sufficient. I can't see her following Polly onto the pier and pushing her – what would be the point? As far as Evelyn was concerned, she'd dealt with the situation. She was cutting off the money, Polly would be thrown out of the flat and Harry thrown out of Pelham Lodge. She would only have attacked the girl physically if she lost her temper, and I just don't see Evelyn shouting and screaming. She's a hard woman – icy and self-contained.'

'Have you forgotten being flung into the ditch? That was Evelyn.'

'She was driving stupidly, but it was an accident.'

'You can't have it both ways, Flora. Why was she driving stupidly, unless someone or something had upset her? Yet, if she's this icy and self-contained woman, driving dangerously in a temper doesn't fit. On the other hand, deliberately driving at someone you want rid of fits the bill perfectly.'

'I still think it was an accident,' she said stubbornly. 'What reason would Evelyn have to hurt me?'

'The same reason that could have led her to push you off the pier. She suspects you know too much.'

He rubbed at his forehead, trying to think clearly, but couldn't stop a small groan. This investigation had become a mess. 'We haven't even begun on Harry,' he said, despondently.

'No, that's the problem. Everyone we've focused on had something against Polly, and the chance to kill her. I thought about Harry Barnes last night and the blackmail he told us about. The letter turned out to be a damp squib, but Harry didn't know that. He'd no idea that his wife was aware of the flat, and he genuinely believed Polly was behind the demand for money. He had a score to settle. Plus he was obviously becoming disenchanted with her, thinking he was being taken for a fool.'

'Which he was.'

'Which he was,' Flora agreed. 'He had motive and possibly the opportunity – to push both Polly and myself off that pier. But in the end, I can't see him doing it. He seems too flabby for anything as dramatic as killing. It would take a lot to stir him into action. I can just about accept he might push Polly if he was in a thunderous temper, but the attack on me? Would the suspicion I might have evidence against him be enough?'

'So... we end up where we started – with Frank.'

'Unless we consider Raymond Parsons. I spoke to him after you left yesterday. He's very cut up about Polly's death. He thinks their quarrel – he sent the blackmail letter when she told him not to – caused her to jump.'

'If he's that cut up, he's not going to have killed her.' Jack couldn't see the logic.

'He could be guilty *and* upset. Plenty of murderers have shown remorse after the event, and Raymond could be disguising what really happened by saying he believed Polly had taken her own life.'

'Why kill her, though?'

'It certainly wouldn't have been rational. A sudden flaring of tempers again? Most likely over the same disagreement they had at Bernie's wake. Raymond saying blackmail was necessary and Polly insisting she could get money from Harry another way. They were two young people who'd spent all their savings on tickets to Canada and were facing a wretched situation with no chance of escape. It's not too difficult to see things getting out of hand very quickly.'

'It's a possibility, but nothing we've talked about is more than that. No one was seen behaving suspiciously when Polly was pushed and no one when you were attacked.'

'The invisible killer,' Flora murmured.

'There is one thing we know for certain – the police will be probing Frank Foster's business dealings, now they have him in custody. Whatever he did or didn't get up to with Polly should come out. The girl might get justice after all.'

Flora gave a small shrug. 'It's a hope, but I'm not confident.'

If only Frank Foster's arrest was the end of the matter, Jack thought, but that tiny snippet from the newspaper had set up a whole new fear. Foster had clearly been under lock and key for days – he couldn't have been the one hurling a missile through the window last night. Could Jack imagine any of the others doing so? Evelyn, Harry, Raymond? What if there was someone out there they didn't know about? Unthinkingly, he'd accepted Flora's list of suspects as definitive – once they'd ticked off each name and absolved them of the crime, they'd be left with their murderer. That was the theory. But what if there was someone who wasn't on that list, someone Flora hadn't considered, with a reason to kill Polly that neither of them knew about?

'You've gone very quiet,' she remarked.

'Sorry. Heavy lunch.'

'I'll leave you to snooze then.'

She walked back to the kitchen and he followed her. Packing the clean plates into Mrs Teague's basket, she said, 'I can drop this off on my way to the All's Well tomorrow.'

'If you're sure.'

She gave him a grin. 'I have to do something for a delicious meal I didn't have to lift a finger for.'

Jack waved her off at the front door, watching her stride homewards along the lane. He felt decidedly uneasy. He realised how much he'd been counting on Foster being the villain. The man played into all the stereotypes and, as a writer, Jack should have known better. It was a lazy assumption. Foster might still turn out to be Polly's killer, but Jack couldn't shake off this new concern, that danger was still out there, in particular, danger to Flora. He'd grown too close to her, that was the problem. Somehow, over the months, he'd become her shield and it annoyed him. Shutting the front door, he turned back into the sitting room, feeling ruffled, unsure of himself.

Dammit, he thought, slumping back into his chair, he wanted to be her shield! Over the next few days, he decided to call at the bookshop regularly and walk past her cottage every evening. With Charlie's help, he'd already made a good start on getting the garden into shape and as for writing the new book, he should in any case put that on hold until they got to Cornwall. They weren't due to leave Sussex for another three months – if there was danger to Flora, it was far more imminent.

TWENTY-FOUR

Despite Michael's loving care over the weekend, Betty seemed particularly grumpy on Monday morning, though Flora herself was in good spirits as she cycled to the All's Well. She was still unsure that Polly would feature in the police enquiry, but delighted with the arrest of Frank Foster, seeing it as a huge step forward. Was it a signal perhaps for her to let things drift for the moment, shifting gears only if it became clear the girl was unlikely to get justice? Flora felt tempted.

Her most pressing concern should be the shop and, apart from the new window display and the newspaper interview yet to be published, she'd done little to improve its finances lately. The situation was by no means as dire as the dreadful days of last October – over those weeks, she'd lost a large number of sales and a good deal of money – but to get back on an even keel, she needed to work harder.

Her customers in the village had gradually trickled back, now her goal must be to attract people from further afield. Before Polly's death, she'd come up with the idea of a special Saturday event, at which several authors would give readings from their work, followed by a book signing. Jack had been adamant he wouldn't take part, hating the idea of being on public display. *They won't want to hear from me*, he'd said. *Try to nab some London authors*. She'd taken his advice, but negotiations with the few writers she'd been able to contact had proved difficult, and so far she had little to show for her efforts.

Small steps, Flora told herself, remembering the new pavement sign, made by the local blacksmith and painted by his talented son. It had been delivered on Saturday just as she was closing and, with Jack waiting in the car to drive them to the golf club, she hadn't had time to unwrap it. This morning would be the great unveiling.

Wheeling Betty to the rear of the All's Well, she unlocked the wide, white-painted front door and, for an instant, savoured the shop's sweet muskiness before making for the parcel she'd stored beneath her desk. The sign was bold. Black and white lettering against a red background and large enough to be seen from a passing car. *All's Well – the bookshop that delivers*, it said. Then lower down in smaller letters, *Pick up a brand new book or browse our beautiful collection of second-hand volumes*. It was her own design and she was proud of it. She hoped Violet would have approved.

Ever since last autumn, Abbeymead had been a popular place to visit, though not always for the right reasons. The village had gained a certain notoriety, and if she could harness that and make it work for her... During deep winter, with snow on the ground, numbers had tailed off, but now spring was in the air and visitors would soon be back. Not the coach trips of gawpers the scandal had attracted, but hopefully people who enjoyed wandering an old Sussex village. People who'd discovered the history of St Saviour's maybe, and that of the Priory. People interested in books.

Feeling a burst of optimism, she arranged the new sign in a prominent position and was about to go indoors when a voice said, 'You probably shouldn't put that on the pavement.'

The remark stopped her in her tracks. 'Pardon?'

It was Sylvia Russell. 'You probably shouldn't put that on the pavement,' the girl repeated. 'There's a law about it, I'm sure.'

'I don't know about any law, but I can't see that it's hurting anyone.'

'I can. People could trip over it.'

Since the sign was two foot high and close up to the bookshop's brick and flint wall, Flora was about to argue her case, but changed her mind. Sylvia's father was ill in hospital, the family had suffered a break-in and their possessions wrecked, and the girl's cousin had died in mysterious circumstances. Even her boyfriend had turned out a disappointment. Life had not treated Sylvia well these past few weeks and Flora decided to hold her tongue.

'If I move the sign a little to the left, will that help?' she asked pleasantly.

Sylvia put her head on one side and surveyed the new position. 'I think that's better.'

There was virtually no difference, as far as Flora could see, but she let it go. 'Tell me, Sylvia, how is Mr Russell?'

'He's doing OK, thanks. The doctors say his heart has been weakened, but he's stable and he's eating well. As well as you can in hospital.'

Flora nodded. 'I'm glad to hear he's feeling better. Do you think he'd be happy to have a visit? I wanted to call in and say hello, but his condition sounded serious and I guessed that only family members would be allowed.'

'You could go if you want,' Sylvia said a trifle off-handedly. 'He's getting a bit bored, he'd probably be glad of the company. I get there most days but it's a bit of a trek from Shoreham.'

'You're in an office there, is that right?'

'For the time being, but I'm thinking of leaving and finding something else. I got spoilt travelling to work from Brighton. The journey was so much easier than from here.'

'I can imagine, and it was a lovely flat that you had.'

'Polly had,' she said sharply. 'But, yeah, I miss Rose Court.'

'I suppose you don't have a date yet...'

'For the funeral? We do. I've just been to see Kate Mitchell to ask her to do the refreshments. It will be Thursday next week. The hospital's promised that Dad will be home by then.'

Flora felt conflicted. It was good news that Polly would be laid to rest, but it signalled, too, that the police were happy with the post-mortem and had closed the official enquiry into her death – Alan Ridley had confirmed as much two days ago. The coroner must be satisfied as well, if he'd released the body.

'Come by and see Dad on Wednesday, if you like,' Sylvia continued. 'It's half-day closing, so you could come after lunch. Visiting hours are two to six.'

'Thank you, Sylvia. I will.'

She was about to walk back into the bookshop, when she remembered. 'I can't make this Wednesday afternoon. I'll be in a rowing boat. At least, I hope so, and not swimming.'

'You're going to learn to row?' Sylvia looked amazed.

'Not me. Mr Carrington. I'm hoping he already knows. We're taking Charlie Teague out for the afternoon – Diggory Moore is loaning us his boat. But what if I came by tomorrow afternoon? I shut at five and if I asked Mr Carrington to drive me, I could be at the hospital well before visiting hours are over. I imagine your father isn't well enough for a long visit, anyway. What do you think?'

'Sounds OK to me. I'll tell Dad to expect you.' She looked at her watch. 'I have to go. They cancelled the first bus to Brighton this morning and I better not miss the next. I'm very late as it is. I can hear my boss yelling from here.'

'It's hardly your fault.'

'I don't much care,' Sylvia said nonchalantly. 'I won't be there much longer.'

Halfway through the morning, Flora felt stupidly hungry, then remembered she'd skipped breakfast. She'd woken late – all that gardening yesterday had had its effect – and there had been no time to toast even a slice of bread. She still adhered to Violet's rule that the All's Well should be ready for customers at least ten minutes before opening time. Even now, she could hear Violet's voice. It was professionalism, her aunt maintained. Would it be a lapse of professionalism if she shot across the road for five minutes and bought a slice of fruit cake from Kate? By the time hunger pangs had twisted her stomach into a tight corkscrew, Flora decided it wouldn't be. Throwing on her wool coat, she locked the bookshop door and ran to the Nook.

The café was empty, except for Kate sitting at a table by the counter, her head in her hands.

'Whatever's the matter?' She closed the café door behind her and hurried to her friend's side.

Kate looked up as she approached, her eyes dull. 'It's Sylvia Russell.'

'Sylvia? What has she done?'

'Nothing really,' Kate said hopelessly.

Flora was bemused and, trying to encourage Kate to talk, she mentioned her own encounter with Sylvia. 'I saw her myself this morning. She walked across the road especially to tell me that I shouldn't put my new and very beautiful sign on the pavement. But how has she upset you?'

'I shouldn't be upset. It's business after all, but another wake... so shortly after Bernie... and before him, my father. It seems like all I'm doing is catering for funerals. And I keep thinking of poor Polly and what she must have felt, dying like that.'

Flora forbore to say that probably Polly hadn't felt anything since she'd not have known she was about to die, but she could see Kate was genuinely disturbed.

'Life will get easier,' she soothed, putting her arm around her friend. 'Spring is coming – it's a most beautiful morning today – and once this awful funeral is done with, there'll be happier times ahead.'

'Sylvia says there's going to be at least fifty people coming. Polly was popular, I know. She had plenty of friends here and must have made more in Brighton.'

'Fifty people is fifty heads you can charge for,' Flora reminded her.

'To be honest, I don't know if I can do it. Bernie's... Bernie's wake was such an effort... in addition to all the work at the café, but this one will be...' She tailed off.

'You have Alice,' Flora coaxed. 'She'll do a lot of the cooking.'

'She's already baking for the Nook and I don't like to ask her to do more. She's having to cook for the Priory the whole of this week-end, as well. The administrators have booked in some society or other for the two days and there's a big dinner on Saturday night. I can't bring myself to ask her to help out again. She did such a wonderful spread for Bernie.'

'I'm fairly sure that Alice will be cross if you don't ask her. She's used to cooking for large numbers so the Priory event won't faze her and, between the two of you, you'll put on a splendid funeral breakfast. You've got Raymond as well to do the waiting. I saw him on Saturday. He was here cleaning up.'

'He's been a good help,' Kate conceded. 'But he hasn't turned up today. He was supposed to help out with lunches.'

'Really? Perhaps you shouldn't depend on him then. He doesn't seem that reliable. He's in trouble at the golf club for walking out when he was supposed to be on duty. Still, I'm sure he'll turn up some time today and he... he liked Polly... he'll be pleased to help at her wake.'

'I suppose so, but...'

Flora gave a silent sigh. More problems, it seemed.

'It's Frank.'

Flora stared at her friend.

'Frank Foster,' Kate prompted. 'You remember, Bernie's friend?' Without waiting for an answer, she went on, 'He tele-phoned me. He was supposed to be coming down at the end of the week to talk to the administrators – about the Priory. He's still keen on buying. I think he'll only come for the day, but he's bound to call in here when his business is finished. Should I mention Polly's funeral, do you think? He asked me to tell him the date as soon as I knew.'

Flora took her friend's hand and squeezed it. 'Frank Foster is one problem less. I don't know when he telephoned you, but he won't be coming to Abbeymead. He won't be going anywhere for a while. He's been arrested and is in police custody.'

Kate's eyes opened wide, staring at Flora in disbelief. 'Arrested? Are you sure?'

'Absolutely. We saw it in the newspaper yesterday. He was arrested last Thursday. He won't be bothering you for a very long time – if ever.'

Kate's expression was confused. Flora could tell she was struggling to know how to feel – upset that a friend of her errant husband had fallen into such trouble, but relief that she wouldn't now have to deal with a man she personally disliked.

The café bell rang, jolting them to attention. A couple Flora didn't recognise smiled a good morning and took a seat at a far table. The first of the spring visitors, she thought, hoping that after eating their fill, they might wander down the road and stop at the All's Well.

Kate had picked up her pad and paper ready to take the couple's order when, still slightly bewildered, she turned and asked, 'Sorry, Flora, can I get you something?'

'Just a slice of fruit cake. I can help myself.'

'Yes, do,' Kate said gratefully.

TWENTY-FIVE

Jack opened the letter from Arthur Bellaby, hoping for the best. His eyes scanned quickly down the page. His agent sounded his usual emollient self, but there was no doubting the tenor of his message. Jack's latest book was a disappointment. He'd be sending more detailed notes later, just as soon as he could get his secretary to type them up. *Dig Ever Deeper* wasn't unrescuable, but it would need work. Quite a lot of work.

Jack threw the letter across the kitchen table. He hated the book. Had hated it from the very first line, and now he had to start over again when all his attention should be on Flora and her safety. Deep down, he'd known that *Dig* wasn't good enough, but he'd wanted to be rid. To start a new chapter, he thought ironically. A fresh beginning in Cornwall and the series Bellaby had championed, devising a crime story to fit the county.

He collected his old tweed jacket, the one with patched elbows, from the hall peg and walked out into the back garden. While he waited for Arthur's suggestions of how to put the wretched novel right, he'd get hot and sweaty. Attacking the soil with a spade was the best thing he'd found to rid himself of low spirits. Why hadn't he known that before? After Helen abandoned him, he could have dug the whole of the Eastern Seaboard – and some more.

By early afternoon, his legs were aching and his back creaking. He'd had enough. A wash and a sandwich, he thought, in that order. Cheese today – he was doing his best to widen his diet. The meal Mrs Teague had sent over yesterday had been brilliant. As well as lending him her son for odd jobs, perhaps he could persuade her to cook for him.

Just before five, he put on his hat and overcoat, locked the front door, and sauntered along the lane from Overlay House to the spinney and, from there, on to the village. Strolling through the woods these days, he was alert to any likely danger, but in mid-February the trees were spare in their beauty, every leaf having fallen long ago. An attacker would be plainly visible. But it wasn't his attacker that concerned him – it was Flora's. Flora as a target. An evening stroll to the bookshop, an offer to accompany her home to her cottage, might ease his mind.

She was counting money from the till when he walked in.

'What are you doing here?' She had a hand full of ten-shilling notes, but stopped counting.

Jack hadn't prepared himself with an excuse and her question took him by surprise. 'Out for a walk, that's all. I thought I'd drop in and fix a time for Wednesday.'

'It will be after one, surely. That's when I close, and we're having lunch, aren't we? A picnic, if the weather holds. I thought it was settled.' She looked quizzically at him.

'Yes, I just wanted to make sure.' He sounded feeble and could have kicked himself, but then she surprised him.

'I'm glad you called. I wanted to ask a favour and you're a difficult man to get hold of. You *still* don't have a telephone. It's so annoying.'

'A favour?' he asked, ignoring the telephone issue. It was beginning to annoy him, too, though he'd always asserted he'd no need for one. He'd had enough of phone calls in New York.

'I'd like to go and see Ted Russell in hospital. Sylvia says he's a lot better now and would be happy to have a visitor. I haven't liked to go before, but he's coming home next week, so a half an hour visit shouldn't tire him too much.' She pushed the banknotes back into the till, scribbled figures on her pad, and shut the drawer.

'We'll need to be careful what we say, though,' she added. 'I'm not sure if he knows about Polly's funeral yet.'

'There's a date?'

'Of course, you don't know either. It's next Thursday, Sylvia told me this morning. She's asked Kate to do the food, which hasn't gone down too well. If we left bang on five, we could be at St Luke's before the end of visiting hours. Unless you're busy elsewhere.'

Jack shook his head. His life was so simple that the thought of being busy elsewhere seemed strange. 'Where is the hospital?'

'You really don't know?'

'Fortunately not. I've never had cause to use it.'

'It's a bit out of the way, that's why a car is important. On the road to Steyning, but you turn right before you get into the town.'

'You can direct me. Are you leaving for home now? I can walk back with you – unless you're on Betty.'

He could see from the crease appearing between her eyes that Flora was suspicious, but all she said was, 'Betty's in the courtyard. I've decided to let her rest until I can take her back to Michael. He did a good repair after the crash, but this morning the saddle started to wobble badly as I came up the high street. I'll be on foot for a while.'

It was nearly dark when they left the All's Well and for most of the way to Flora's cottage they walked in companionable silence, Jack's torch lighting the way.

'This is a long way round to Overlay House,' she said at last. 'The spinney would have been quicker.'

'A walk is a walk,' he said blandly.

'Hmm,' she muttered. 'I'll see you tomorrow.'

* * *

The journey to St Luke's was easily accomplished and they arrived at the hospital to find the small car park almost empty. The few visitors they saw were leaving rather than arriving.

'We're latecomers,' Jack said.

'That was always going to be the case, but I think it was right to come. I don't suppose too many people from the village have visited – Ted's liked well enough, but St Luke's is difficult to get to. Sylvia said her father was bored.'

'Then we're just the people to amuse him,' he said drily.

She poked him in the ribs. 'Be serious. We must do our best.'

St Luke's grey stone mass was austere. Late Victorian in design, it rose four floors high with a roof built to form a series of vertical points. A few Dutch gables were sprinkled in between, and below them windows that couldn't decide whether to be arched or square. Two pentagon-shaped towers flanked the sprawling building on either side.

'A bit of a mess,' Jack observed.

'It's what's inside that matters.'

In his view, what was inside was little better. Wards containing at least twenty beds, windows that stared back uncurtained, and a linoleum floor so highly polished that it posed a danger to both patients and nurses.

They found Ted Russell in the third ward along the corridor, his bed pushed against the far wall. He looked doleful, as well he might, Jack thought. There had been some attempt to make him comfortable. A vase of early daffodils sat on his bedside table, along with a half-drunk bottle of juice and several magazines, but he lay in a bed that would not have been out of place in a military institution, its sheets pulled so tightly beneath the thin mattress that Jack wondered the poor man could breathe.

'Hello, Mr Russell.' Flora's voice was at its sunniest. 'I hope you're not too tired to have a chat. We won't stay long.'

The words brought an immediate change. Ted's expression visibly brightened and he began pulling himself upright against the mountain of pillows, a slow smile spreading across his face.

'Flora, Flora Steele! Well, aren't you a kind girl. And Mr...'

'Carrington,' Jack said, wondering if there would ever be a time when people in Abbeymead remembered his name. His years tucked away at Overlay House had a lot to answer for.

'Pull up a chair, my love,' Ted said, gesturing to a metal seat rammed against the wall to one side of his bed. 'And...' He looked hopelessly around for a second chair.

'Don't worry,' Jack said. 'I'll borrow one – there are plenty spare. How are you feeling?'

It was the obvious question, though Jack could see for himself. The man's face was still far too pale and he looked as though he'd lost weight in the days since being admitted.

'Not so bad, you know. Goin' home next week, if all goes well.' There was a pause. 'Not that it's much like home any more.'

'You'll soon have the house put to rights,' Flora said rousingly. 'I'm sure Sylvia will have made a start already. The good thing is that nothing was stolen, so it's mostly a case of tidying and that shouldn't take too long.'

'You're right. I'm being a miserable old bu— It's bein' in here that gets you down. Makes you think the worst.'

'Then it's just as well you'll be leaving very soon.'

Jack swore he could see the pale cheeks brighten at the thought, but almost immediately Ted's eyes dimmed. 'It's Sylvia I worry about,' he said unexpectedly.

'She'll be glad to have you home.' Flora sounded as puzzled as Jack felt. Was Ted Russell worried he'd be a burden on his daughter? 'Sylvia will be fine,' Flora said. 'She's young, energetic. She'll look after you well and have the house shipshape in no time.'

'It's not the house. It's that young man.'

'Sylvia's young man?' Jack asked.

'He's made her unhappy, poor girl.'

'There's not much you can do about it, Mr Russell.' Jack knew that kind of unhappiness only too well. 'It's out of your hands.'

'I know. I tell myself that, but Sylvia... well... I've always spoilt her a bit, what with her mother disappearin' when she was a little'un. Always tried to give her everythin' she wanted. Within reason, of course, I'm not a wealthy man.' He tried to laugh and ended with a splutter. 'But this Raymond, he's somethin' I can't give her.'

'No, you can't.' Flora patted the starched white sheet, as if to emphasise her point. 'I'm sure you've done everything you can, but you can't make people feel the way you want them to.'

Ted gave a long sigh. 'True enough. I remember wantin' Dolly to go on feelin' the way she did when we were first married. Wanted it very badly, but it didn't happen.' He fell silent for a moment. 'We had some grand times together, you know, Dolly and me. Even when we were workin' ten hours a day. We ran the sweet shop in the village – you remember, Flora?'

'I do. Four ounces of sweets a week. That was the ration. I always chose jelly babies.'

'They were a lot of kids' favourites. I kept the shop on for a while after Dolly left, but in the end my heart wasn't in it. It was a good life, though, while it lasted. We knew every child in the district and every family. Sylvia got invited to all the parties that were goin'! And Dolly and me, we'd often be asked to dress up and do the entertainment. All free, mind. There wasn't much doin' during the war, or even after it, so you made your own fun. We'd have a different costume for every party. We were lucky – belonged to the local am dram society. They had a whole wardrobe and they let us borrow the costumes we wanted.' He gave another long sigh. 'Yes, they were grand times.'

'It's good to have wonderful memories,' Flora said gently. 'And you'll make plenty more once you're on your feet again.'

'I hope so, my dear. I don't ever want to be back in this place. Hello, Sister,' he said brightly, his voice changing as a starched nurse crackled by. 'Nice enough women. Carin', you know, but it's not home.'

'Think of next week – it's coming,' Flora urged.

'Only seven more days,' Jack added.

Seeing Ted sink a little into his pillows, he took the hint.

'Supper will be round soon, I imagine. It's probably time for us to go.'

Despite his tiredness, Ted gave a throaty chuckle. 'Supper? Not on your life. That'll be my bedtime drink.'

Walking back to the car, Jack's thoughts stayed with the frail man they had left behind. Ted Russell couldn't be more than twenty years older than him, but it felt as though the poor chap belonged to a different era.

Flora, walking beside him, squeezed his arm understandingly. 'Ted will be better once he's home,' she said.

TWENTY-SIX

From the moment the shop opened the next morning, Flora was kept busy. It was as though all her regular customers had decided to buy a book before the All's Well closed at lunchtime.

Miss Lancaster led the charge and was already waiting outside the locked building when Flora hurried up the main street. For the first few weeks of ice and snow, she'd managed to hand-deliver several of the books Miss Lancaster had ordered – Fern Hill wasn't the easiest to navigate in snow and there was no way Betty would have managed the climb. But as the bad weather continued, Flora had been forced to ask her customer to collect any remaining orders. She'd felt bad doing so, but it seemed that Miss Lancaster had developed a taste for the walk into Abbeymead and enjoyed spending an hour browsing the All's Well's shelves.

Betty would be delighted that Fern Hill was no longer on her route. The newly mended bicycle was safely stowed in the courtyard behind the shop after Michael had called at the cottage last night with the wooden planter Flora had ordered earlier, and gone straight round to the bookshop to fix the errant saddle. She intended to cycle back to the cottage once the boat trip was over, wanting Jack to have no excuse to see her home again. That's what he'd been doing on Monday evening, she was certain, and yesterday he'd driven her to the cottage straight from the hospital. He was on edge, she could feel it, but she wasn't sure why.

The attempt to push her to her death – was that his worry? But it had been days ago, and now Frank Foster was in a police cell, what was there to fear? They'd agreed he was their main suspect, and who else could be fretting Jack? If the formidable Evelyn had intended to kill Flora, she would have finished the job by now and, as for her husband, it would be easier, Flora thought, for her to push *him* off the pier rather than the reverse. As for the missile through Jack's window, she'd decided after some thought that it must be unconnected. A naughty boy from the village, perhaps, passing Overlay House and tempted to pick up a flint from the ditch – there were plenty lying around – and practise his aim. A young boy was unlikely to consider how dangerous that could be.

After Miss Lancaster, there was a constant trickle of villagers, stocking up for the weekend. They'd heard the weather was likely to be stormy and decided a good book beside a bright fire was the best way to spend it. Hot on their heels came an influx of visitors. It was after the fourth or fifth unknown customer that Flora remembered the monthly market was back, held on the village green. There had always been weekly stalls selling fruit and vegetables, much of the produce coming from villagers' own gardens, but during the summer last year the vicar had set up a Bring and Buy stall outside the church to raise funds for St Saviour's. A young woman, who owned a clothes shop in Steyning, had asked the village council for permission to run a stall selling blouses and skirts, and another shopkeeper who kept bees in his back garden wanted to offer honey. Gradually, the monthly market had grown in size, only ceasing to operate in the middle of winter. Today was the first time it had opened for several months, which explained the sudden increase in the bookshop's trade.

Flora was feeling buoyant when, at the end of the morning as she was getting ready to close, Alice Jenner walked through the door.

'Hello, my love. Did you do well this mornin'?' She pointed to the books scattered across the central table, one or two open on the bench that Flora kept by the window, and several hanging part the way off shelves.

'It's been a profitable few hours. Have you come to buy, too?' she asked jokingly.

'I have. Not for me, though. For Kate. She ordered a recipe book a while back.'

'That's right. It arrived yesterday– the *Constance Spry Cookery Book*. Kate was coming to pick it up. I'll fetch it for you.'

The layout of the cellar followed the same higgledy-piggledy pattern of the sales floor, the walls twisting and turning in dizzying fashion, often ending in a dead end. Storing goods in any kind of order was almost impossible. Books had to be stacked where they would fit and it wasn't until Violet established a labelling system that they could be sure they would find everything a customer had ordered. The books, as they arrived, were placed beneath a separate ticket for each name. Flora had tucked the cookery book at the bottom of the stairs – it was an expensive volume and she'd double-wrapped it in paper.

'Here it is.' She was panting a little from climbing the steep flight of stairs. 'Kate hasn't actually paid,' she said a little awkwardly.

'I know and that's why I'm here. I'm buyin' it for Kate. She's lookin' a lot better now, but the lass still has her black moments. A little treat might help.'

'That's a lovely thought,' Flora said, rewrapping the book and ringing the price up.

'This funeral breakfast for Polly.' Alice shook her head. 'It's worryin' the girl.'

'Has she asked you to help?'

'Didn't have to ask, my love. I offered soon as I heard Polly was bein' buried next week.'

'I knew you would.'

'The thing is' – Alice leaned forward – 'we can do the cookin' between us. That's not a problem, it's more the memories it brings back.' She tutted. 'Still mournin' that no-good husband of hers, but what can you do?'

'Perhaps Kate should have said no to Sylvia.'

'She don't want to turn down business. Word gets around and then no one comes askin' her to cook for them. I hear Ted Russell will be back soon, in time for the service. That's a bit of good news, leastways.'

'I went to visit him in hospital yesterday. Jack drove me over.' She ignored the tiny smirk appearing at the corner of Alice's mouth. 'He looks pale and thin, poor man, but it seems he's well enough to go home or they wouldn't be discharging him.'

'Let's hope he's all right when he gets home.' Alice packed the book away in her wicker basket.

'He has Sylvia.'

Her friend gave a loud sniff. 'He better not be dependin' on her. He should know better than that.'

'You don't think she'll look after him well?'

'Spoilt rotten, that's what she is. Ted Russell's been a fool with her for years, but there, you can't really blame him. No mother to care for her, just her dad. He did his best, but he indulged her too much.'

'Ted said as much. What happened to his wife? I didn't like to ask. He spoke glowingly of her.'

'Well,' Alice said judiciously, 'it did seem a good marriage. They always looked happy, but there, you never can tell. Dolly Russell vanished after the war. Went off with a GI, back with him to America. That was the rumour anyways. Whatever the truth, the woman never came back to Abbeymead.'

'How old was Sylvia when her mother left?'

'A bitty little thing. No more than nine, mebbe ten years old.' Alice nodded sagely. 'You can't get away from it, a girl needs her mother.'

She's forgotten that I didn't have one either, Flora thought, wondering how well Sylvia remembered the lost woman. Memories of her own mother were sparse. Of her father, too. Occasionally, the smell of cigarette smoke on the street or the fragrance of a jasmine bush in someone's garden would trigger something deep inside – a painful ache – but of true remembrance Flora had little.

'I'm sure Sylvia will do everything she can,' she said briskly. 'Though it's sad the girl hasn't someone to share the burden. Sad that it hasn't worked out with Raymond.'

'That boy! Just as well for Sylvia, I'd say. Unreliable. You don't want that in a husband. The lad was supposed to be workin' at the café this week, but there's not been a sign of him.'

Flora frowned. 'That's strange. When I saw him on Saturday, he was expecting to work at the Nook. He'd called in to check his hours, I remember him saying.'

'If he was, he hasn't turned up. I told Kate to tell him, when he does, not to bother again. She should find someone more dependable.'

Flora crossed to the bookshop door and turned the notice to Closed.

'Sorry, my love, am I keepin' you?'

'Of course you're not. I don't need any more customers this morning, that's all. We're taking Charlie Teague for a picnic lunch – and a row on the river. To make up for the mess the Brighton trip turned into.'

'And who's "we"?'

'I'm meeting Jack in a few minutes,' she said airily, and saw the tiny smirk make its reappearance.

Her friend craned forward, looking hard into Flora's face. 'What's that you've done to your eyes?'

Flora flushed slightly. 'It's called eyeliner.'

'I've never seen you do that before.'

'I read about it in a magazine. You draw a line along your lashes and then give it a little outward flick. It's supposed to look like a cat's eye. I like it.'

Alice gave a muffled snort. 'You'll be dabbing on the rouge next.'

TWENTY-SEVEN

Flora fastened the scarf around her neck. It wasn't too bad an afternoon to eat outside, as long as you wrapped up warmly, but it would probably be wise to make the meal a brief one. Even with the sky a limpid blue and the sun trying hard to shine, the chill was ever present. She'd arranged with Jack to meet at the Teagues' house, and found the Austin already parked outside when she arrived. Charlie was jumping on and off the grass verge, excited or impatient, or most likely, both.

Mrs Teague emerged from the side door at that moment and waved to Flora. 'I've done up a few things for your picnic,' she called out, walking to the front gate. 'Let's hope the sun keeps shining.'

Flora took the basket the woman handed her. 'That's very kind of you, Mrs Teague. Jack was going to—'

'Jack did.' Their driver for the afternoon appeared from behind the car. 'But his expertise is sadly limited – mainly to buying sausage rolls and lemonade.'

'You'll find some beef sandwiches in there.' Mrs Teague pointed to the basket. 'A real good hunk of cheddar, and an apple for each of you. Oh, and a flask of tea. You don't want to be drinking lemonade in February, that's for Charlie.'

'Wonderful.' Flora smiled back at her. 'We'll be off then.'

Charlie gave a loud whoop and piled into the back of the car, but not before his mother had taken hold of the rear door and held it open. 'You behave yourself, Charlie Teague,' she said severely. 'This is the second treat you've had in a month. Make sure you're grateful.'

Jack started to protest that it was only what Charlie deserved, when his words were drowned in a wail from the back seat. 'Can't we go?'

'I think we'd better,' he conceded. 'Many thanks, Mrs Teague.'

They bumped their way along the lane and out onto the main street, then turned right for the Brighton road and the flat pasture-land that characterised the area, grazed today by several large herds of brown and white cows.

As they reached the outskirts of Steyning, Jack slowed the car and peered through the windscreen. 'It was somewhere along here that Diggory said to look out for a left turn.'

'There it is, Mr Carrington,' Charlie said eagerly. The boy was sitting so far forward that Flora could feel his breath on her neck.

Jack swung the car into the minor road. A few yards further on, it divided into two and, following his neighbour's instructions, he took the left-hand fork into what was little more than a lane.

'This is what Diggory gave me,' he said, passing Flora a crumpled sheet of paper. 'We're going in the right direction, but where we find the actual mooring is a bit of a mystery.'

Flora studied the paper, then pulled from the glove box the map Jack had begun to carry in the car. 'I think we're nearly there,' she said slowly, her finger following the map. 'See, there should be another small lane on the right-hand side, a bit further along. It seems to run near to the river, but then bends away. I don't think there's a track allowing you to drive any closer.'

'No, Diggory said not. There's some kind of parking space by a farmyard, and a right of way that should take us down to the river.'

It wasn't long before they pulled up outside a ramshackle barn, one of the many outbuildings belonging to what looked to be a large farm. Flora was the first to spot the weathered sign indicating a footpath.

'I think you've found the right place. Well done, Jack.'

'You sound surprised.'

'I'm impressed. For someone who was a hermit for years, you're quite adept at finding your way around Sussex.'

'No more chitter-chatter,' Jack said sternly. 'We need to get going, or what sun there is will have disappeared over the horizon.'

Flora climbed out of the car to see Charlie already heaving the two baskets from the boot.

'Give me those,' Jack commanded, as Mrs Teague's flask of tea looked in danger of toppling to the ground.

'How about one basket each?' Charlie asked.

Jack gave in with a good grace and handed back the lighter of the two. 'Let's hope we end up with some food,' he said in Flora's ear. 'Can you take the blanket?'

It was a longer walk than she'd expected, over half a mile, but she smelt the river – the muddy flats, the vegetation, the crisp, cold aroma of a fresh stream – before she saw the ribbon of water ahead. The tributary to the Adur ran calmly this afternoon, almost silver beneath the pale sky, hugging itself to the earth and protected by high banks of green.

'We're here, and there's our transport.' Jack pointed to a bright red rowing boat bobbing in the shallows and anchored to a wooden post where the river bent sharply. '*Mabel*,' he read. 'That's her.'

'She can wait.' Flora spread the blanket across a smooth expanse of bank. 'Let's eat. I'm starving.'

'Me, too.' Charlie burrowed into the baskets. 'I had my lunch really early.'

'You've had lunch already?'

'It was hours and hours ago, Miss Steele,' he said, and began laying out plates of sausage rolls and sandwiches, together with the chunk of cheese, knife provided, and apples. Three large slices of sponge cake were last to emerge.

'Mum's done OK,' he said.

Jack smiled at him. 'She has, and we'd better do the spread justice.'

Charlie needed no further urging and, within seconds, had filled his plate to the rim. For the moment, his hosts made no attempt to follow, simply enjoying the peace of the riverside.

It was blissfully quiet and Flora felt herself cocooned, a silent Jack by her side and Charlie having stopped talking to eat. The only sounds were the breeze filtering through bushes on the opposite bank and the gurgle of water over a stony riverbed. She looked down. The water was enticing, running clear and crystalline and, on impulse, she leaned over, bending almost double to scoop up a handful. It was ice cold.

'Better stick to the tea,' Jack advised.

Charlie was naturally the first to finish his lunch. 'Go and look at the boat,' Jack said. 'Choose where you want to sit.' He turned to Flora. 'We won't have a second's peace till we're out on that river.'

'I'm afraid not,' she said, with a small sigh.

She would have been content to stay where she was, cosy enough in hat, scarf and winter coat. Though it was still chilly, the sun was at its best. She turned her face to its rays, drinking in what warmth she could, allowing herself to sink deep into the silence.

'I liked your opening,' she said, remembering suddenly that she still had Jack's manuscript to finish.

'Honestly?'

'Would I lie? It's a really pacey beginning.'

'Let's hope Arthur thinks so, too.'

'He's bound to.' She propped herself up on her elbow and looked at him. 'Are you worried about it?'

'A little,' he confessed. 'Arthur wasn't happy with the last book.'

'The one you were writing when—'

'When you decided to investigate one too many times. I have to do "work" on it apparently. If I'm truthful, I knew it was a problem book when I sent it to him.'

'How much does he want you to change?'

'I don't know for sure, but I suspect it's pretty much a rewrite. I've time to get it done before the Cornish trip, but I'd rather have spent the hours doing something else.'

He broke off a piece of grass and chewed on it. 'I never asked you about your newspaper interview – with all the stuff that's been happening, I completely forgot – but did the All's Well get its moment of fame?'

'Jim Hargreaves rang me this morning. The article will be in next week's edition of the *Worthing Echo*.'

'I must make sure I buy a copy.'

'Let's hope half of Sussex does and I see more customers as a result. The window display has attracted a few browsers, and then the market this morning, but I'm still struggling a little.'

'It seems like we'll both be busy for next few weeks.'

'Just as well then that Helen left for Bournemouth,' she remarked as casually as she could. Helen Milsom was still a niggle that bothered Flora. 'Have you heard from her?' She crossed her fingers he wouldn't find the question tactless.

'No,' he said briefly, though his tone wasn't discouraging.

'It was strange, her turning up like that,' she ventured.

There was a pause while Jack appeared to gather his thoughts. Eventually, he said slowly, 'I have no idea why Helen thought it a good idea to come here. Well... that's not strictly true. She told me she'd lost her job recently, along with the man in her life. That seems to have been enough to persuade her to get on a plane for England.'

'She's not with your... your friend any longer?' It was what Flora would expect from the woman. Lose your current boyfriend and bounce back to your first, if he'd have you.

'The one she ditched me for? Apparently not,' Jack said easily. 'I'd always imagined they would have married, but they didn't.'

Flora trained her gaze on the river before she asked, 'Did she come here hoping your marriage might still be on?' It sounded brutal, put like that, but Jack didn't appear to mind.

'She might have. To be candid, I've no idea what was in her mind. But if she thought it, she was disappointed.'

'She's very beautiful.' There was a wistful note in Flora's voice.

'I agree, but it doesn't make me want to marry her.' He gave a twisted smile. 'You know, when I opened the door and saw who was standing there, I was floored. Devastated wouldn't be too strong a word. But now, I think it was probably the best thing that could have happened. I've carried her image around in my head – in my heart, too, if I'm honest – for the last six years. Now, at last, I feel free.'

'Are you sure? She's only gone to Bournemouth. It's not a million miles away.'

'Quite sure.' He leaned back, cushioning his head in his arms, and stretching out a pair of long legs. 'We have nothing to say to each other. Not any more. And where Helen goes after Bournemouth, what she chooses to do, holds no interest for me.'

'C'mon, let's go.' Charlie bounced up to them and started to shovel empty plates, and what food remained uneaten, into the baskets.

'Tranquillity is officially cancelled,' Jack announced, scrambling up and helping her to her feet.

She gave a rueful nod. 'Be careful,' she warned the boy, at the continued sound of clashing plates. 'We don't want to return with a heap of broken china.' She folded the blanket and stowed it on top of the baskets in a neat pile. 'We can leave these here. They'll be perfectly safe.'

Charlie led the way along the bank to the boat. 'I've bagged this seat,' the boy said, grabbing the side of the vessel to pull it further into shore, before climbing in. He settled himself on the rear bench.

Jack turned to her. 'Sorry, looks like you're in the bow.'

'As long as I don't sink, I'm happy anywhere.' She followed Charlie's example, making sure she kept her feet dry.

Unloosing the oars, Jack pushed off from the bank. 'Where to, Captain?' he asked Charlie.

'Down to Brighton,' the boy shot back immediately. 'Then we can go to the waxworks again.'

There was horror on Flora's face and Jack was quick to say, 'That's an awful long way. I'd never make it that far and, even if I did, think of all those boats in Shoreham harbour. I'd make a complete hash of navigating.'

'Let's be content with rowing downstream for a mile or two.' Flora waved a hand expansively. 'The scenery here is beautiful.'

Primroses and wild violets were scattered across the river bank – it was easier to appreciate them now they were on the water – and beyond, there was meadowland, its green occasionally broken by the delicate beauty of golden saxifrage. At the edge of her vision, the swoop and hollow of the Downs rose hazy in the soft winter light.

They had been rowing a while when Charlie began to fidget. 'Can I row now, Mr Carrington?' he asked.

Flora smiled to herself. A twelve-year-old boy's interest in scenery would be minimal.

'You're a strong lad, Charlie,' Jack said, 'but I'm not sure it would be a good idea. These oars are mighty heavy.'

'I'm definitely sure it's not a good idea,' Flora put in. 'The river seems a lot rougher here.'

It had certainly widened and, beyond, she caught sight of the water bubbling and frothing over some kind of obstacle below the surface, then the river falling away into a deep gulf. It looked almost like a miniature waterfall.

'Jack, do you think we should turn round?' she asked urgently. 'It doesn't look too safe ahead.'

He glanced behind him. 'God, I didn't know that was there. I'll turn round now.'

With his right hand, he thrust the oar deep into the water and the boat began to move in a circle.

Flora had started to relax when Charlie suddenly piped, 'My feet are wet.'

She twisted herself around to look. There was water on the

floor of the boat and the boy's feet were dangling in it. As Jack turned the boat further in the circle, the river abandoned its slow seep and began to rush in, deluging her own feet.

'We've a leak,' she said, trying not to sound panicked.

Another surge and the water was over their ankles.

'What the hell!'

Jack stopped turning the boat and instead began paddling furiously towards the nearest bank. But the current at this point had become too strong and for every stroke of the oar they moved no more than an inch. Meanwhile, the boat was filling steadily with water.

Flora shifted backwards, her hand reaching down to the floor of the boat. Almost immediately, she struck rough wood and, with her fingers, traced a clear gap in the boat's wooden hull. It must have been filled with broken wood to keep it afloat, she thought, but their passage downstream and the turn Jack had been making, had shaken the pieces free.

It was then that Charlie announced, 'We're sinking.'

TWENTY-EIGHT

The boy was right. The boat had dipped so far down into the water that it was now impossible for Jack to use the oars.

'Can you swim, Charlie?' he asked.

The boy shook his head. 'No, Mr Carrington.' His voice had a quaver to it.

She couldn't swim either, but Jack must rescue the child first.

'I'm going to jump in,' he said calmly. 'When I jump, Charlie, you're to jump, too, and take hold of me. I'll swim to the bank with you, then I'll go back for Miss Steele.'

He looked across at her. 'I'd tow the boat if I could with you both on board, but it's too big and in this swell, too heavy.' She knew what he was thinking. By the time he got Charlie to shore, the boat might well have gone under.

Jack pulled off his coat along with his shoes, dumping them into the swell of water that now filled the boat. Plunging into the river, he made sure that Charlie had hold of him, before striking out for the bank. He was swimming hard against the current, but even so it seemed an age to Flora before he reached a grassy spur of land. At Jack's urging, Charlie reached up and grabbed a handful of coarse grass, heaving himself onto dry land.

As soon as he saw the boy safe, Jack turned back, swimming as fast as he could towards her but making little headway. The boat was sinking and, at the same time, drifting ever closer to the water-fall. Flora could see that if it toppled over, there was no way he would get to her.

He must have seen it, too. 'Jump!' he shouted over the increasing noise of pounding water. 'Jump, Flora, or you'll go over with it.'

She took hold of the side of the boat that was now tossing badly, and pulled herself upright. Stripping off her coat and shoes as Jack had done, she took a deep breath, trying to still limbs that were trembling. Then she stepped off the sinking boat – it was now so low in the water she had no need to jump – and into a mael-strom of churning river.

The intense cold almost stopped her breath and, for an instant, a deadly numbness took hold until, by instinct it seemed, her arms and legs began to thrash the water, trying to keep herself afloat long enough for Jack to reach her. He was tantalisingly close, swimming hard against the current, but not yet close enough. She felt the water bubble around her mouth and her thrashing became wilder. Then she was beneath the surface, floating downwards to the river bed. The impulse to give up, to simply let the river take her where it would, overwhelmed her for an instant.

But only an instant. The next moment she was kicking her legs frantically, and sculling upwards with her hands through a tangle of river weeds. When she surfaced, Jack was an arm's length away, and with one long stroke, he pulled beside her. Girdling her waist, he held her fast as the boat tumbled into the gulf, the sound of wood breaking on rocks clearly audible. For a minute he trod water with her, trying to get his breath back, but the current was too strong to stay still, pulling them always and inexorably towards the fall.

'Hang on to me,' he said. And she did.

Once more, he struck out for the shore, at a point further downstream now than the spur on which he'd landed Charlie. It appeared to Flora that they slid sideways as fast as they moved ahead. Endless minutes, it seemed, before she felt Jack slow his stroke. He steadied himself, treading water again, and then with one desperate lurch, made a grab for the bank above. A dripping Charlie ran towards them, kneeling on the bank and bending down to hold his hand out to Jack.

'Not me – Flora!' Jack yelled to the boy.

She knew what she was supposed to do and, though her grip on Jack felt the only small safety she had, she let go, and reached up for Charlie's hand. He was a strong boy and within seconds had helped pull her up and out of the river. Now free of his burden, Jack made a grab with his other hand for a clump of grass and slowly and agonisingly pulled himself clear of the water, collapsing prostrate beside her.

Wet clothes stuck to every inch of Flora's skin and ferocious shivers took hold of her. She had never thought that teeth chattered, but it was exactly what they did.

'We need to move,' Jack managed to say, his breath coming in spurts. He sat up and, as best he could, wrung the water from his trousers and shirt.

'Have you still got your shoes, Charlie?'

'Yes, Mr Carrington.' The boy was shivering badly, too.

'Then you must run ahead and try and get help from the farm where we parked the car.'

'Yes, Mr Carrington.'

'We'll follow,' Jack assured him, 'but we'll not get there as fast on stockinged feet.'

Still the boy made no move. He appeared frozen to the spot, as scared as he was bedraggled. 'Charlie,' she said quietly, 'you must run as fast as you can to save us all from pneumonia.'

The boy nodded gravely and, with a brief look at them, turned and ran back along the bank and onto the footpath they'd wandered along so carelessly a few hours before.

Jack took hold of her hand and pulled her to her feet. Then his arms were round her, and he tightened his grip. 'I thought you were gone,' he whispered.

She tried to laugh, but it came out muffled and distorted. 'I thought so, too.'

He let go of her, reluctantly she felt, and together they limped back to the spot where they'd picnicked. Baskets and blanket still sat in a tidy pile. Ignoring them, they began the painful walk, shoe-less, along the rutted path. They were halfway back to the farm when they heard the roar of a motorcycle and, for the first time, raised their heads from the track.

'Hop on, the pair of you.' A weather-beaten face smiled at them from beneath a pair of fierce eyebrows. 'We'll have you warm in two shakes of a lamb's tail. Name's Lenister, by the way.'

Flora's limbs were ice-cold, but somehow she clambered onto the motorbike with Jack behind, scrunched tight against her. Swaying dangerously, as the bike weaved a path around the track's bumps, lumps and potholes, they arrived at the farmhouse door to find Mrs Lenister waiting for them.

'Your lad is in the kitchen having a hot wash,' she said. 'He was frozen to the marrow, but we'll have him dressed and dry in no time. Lucky, we've still got some of our son's old clothes. And Dad will find you something,' she said, addressing Jack. She turned to Flora. 'You come with me, my love. I've a skirt and jumper you can have. No shoes, I'm afraid. A pair of boots will have to do. I've put it all in the bathroom – you'll find plenty of hot water up there.'

Within half an hour, they were sitting at the farmhouse table with mugs of tea and a plate of Mrs Lenister's plum-heavy cakes straight from the oven. Their sopping clothes had been funnelled into a large straw basket the farmer's wife had dug from the depths of a kitchen cupboard.

Flora took a cake and looked around the table at their strangely dressed party. The sight would normally have her laugh out loud, but right now hysteria lurked too close to the surface. She must concentrate on being warm and safe and immensely grateful for being given back her life for the third time in the last few weeks.

'Can't do nothin' about your coats and shoes,' Mrs Lenister said sadly. 'They're good and gone.'

Flora's had been her second-best coat, bought only three years previously, and its loss grieved her, but a far bigger grief had been averted – the tumble into that gulf and the watery hell that awaited. She forgot about the coat.

They were finishing their cakes when Mr Lenister walked in with the picnic baskets and blanket. 'Shame for a nice outin' to end like that,' he observed. 'And Diggory's boat broken to pieces, no doubt.'

Jack looked glum. 'I have to tell him that he's lost *Mabel*, and after he was kind enough to loan her to us.' He passed a hand through his still damp hair. 'I don't know what happened – one minute we were bowling along, the next we were sinking.'

'There was a hole,' Flora said, and then wished she'd kept quiet.

All eyes were on her. 'A hole?' Mrs Lenister queried. 'You mean Diggory let the boat go out with a hole in it?'

'He wouldn't do that,' her husband protested.

'Mebbe he didn't know.'

'He'd have to know,' the farmer said. 'He's been here these last few weeks doin' her up. Painted her nice and proper, too.'

'Could the hole have been made since then?' Flora asked tentatively, careful not to suggest deliberate sabotage.

'I wouldn't think so. Unless it were someone who meant mischief. Some hooligan with nothing better to do.' Mrs Lenister frowned at the thought and looked over at her husband.

He nodded. 'Could be. Now I think of it, there was a bit of a commotion t'other evening. We were sittin' listenin' to the wireless, weren't we, Mother, and all of a sudden Benji, he's our best dog, started barkin' for all he was worth. I went out with a torch to see what was gettin' him excited, but I couldn't see anythin'. Still, it was a while before he stopped his barkin'.'

'It a queer one.' His wife shook her head. 'We don't see many people round here. We're a long way out. Who'd have come by and done a thing like that?'

'Who'd have even knowed Diggory had his boat moored there?' her husband put in.

'It must have been chance. Someone from Brampton.' She named the nearby village. 'Got drunk in the pub and thought they'd have a lark. Mebbe took the boat out and messed it up.'

'Has to be.' Mr Lenister had started to nod in time with his wife. 'We've not seen a soul since Benji had his fit.'

'I did,' Charlie said unexpectedly.

During the conversation, the boy had been completely silent, too busy devouring at least three plum-heavies, washed down by Mrs Lenister's home-made lemonade.

'I did,' he repeated, when everyone turned to him expectantly. 'When we were in the boat. A bit after we started off. I was at the back and I turned round to look at the way we'd come. There was someone in the bushes.'

'Well, I never!' Mrs Lenister was scandalised.

'Did you get a good look at them?' Flora asked, leaning towards him.

'Not that good. They were in the bushes, like I said. It looked like they were hidin', but they were in bright colours. I saw the colours.'

Jack flashed her a look which said plainly, *leave it there*. He was right. It was best not to involve the Lenisters any further in what appeared another step in the murky game they'd been playing.

After a heartfelt thank-you to the farmer and his wife and a promise to return the clothes as soon as they could, they clambered back into the car. Driving down the narrow lane they'd arrived by, Jack's face was set. Flora guessed he was thinking of Diggory and the confession he had to make. She hoped the old man was insured, but if not they would somehow have to find the money to replace *Mabel*. It was clear the boat had been deliberately damaged. Was that by the person Charlie had seen? It might, of course, be coincidence that there'd been a walker on the river bank at the time. Or, it might not. The figure Charlie had spotted could have been hiding in the bushes, waiting for them to take the boat out and keen to see the result of their handiwork.

She twisted round in her seat to speak to the boy.

'The figure you saw, Charlie? You said they were in bright clothes. What kind of clothes? What kind of colours?'

It was a shot in the dark, but anything he could remember might be of help.

'Red,' he said firmly. 'I saw red. And black, I think. All kind of mixed up.' He thought for a moment. 'Like those actors on the pier.'

She felt Jack beside her give a small shrug. Colours, actors, pier – they were trifling details to set against a ruined boat.

TWENTY-NINE

They dropped Charlie at his house with only a brief explanation to Mrs Teague of why her son was dressed in a jumper and trousers two sizes too big, before handing over the still sodden clothes he'd left home in. Charlie would no doubt tell his own story.

'The cottage?' Jack asked, starting the car.

'Please. Mrs Lenister was extremely kind but I can't wait to take these boots off. How about you?'

'"Dad's clothes" are uncomfortably itchy. Farmers must be a tough breed.'

Within a few minutes, they'd pulled up outside Flora's house but before she could say goodbye, he placed a detaining hand on her arm.

'We're in trouble,' he said simply.

He needed her to realise the seriousness of the situation. Frank Foster hadn't been around to throw a flint through his window and he hadn't been around to sabotage *Mabel*. They had an unknown enemy. A ruthless enemy, who had somehow discovered they'd planned to take the boat out today.

'Not that much trouble, surely,' Flora said, her head to one side, as though judging the situation. 'We've made some progress.'

Jack felt exasperated. Her sunny optimism was something to

cherish, but when it was as misplaced as it was at the moment, he could have happily wrung her neck.

'You're not going to tell me that the picnic has been some kind of sleuthing triumph?'

'Not triumph, no. But we've started to flush out the villain. He or she is no longer invisible. Not quite in sight yet, but it's given me hope.'

Jack glared at her. 'You and I nearly drowned this afternoon. Charlie, too. How has that in any way flushed out the bast— the guilty person?'

'Someone risked a lot when they attacked that boat, Jack. Mr Lenister could have discovered them the evening they took a hammer to *Mabel*. If he'd investigated a little further than his farm-yard, he would have caught them red-handed. And today was another big risk. If the figure Charlie saw on the bank was there to watch our destruction, to make sure we perished, they could easily have been seen by others. The river path is a local walk and an enquiry into our deaths would have looked for witnesses. There weren't any, as it happened, but our enemy wasn't to know that.'

He tightened his grip on her arm. 'I can't see that makes for anything good. Your optimism is false. This person, whoever they are, was willing for a child – a *child*, Flora – to drown, in order to make sure that we died.'

She struggled free from his grasp and swivelled round to face him. 'But that's my point. They're desperate. It means we're getting close.'

He stared through the windscreen at the gathering dusk. 'You don't need me to remind you of the obvious. Desperate people do desperate things, and we're in the firing line. You, particularly. There's already been an attempt on your life before today's. Maybe two attempts.'

'My crash on Betty was the result of bad driving,' she argued back.

'Only according to you. As for us getting close to the villain's identity, why would you think that? We're no closer now than we were at the very beginning. It must be clear, even to you, that Frank Foster isn't our man. He's in a police cell, not rampaging along the Adur. That leaves us with who? Harry Barnes – do you really see him finding his way to the riverside in the dark and taking a hammer to *Mabel*?'

'I could see Evelyn doing it,' she countered.

'So could I, and she was driving the car that ran you down. But she has alibis for the day that Polly died. We've no chance of checking, but I'm pretty sure they'd hold – and we have no idea if she was even in Brighton the day *you* were pushed from the pier.'

His fingers beat a tattoo on the steering wheel. 'We have to admit we've reached a dead end. Each of the people we've listed as suspects could be guilty of one or other of these incidents. None of them could be guilty of them all. That has to mean we're looking for another person entirely. Except, we mustn't. We're flailing around with no real idea who to look for, while the unknown killer knows exactly who *they're* looking for. What does that say to you? To me, it says danger, pure and simple.'

He waited for her response. Surely, she could see the truth of his words?

'Raymond,' she said suddenly.

'Parsons? What has he to do with it?'

'He's gone missing. He left the golf club and hasn't been seen at the Nook since last Saturday. Alice is furious that he's let Kate down so badly. *And*,' she continued, 'look how wretched he's seemed these past few weeks. A completely changed man.'

'He's bound to look wretched. He's lost the woman he loved.'

'He could love her but still kill. I've said so before and I believe it. Lovers can quarrel. They did quarrel, we saw it for ourselves, and I have only Raymond's word that he would never harm her. He could have been in Brighton on both the days in question. If my bicycle crash was an accident, and I believe it was, there's only the sinking of the boat to account for. And I *can* see him making his way to the river with a hammer in his hand. He's a country boy. A footpath in the dark, a river at night, neither would bother him.'

'In that case, all we need to discover is whether he's partial to wearing red and black.' Jack said it half-jokingly, though he didn't feel at all like joking.

'He could have adopted a disguise at the river.' For the first time, her tone was uncertain.

'You don't sound too sure now.'

'I like Raymond. I don't want it to be him. But I can't think of a single other person it could be.'

'Why don't we bow out now?' he asked, in what he hoped was his most coaxing voice. 'Polly's death will be registered as an accident. That's much better for Ted Russell than either suicide or murder. It's important we think of him. He's a very sad man and next week will be worse for him when he buries Polly. After that, given a chance, he can begin to mend, and the sooner this business is wrapped up, the better for him.'

Jack could see she was unconvinced and redoubled his efforts. 'Leaving aside Ted, we're both of us exhausted and not making much sense at the moment. At least, let's agree on no more investigating until we've had a chance to talk this through properly.'

'OK,' she said reluctantly. 'I agree, but only for the moment, and only because all I can think of right now is a hot bath.'

'Enjoy it to the full. And make sure you keep out of trouble until I see you again.'

She climbed out of the car and he watched her walk up the front path and let herself into the cottage. At the doorway, she paused and waved to him, her figure silhouetted against the hall light. Satisfied that for the moment at least she was safe, he restarted the car and made for Overlay House.

* * *

Flora lay back in the bath, luxuriating in its warmth, a clean nightdress on the bathroom stool and Mrs Lenister's clothes in the laundry basket. How kind the farmer's wife had been. She must think of something nice to take her when she returned the clothes.

A book? she wondered. No, flowers most probably. A beautiful, large bouquet from the florist's in Steyning.

She yawned and then yawned again. It had been a very long day. The busy morning she'd spent in the shop felt an age ago, and even their walk to the river seemed to have happened in another world. Terrible danger had obliterated all else, possessing Flora's thoughts and feelings completely. No wonder she felt exhausted.

She would sleep like a log, she decided, when later she sat by the fire, sipping a mug of cocoa. She hadn't made cocoa since her aunt died. It had become a favourite with Violet in the last year of her life, a warm and comforting end to each day, even during summertime. For a moment, she felt her aunt beside her, sitting in her treasured chair, a woollen blanket across her knees. Violet would have disapproved of what her niece had been doing, disapproved of her involvement in a murder hunt. She would have insisted that Flora thought only of the bookshop, of making it a success after the months of struggle.

'I've tried,' she said, hoping her aunt could hear. The window display had been admired way beyond the village. The new bookshop sign was bold and inviting. The article in the *Worthing Echo* would appear very soon. Some of it, at least, should lead to more customers.

She breathed out forcefully. She was making excuses for herself – it wasn't enough. The All's Well's fortunes were looking better, but she had to confess she'd allowed her focus to slip since Polly's death. She didn't want to admit it, but Jack was right. She should get back to what was important and let the girl go quietly to her grave. Agree with Inspector Ridley that Polly had suffered an unfortunate accident and allow Ted Russell to lay his niece to rest without further worry. Finishing her cocoa, she took the cup into the kitchen, then climbed the stairs.

As she'd foretold, she had no trouble falling into a heavy sleep. Until the early hours, when she began tossing and turning, throwing herself from one side of the bed to the other, the sheets and blankets pulled into disarray. She could feel the glacial water climbing ever higher, the reeds around her legs, a tangle of waving green, her body being pulled under and under and under. The water had closed over her head, pressing so heavily on her that her breath had stopped and she hung, limpid and suspended, while all around were flashes of darting fish, red and black. Had they come to see her drown? Now, there was thunder in her head and she was no longer simply hanging, but being dragged unresistingly towards the noise. No! she screamed out. No!

With a bang, she landed on the floor. She had fallen out of bed, so violent had been the nightmare. Still terrified, she pulled herself to her feet, collapsing onto the mattress. She was sweating, her forehead laced with water, her pulse beating so hard it filled her ears. Switching on the bedside light, she shuffled her feet into slippers and padded into the bathroom to wash. Her face in the mirror was drained of all colour. Trying to shake herself free of the fear that still had her in its grip, she went downstairs to the kitchen, putting the kettle on to boil. She was still shaking as she made tea.

Gradually, the warm liquid soothed her and she felt her pulse return to normal. Dawn was breaking and ahead of her was a long day in the shop, but there would be no more sleep for her tonight – instead, she would rest until it was time to rise. Settled once more in bed, though, she found her eyelids closing and within minutes she was fast asleep.

It took the rattle of milk bottles to wake her. A quick glance at her bedside clock, and she jumped out of bed and rushed to the bathroom for a quick wash. She was going to be late opening the All's Well. Pulling a skirt and jumper at random from the old oak wardrobe, she dressed quickly and ran down the stairs to the front door.

There was milk to collect from the doorstep before she could leave. Hastily, she stowed the bottle in the larder, where the sad eyes of the trout she was to have eaten last night looked reproachfully back at her. A memory was triggered and not one she wanted. The memory of river fish. Fish that were red and black. Suddenly, she stood stock-still, her hand arrested, her whole body frozen.

Red and black. Clothes in red and black. Like the actors on the pier. That's what Charlie had said. And in that instant, she knew who had plotted their death yesterday, who had pushed her from the pier, who had attacked Jack. Who had succeeded in killing Polly Dakers.

Abandoning all thoughts of the bookshop, she threw on the coat she'd worn to Brighton and raced out of the house, running like a demon to Overlay House and Jack.

THIRTY

Jack was wiping the shaving cream from his chin when there was a loud bang on the front door. The noise was familiar, but surely it couldn't be Flora? Not at this hour – she had a bookshop to open.

Hastily, he tugged a shirt over his head and ran down the stairs.

'I know who it is,' she said breathlessly, as he opened the door.

Jack found himself staring. Her coat was unbuttoned, her long hair tumbled across her face, and was that a smear of toothpaste on her lips?

'You'd better come in,' he said calmly, resigned to whatever new leap of imagination had taken her by storm.

He led the way into the kitchen. 'I haven't had my breakfast yet. Do you mind if I toast some bread?'

'Go ahead. You could do some for me, too.'

Then, as his hand reached out for the bread bin, she rushed over to him and grabbed him by the waist. 'I know, Jack, I know,' she repeated, bouncing up and down.

'Stop that!' he protested. 'I realise you're excited, but I wake up slowly. I need time to meet a new day. I'll make the toast – I've even got some decent coffee – and you can tell me the great new idea.'

'It's not an idea. It's absolutely rock solid.' She was still bouncing.

Trying not to mutter too loudly, Jack spooned coffee into the new percolator Arthur Bellaby had sent him and filled it with water. *Straight from Italy*, his agent had written. *And coffee to go alongside. You'll love it.*

'So... sleuth extraordinaire... who is it?' He couldn't help smiling. She was exhausting at times, but he had to admit, she was fun to be with.

'Sylvia,' she announced. 'Sylvia Russell.'

He stared at her. 'I know you sometimes lose the plot, but Sylvia Russell—'

'I know. That was my first thought, too. But only for an instant. My second was that it all made sense. The figure that Charlie saw yesterday? What stuck in his mind, the primary thing he remembered? It wasn't whether it was a man or a woman, young or old. It was the colours the figure was wearing. And he was specific – red and black, he said.'

'I don't see the significance.'

'I didn't expect you to. But I do,' she crowed, delving into her coat pocket and bringing out the red woollen bobble. 'Remember this? It came from a Harlequin costume – we established that much at least. When I thought about what Charlie had said, I knew. The figure on the river bank was wearing a costume like the ones worn by the actors on the pier. And this bobble is our proof.' She waved it excitedly in the air.

Leaving aside the surreal thought that someone would dress up in a Harlequin costume to murder, he pointed out the obvious problem. 'You went through the theatre company's wardrobe. Nothing was missing. Not even a bobble.'

'That's because the costume didn't belong to the theatre company,' she said triumphantly. 'It came from Ted Russell's wardrobe! He told us at the hospital how he and his wife used to put on shows for the village children at their birthday parties, how they wore costumes they borrowed from the local amateur dramatic society.'

'"Borrowed" being the operative word.' This was going to be

one of Flora's magnificent hunches, based on absolutely no evidence. He could feel it.

'Permanently borrowed if he forgot to give a costume back,' she countered. 'What if he borrowed the Harlequin – it would be just the thing for a children's party with the bells and the rattle – and then never gave it back?'

'It's that familiar "what if" that bothers me. You're saying that Ted Russell kept a costume in his wardrobe, a costume he should have returned, how long ago? Fifteen years?'

Flora was about to plunge in again when, determined to bring her down to earth, he went on, 'Then, his daughter finds the costume and thinks it's just the thing to wear to murder her cousin? Why would she want to murder Polly, in any case, and why on earth would she dress up to do it?'

'Why dress up? That's simple – disguise. There were several actors playing Harlequin in the panto, understudying each other. At dress rehearsals and during the performance, they were in costume, in case they had to go on stage at very short notice. While they were waiting for a call that didn't come, they wandered around, went outside for a cigarette. Smoking wasn't allowed in the theatre, I saw a notice. It's not usual but the building is very old and built of wood, so maybe it's a fire regulation. Those actors were in and out of the theatre door. They told us that over tea, the afternoon I was attacked. Think of it, Jack, actors dressed as Harlequin trotting in and out of the theatre. The few witnesses that were on the pier when Polly died told Inspector Ridley and his men the same thing – the only people they'd seen had been actors.'

'You're suggesting Sylvia mingled with the actors?'

'Exactly. They were drifting around, in and out of the theatre. Who would be counting how many Harlequins there were? How could you distinguish between one or the other when they all looked the same? It's a perfect disguise.'

Jack supposed there might be some truth in what she was saying. A sliver of truth at most, though. He wasn't convinced. 'That may have worked on the pier but what about yesterday?

Why would she have worn the costume to walk along the river bank? Frankly, that's bizarre.'

Flora pursed her lips. 'I don't know for sure. It could have been disguise again. If she was spotted, she wouldn't want to be recognised – and wearing the costume could have spooked anyone who saw it, ensuring they steered clear. It certainly made an impression on Charlie. And perhaps she felt it would bring her luck. She'd been successful at getting rid of Polly wearing it, and almost managed to get rid of me. Yesterday afternoon, she set out to get the job done – on both of us.'

There was a long silence, until she said, 'I think the toast is burning.'

Frantically, he pulled the pan from under the grill, and waved a hand over the blackened bread, while smoke filled the kitchen.

'Damn,' he said, followed by several less audible curses, and rushed to open the window.

'We'll have to go without,' Flora said firmly. 'We don't have the time. We need to get going.'

'What do you mean, we need to get going?'

She stared at him, a blank expression on her face. 'It's obvious, isn't it? To the Russells' house. We need to find that costume. And the shoe this comes from.' She waved the bobble at him again.

'We're breaking in? No, Flora. I won't do it.'

'Then I will. Anyway, we won't need to break in. Not technically. The key will be under the flower pot by the front door. It always is.'

He shook his head, still bemused by the ways of country dwellers, despite having lived in Abbeymead for well over five years.

'Everyone knows the key is there?'

She nodded.

'So what's the point of hiding it?'

'It keeps it safe,' she said inexplicably.

He gave up. He wouldn't get a logical answer, but as far as he was concerned, walking into another person's house without permission was breaking the law, however you did it.

'You want us to walk into Ted's house and start ransacking his wardrobe? I'm not doing it.'

'You have to, Jack. Or I have to, alone. We've solved the crime and once we have the costume in our possession, we'll have the evidence to prove it. You can tell your inspector who to arrest.'

He didn't look at her but began walking up and down the kitchen, between table and window, window and table.

'Why is it such a problem for you?' she challenged. 'Ted is still in hospital. He won't be discharged until the weekend, and Sylvia is at work in Shoreham, miles away. We'll be completely alone. We go quietly into the house, find the costume – it will be stuffed into Sylvia's wardrobe, I reckon – then take it to the Brighton police station and ask for Alan Ridley.'

Jack slumped down onto a kitchen chair, feeling the energy sucked out of him. Could she really be right? When they'd visited the Russells after Polly's death, Sylvia seemed to have little affection for her cousin and, if she suspected Polly's involvement with Raymond, she would have even less. But to push the girl to her death and then return to typing letters in a Shoreham office... it seemed ridiculous.

He jumped up. 'Before we go anywhere, I'm ringing Ridley,' he said decidedly.

Flora caught at his arm. 'If you do that, we could be arrested before we even get to Ted's house.'

'We'll have to take the chance. I'm not going into that house without someone knowing where we are, and preferably someone in authority. If you're right, and it's still a big "if", the girl is highly dangerous.'

'I think you're making a mistake.'

'If you want me with you—'

'You win,' she murmured, but it was plain her mind had travelled on. 'I wonder why Sylvia took the costume to Brighton in the first place? Was it serendipitous, d'you think? Or had she planned the murder weeks in advance? And how did she remain undetected?'

'Questions and more questions – and we're to find the answers by breaking into her house?'

Flora buttoned her coat, impatience written across her face. 'Well, are you coming?'

* * *

They were nearing the estate where Ted Russell had his house. 'I think it's better if we park on the main road and walk the rest of the way,' she suggested.

'That's exactly what I intend to do. I've no wish to incriminate myself any more than necessary.'

'Now you're being grumpy. This is our big moment, Jack.'

She felt exhilarated. Ever since that astonishing revelation in the larder, her brain had been buzzing. It all fitted so brilliantly. Sylvia's obvious jealousy of her cousin, the glares Flora had intercepted way back at Bernie Mitchell's wake. If looks could kill! And then later her insistence that Polly must have slipped off the pier. She had been cunning, pretending it was best for Ted to think his niece had slipped, rather than have him believe Polly had thrown herself to her death. Of course, an accident was preferable to suicide, but the other possibility – murder – had been craftily excluded.

'If the key isn't where you say, do we creep around the back and throw ourselves over the garden fence?' Jack enquired.

His tone was deliberately satirical, but she refused to rise to the bait.

'The key will be there,' she said calmly. 'We walk up to the house and let ourselves in, as though we'd been asked to check on something while Sylvia is away. If you don't act suspiciously, people won't suspect. You should know that. I read one of your books at Christmas, *A Stranger in Tangiers*, and the hero definitely does some very questionable things, but no one blinks an eye, simply because he does it with an air of insouciance.'

'How's my insouciance doing?' he asked, smiling despite his misgiving.

She looked at him critically. 'You still look a bit furtive. Keep trying.'

Striding up the garden path, she kept a watch for any neighbours out walking who might be tempted to stop and talk. Fortunately, the residents were either at work or hadn't yet left to do their shopping. Fortunately, too, the key was just where she prophesied.

Unlocking the door, she let herself into the hall with Jack following closely behind.

She sniffed the air. It felt close and stale. 'I know my cottage has draughts and the occasional leaking pipe, and the water doesn't always run hot,' she said, 'but I'd hate to live in a house like this. It feels so... so cloying.'

'You're not thinking of living here, are you?' he said briskly. 'Let's get on with the search and get out of the place as soon as we can.'

'Upstairs then?'

They walked up in single file, every step emitting an eerie creak.

'The staircase isn't too solid, is it?'

'Quit the house critique, Flora. Let's find the bedrooms and be done.'

Jack was right. They needed to be swift. 'You take Ted's,' she said, suddenly businesslike, 'and I'll search Sylvia's wardrobe.'

'How fair is that? You're the one who'll get first prize.'

'Ah, but I've got the bobble,' she pointed out.

Two of the bedroom doors were open and it was easy to decide whose bedroom was whose. A third door was closed. 'We don't need to go in there. It will be a boxroom,' she said knowledgeably, having been in several such houses in Abbeymead. 'There'll be barely room for an arm and a leg.'

Walking into Sylvia's bedroom was to take a journey back in time, at least ten years. Nothing could have changed since the day Dolly Russell had marched out of the house and into her new life in America. The curtains were almost threadbare now, but Flora could see that once they had been a girlish pink. A pink lampshade hung from the ceiling, its pleats crumpled, and a grey bedspread with appliqué pink elephants covered the bed. There were photographs on the tiny wooden dressing table, one of Sylvia taken at school, one of Dolly, she imagined. And one with all three of them – Sylvia, Dolly and Ted at the Victory in Europe party that had been held on the village green.

Flora remembered it well. She'd been an awkward sixteen-year-old, commandeered to fetch and carry tables and chairs and anything else the good ladies of St Saviour's needed on the green. But it had been the most wonderful day and, when she and her aunt had arrived home that night, tired and still drunk with joy that the war was finally over, Violet had given her a silver charm bracelet. *Wear this to remember*, her aunt had said. *Wear it in hope of a better future*. And Flora did. Still wore it. Still added charms when she could afford to.

She pulled herself out of her reverie and walked across the room to the single wardrobe which stood in an alcove. A child's wardrobe. It was uncanny and Flora felt a prickling in the nape of her neck. Opening the cupboard door, she saw a meagre collection of hangers. There were several office-type skirts, one or two blouses, the dress Sylvia had worn to the wake. But nothing else. Disappointment coursed through her. The costume had to be here.

She lowered her glance to the floor of the wardrobe. Slippers, a scuffed pair of court shoes and a pair of boots – mud-caked. Flora's interest quickened. She knelt down and peered beneath the hanging clothes, then delved her hand deep into the back of the wardrobe and brought out a tangle of red and black cloth. Yes! Another fumble and here were Harlequin's slippers, one of which was bereft of its decoration. Dragging it into the light, she took the bobble from her coat pocket and placed it in the middle of the slipper. A wide smile spread across her face. A perfect fit.

'A perfect fit,' she said aloud.

'Yes, isn't it?' a voice said in her ear, and Flora felt the prick of thin steel against her neck.

THIRTY-ONE

'Nothing in Ted's wardrobe,' Jack called from the landing. 'Any luck for you?'

Flora couldn't answer. She dared hardly breathe. The tip of a very sharp knife was digging into her skin and she could already feel a trickle of blood making its way down her neck.

'Come in, Mr Carrington,' Sylvia said over her shoulder. 'Don't be shy.'

Flora heard the creak of Jack's feet on the floorboards and his harsh intake of breath as he walked into the room.

'No trying to disarm me,' Sylvia said, still kneeling beside Flora, 'or your girlfriend will end in a mess.'

'We... we can talk about this... this problem, I'm sure.' Jack's voice was strained to breaking point.

'You have the problem, not me,' the girl pointed out, getting to her feet. 'And really, I've far too much to do to waste time talking. I'm sure you'll understand. At least, you would if you busied yourself with your own affairs and kept out of mine. You've been a trial to me, the pair of you.'

She glared from one to the other. 'I knew something was wrong from the time you first called here – it was the way you spoke to me, Flora Steele. You sounded suspicious and I reckoned then that

you'd need watching. So that's what I did. It was easy enough –
you didn't go far. It meant taking days off work, pretending I was
sick, but I really didn't care. I was leaving that miserable job as
soon as I was sure neither of you would cause me trouble. But you
did – going round asking questions, talking to that policeman.'

While Sylvia talked, Flora had slowly moved her feet so that
the tips of her toes were on the floor. From this crouched position,
she reckoned it might just be possible to spring upright when the
girl's attention was distracted and knock the weapon from her
hand.

Almost immediately, a sharp sting as the knife was pushed
further into her neck destroyed the idea.

'I was following you the Saturday you collected the cases from
Rose Court,' Sylvia continued musingly. 'I knew you'd keep to the
arrangement you'd made with Dad – it made sense, it being half-
day closing and, sure enough, I watched Mr Carrington collect you
from the shop. Then I got into the taxi I'd booked and followed you
to Brighton. I thought you might poke around in the flat, maybe
find something you shouldn't, but instead you went to Annabel's.
The girl behind the desk was looking something up for you and it
seemed you weren't at the salon to make an appointment, so I kept
following you. You had no idea I was there, had you?

'As soon as I saw you go towards the pier, I knew for certain
that you were on to me, and that I'd have to take action. I rushed
back to the flat to change – I had a second key no one knew about.
It was quite amusing. There you were poking around the theatre's
costumes, and there was me dressed as Harlequin. I decided I'd get
rid of you there and then and deal with Mr Carrington later.'

'But you didn't get rid of me,' Flora said. 'Nor Jack.'

'More's the pity. After that, it took a while to see how to do it,
but then you were stupid enough to tell me about Diggory's boat
and I thought why not drown you in the river rather than the sea. It
was a pity about the kid, but I couldn't let it worry me too much.'

This woman was evil, Flora thought, or insane. Or perhaps
both. For the first time she looked at her attacker closely. Sylvia's

hair had been swept into an elegant French roll, her deep-set eyes were ablaze with a dark excitement and was that Polly's dress she was wearing – the one her cousin had worn to Bernie Mitchell's wake? In her mind, had she become Polly?

'Get up,' the girl ordered abruptly, jabbing Flora in the back with her knee.

Flora shuffled to her feet. Held tightly around the neck, the knife still cutting deep into her skin, she was pushed forward.

'Sylvia,' she said hoarsely, in a desperate attempt to communicate with the girl. 'Please don't do this. It will only make things worse for you.'

'Worse? Hardly. Unless you think a life of freedom in a new country is worse than the hangman's noose. Now get going.'

There was another sharp jab to Flora's back, but she dug her feet into the rug and held fast. 'Before I do, tell me why?' Her own mind was clear as to why, but she wanted to hear it from Sylvia.

'Why Polly? You're supposed to be the brainy one, Flora. Work it out for yourself.'

'Jealousy. Has all of this been about jealousy?'

'Such a simple word, isn't it? But look what's beneath – anger, resentment, bitterness. I'm full of it.' There was pride in her distorted announcement. 'My mother didn't love me enough to stay. She walked away and left me as a small child. My father tried, but in the end he didn't love me enough either – at least to pretend I was special. *He* walked away to pet and spoil another girl. Polly was the daughter he wanted.'

'I'm sure that's not true.'

'What do you know about it? About anything? You've never had a mother or a father. Just a fusty old aunt. And you don't even have her now. You know, my father idolised Polly,' she said, as though they were talking over the teacups. 'Polly was beautiful, Polly was clever, Polly was going places. While Sylvia, she wasn't a bad looker but no competition, and not too much up top either – just enough to keep her typing other people's letters for a pittance.

'I haven't had a holiday for years, there's not a decent piece of clothing in my wardrobe. You've seen that for yourself. Yet Dad could find money to pay for stupid photographs that would make my beautiful cousin even more beautiful. And when he didn't have enough money, he found someone who did. That sleazy old fool, Barnes. Harry lavished everything on her. Fur coat, diamond earrings, the flat in Brighton – you saw how expensive it was. All for Polly. I was allowed the smallest little piece of her good fortune, the poor relation acting as chaperone and expected to be grateful. So jealousy? You don't know the half of it.'

'Obviously not,' Flora said, drawing in a deep breath. The three of them had stayed completely immobile during Sylvia's diatribe, and she wondered if this was the moment to try and break free. Could she somehow duck beneath Sylvia's hold, escape the razor-edged blade thrust into her neck?

'You've been unhappy for such a long time,' she said, trying desperately to distract the girl, 'so why take action now?'

'You're right. A lifetime of hurt which got a whole lot worse when Polly Dakers moved in. I didn't want her in the house, but what do I count? Once her parents left for New Zealand, Dad couldn't wait to adopt her.' There was a moment's silence until she said roughly, 'We're wasting time. Now move!' She dug the knife deeper, causing Flora to jerk her head in pain.

Jack started forward. 'Don't!' the girl ordered, twisting the knife, and Flora saw him fall back, his face as rigid and pale as marble.

'Don't be scared of the knife,' she said to Flora. 'You'll find it's quicker than drowning. So why now? It's usually a simple thing that breaks you, isn't it? I asked my dear cousin for the bracelet Frank Foster had given her. It was beautiful, Flora, sapphire and pearls. The most beautiful thing I've ever seen. Polly had a drawer full of expensive jewellery at Rose Court, stuff that Harry had thrown at her, and all I was asking for was one small item. I asked her just before I left for the hairdresser's that morning, and she refused. She didn't even like Frank, so why not give me the bracelet? But she wouldn't. Instead, she laughed and said,

"You're going to have to wait, Sylvia." As if I hadn't waited all my life.

'When she said she was going to the pier, I knew what I had to do. We'd walked along it the previous week and seen the actors. It's what gave me the idea of wearing the Harlequin costume. When she said she was going there that morning, it was the best present I could have had. Why not wear the costume and do what I'd wanted to do for months? So I followed her.'

'You walked along the seafront in a Harlequin costume?' Flora couldn't keep the amazement from her voice.

'Don't be stupid. I wasn't about to advertise my presence. I wore a winter coat, then dumped it behind the bench outside the theatre. That early in the morning, there were only a few people on the pier and all they saw was another Harlequin. Clever, don't you think? When I'd seen Polly off, it was easy enough to retrieve my coat without being noticed.'

An intense silence filled the room. Flora was dumbstruck at the depth of bitterness, the sheer wickedness that lived in this girl.

'Now get going!' Sylvia ordered. 'There's been far too much gabble and you've made me late. I'll spare myself the bother of killing you – I really don't have the time – but only if you behave. You and your shadow here. I'm going to lock you both away – with a friend of yours. You can keep him company.'

Flora's stomach did a wild somersault. She was beset by the worst foreboding. 'Do you mean Raymond?' she asked, hoping she was wrong.

'So you do have a brain. Yes, dear Raymond. Wicked, weak Raymond, who couldn't resist Polly's charms either. She wasn't content with taking my father from me, she had to take my boyfriend, too.'

'Polly's no longer here,' Flora said, in a last attempt to reason with madness. 'But you are, and so is Raymond. In time, he'll see how foolish he's been. You and he could become friends again.'

Sylvia gave an explosive laugh. 'You really think so?'

'I do,' Flora said earnestly, trying to build another section of the bridge she'd begun. 'Raymond could be there to support you in the months ahead. You'll need all the help you can get.'

'You're a fool, Flora Steele,' the girl said derisively. 'If you don't stop talking claptrap, it will be you who needs help. I found the tickets. You must know I would, it's why you asked me if the cases had arrived. I hadn't unpacked them at the time. I only did it a day or so ago, and that's when I discovered that the man who was supposed to be my boyfriend hadn't only looked at another woman, but was leaving Abbeymead with her. For good. Leaving with my adorable cousin, without saying a word. That's when I decided.'

The darkness in Flora's mind intensified. Decided what? To kidnap Raymond! The ugly truth was there in front of her. It was why Raymond had never returned to work at the golf club, why he'd never turned up for duty at the Nook. He had been locked away in this house and they were about to be locked up with him. A sudden wash of coldness hit Flora, deep in her core.

'This has gone on too long,' Sylvia said in a bored voice. 'It's more than time that I left.' She gestured to a bag that Flora hadn't noticed before, sitting beside the bedside table. From the corner of her eye, she saw the girl's mouth stretch into a frightening grin. 'Can't let a ticket go to waste, can I? Now walk!'

Still holding the knife at Flora's throat, she shoved her forward.

'Don't try anything,' she warned Jack, as they approached the door. Flora had seen him tense, making ready to pounce. 'Just one more stab and she's gone.'

'Do as she says, Jack.'

He gave a grim nod and together they were hustled out on to the landing and pushed towards the closed door.

'Open it!' Sylvia commanded.

He turned the door knob with ease and Flora gave a small gasp. The door hadn't been locked, so why hadn't Raymond taken the chance to escape? Sylvia must have bound him so tightly, it was impossible to wriggle free.

With a final thump in the back, Flora was propelled forward, cannoning into Jack and, together, they were sent flying into the room. The door banged behind them and the key ground in the lock.

Jack was on his feet first and Flora, looking up at him from where she'd landed, saw him white-faced and staring. 'Don't look,' he said.

But it was too late – she had turned her head. Raymond would keep them company. Not tightly bound, as Flora had surmised, but lying sprawled in a corner, a crimson stain spread wide across his chest.

THIRTY-TWO

Jack had rarely felt such profound gratitude as when, minutes later, he heard bells. The bells of police vehicles arriving in Mulberry Crescent. Alan Ridley had responded to the phone call Jack had made earlier and mobilised his force. Rescue was on its way.

'It's going to be OK,' he said, fishing a handkerchief from his pocket and folding it into a thick pad to hold against Flora's neck. Thankfully, the blood had stopped seeping from the wound and was now no more than a dribble. But when she turned her face to his, there were tears trickling down her face.

'Raymond,' she said, her voice breaking.

'The police are here, Flora.' He wasn't sure if she'd even heard the bells. She seemed to have retreated into a world of her own. 'They'll look after Raymond.'

There were heavy footsteps on the stairs, then a loud thud as a hefty shoulder was thrust against the door. The sound of tearing wood echoed around the room before the door fell in, one side hanging lopsidedly from its hinges.

The two policemen who stood in the doorway took in the scene with a glance, one of them sweeping Flora from the floor and into his arms, while the other offered a hand to Jack. They cast an appalled look at Raymond's crumpled body before escorting their charges down the stairs and into the front garden.

A small crowd had gathered to watch. It wasn't every day that a convoy of police cars arrived in Mulberry Crescent, or every day that one of their neighbours was arrested. Framed in the window of a police van, Jack saw the stony face of Sylvia Russell.

When the officer who had carried Flora down the stairs lowered her gently to her feet, a policewoman came forward to take her hand. Flora was safe, Jack thought.

Alan Ridley left his men and came over to him. 'We'll do the questions later,' he said quietly. 'We need to get Miss Steele to the doctor. My chap tells me it's a deep wound and needs looking at. And what about you, Jack?'

'In one piece,' Jack said, trying to sound unconcerned, but his body was stiff with tension and he could hardly move. 'I've a car parked round the corner. I'll drive home.'

'If you're sure.'

He could see Ridley was worried and tried to conjure a smile. 'I'll be fine,' he assured him.

He was far from fine, and when he once more slid behind the wheel of the Austin, his hands were shaking so much he could barely push the starter.

* * *

Two days later, he parked the Austin in Bartholomew Square, having memorised Alice's directions, and gazed up at the neo-classical façade of Brighton Town Hall, its once honey-coloured stone faded to an indeterminate grey. The clock on the dashboard told him he was right on time. Locking the car door, he walked to the rear of the building, looking for the basement entrance. This was where Brighton housed its police station and he'd come to give a statement.

The policewoman who'd accompanied Flora to the doctor had taken down her account of events, Ridley indicating that Flora's brief statement was all they would need from her. It would be Jack's job to give the police a detailed account of exactly what had happened at the Russell house. According to Dr Hansen, Flora had been lucky. The knife had punctured her flesh deeply, but had missed the artery by a tenth of an inch. A painful half hour in his surgery had involved stitches and a thick dressing but, though the wound would sting for a while, the doctor was confident that within days it would heal well.

Yesterday, Jack had walked round to the cottage to see her and, though subdued, she'd seemed composed. They'd been careful to avoid speaking of the previous day's events. It had seemed safer to say nothing until the horror had faded a little. The bookshop remained closed for the moment, but it was encouraging that Flora had spoken of reopening in a day or so. Life needed to return to normal as soon as possible and his statement today would be a step on the way.

Jack followed the signs to the basement. At the reception desk, he gave the sergeant on duty his name and waited. He hoped whoever was to take his statement wouldn't be long – the only chair the police offered was wooden, straight-backed and uncomfortable. A barrage of shouting started up from a corridor on his left and he turned his head to look.

'The cells are along there,' the desk sergeant explained. He was smiling, as though the racket was no more than business as usual. 'A right old scrum last night. Two groups of Teddy Boys scrapping outside the Regent. D'you know the dance hall?'

Jack shook his head.

'Nice place,' the sergeant said. 'Elegant, you know. Gotta keep it that way.'

'Jack!' Alan Ridley arrived from the opposite direction. The inspector greeted him with a slap on the shoulder. 'Good to see you. I'll get one of my men to take an official statement in a moment, but come into my office first.'

He led the way into a small box of a room which seemed more like a store cupboard to Jack than an office. There was paper everywhere: files filling the shelves on every wall, stacks piled high in every corner and a desk hardly visible beneath the mounds that swamped it. The air hung thick and heavy as though the paper had sucked from it any hint of freshness.

'Take a seat,' the inspector said, nimbly swiping yet another pile of paper from a chair. 'Good to see you looking well – after that malarkey. You do seem to attract trouble, old chap.' He picked up his pen, and rifled through the papers on his desk to find a blank pad. 'Now, tell me, what were you doing in Mulberry Crescent? Your phone call sounded urgent but was light on details.'

Jack had primed himself and was ready with an expurgated version of their visit, stressing the sudden impulse that had made Flora sure the red bobble she'd picked up on the pier the day Miss Dakers died might belong to the Russells. It had been Ted Russell talking about costumes that alerted Flora and made her want to return the bobble to where it belonged. They'd gone to Mulberry Crescent, hoping to speak to Sylvia, ask her whether her father had a Harlequin costume from his theatrical past, but they hadn't been able to make her hear. The door had been open, which they'd found strange, but they'd taken the liberty of going in and calling her name.

Ridley had begun to look sceptical and Jack could guess why. His explanation hadn't touched on why they had then walked up the stairs when it was evident no one was at home.

'The next thing we knew,' Jack went on quickly, 'was Sylvia Russell had a knife to Flora's neck. It happened so suddenly that it took us both completely unawares. I felt helpless – any move I made could have meant Flora's death.'

The inspector nodded sympathetically, but then the inevitable question. 'What made you go upstairs?'

'Flora wondered, we wondered whether Sylvia was all right. The door was open but no one answered. We thought we should check.'

'Yes, of course,' Ridley said, and Jack felt proud of himself. It was an element he'd forgotten to work out, and he'd had to think on his feet. He hoped Flora would appreciate it.

'In a situation like that, very wise not to attempt anything,' the inspector went on. 'The court will decide on the girl's state of mind when the case comes to trial, if it ever does, but it's my belief she's unbalanced.'

'She's admitted to killing?'

'Oh, yes.' For the first time Jack could remember, Ridley looked shocked. 'Not only admitted to murdering her cousin and young Parsons, but appears to be proud of it. And, as you suspected, she'd tried earlier to kill Miss Steele in Brighton.'

Jack knew that at this point he should mention the gaping hole in *Mabel* and their near drowning on the river, but decided against. The less he said, the fewer questions there'd be. He didn't want the inspector probing their role in the affair too deeply.

Realising he'd be grilled by Flora when he got back to Abbeymead, he had a question of his own. 'Did you get to the bottom of the Harlequin costume?'

Ridley gave a loud laugh. 'She wore it as disguise, of course. Ingenious, really. Stole it from her father without him knowing, and took it to Brighton with her. I asked her if it was a part of a deliberate plan. Had she decided to murder her cousin way back? But apparently not. The two of them had been invited to a fancy dress party some swanky friend of Harry Barnes was throwing, out at Rottingdean. Sylvia had nothing to wear to such a posh do, so she sneaked the Harlequin costume when she was home for the weekend.'

'Did she get to wear it at the party?'

'No, she didn't. Polly decided she was too tired to go in the end, so no party for Sylvia. One more black mark against her cousin. Still, at least the girl won't be hurting anyone else,' Ridley said comfortably. 'She's locked away safe and sound until she sees the psychiatrist. He'll be the judge as to whether she's fit to stand trial.'

'What's your opinion?'

The inspector shrugged. 'You can never tell what these shrinks will decide, but if it were up to me I'd find somewhere secure for her. If she goes to trial, she'll end up with the hangman for sure, and I'd rather not see that. Her father's the one I feel sorry for – as if he doesn't have enough to deal with.'

Jack was silent for a moment, thinking of what Ted Russell would face once discharged from St Luke's, but when he spoke, it was to change the subject.

'Did you hear anything more about Frank Foster? From your colleagues in London?'

'Ah, yes, I was going to pass on the news. I know you're interested in the bloke – one of your suspects, wasn't he? By the way, that list you gave me was well off beam.' He gave a smug laugh. 'Anyway, Foster... when they first arrested him, it was for money laundering – he's part of a gang making a hell of a lot of cash out of the operation. But, since then, the London chaps have raided the Blue Peacock – that's his nightclub somewhere in the West End – and found a stash of jewellery. All stolen, of course. Foster wasn't content with money laundering, he was working as a fence as well. Receiving stolen goods has been added to the charge sheet.'

Jack wondered if he dared ask about the doomed bracelet. It wouldn't do to reveal how involved he and Flora had been in the investigation, then decided that Ridley was in a good enough mood to chance it. 'Sylvia Russell mentioned that Foster had given her cousin a bracelet. Was Polly wearing it when you brought her out of the water, do you know?'

'She hadn't any jewellery on, as I recall. Just a watch. But now you've mentioned it, there is something interesting, for us at least – we found the bracelet when we searched the Russell house and sent it to London on the off-chance that it matched an item they'd told us about. The boys there were delighted. It was stolen, naturally, not that Miss Dakers would have known. It's got the poor kid's fingerprints on it, but also Foster's. He won't be able to wriggle out of that one.'

Jack was intrigued. 'Where did you find the bracelet? Foster—' He'd been going to say that Foster had searched the Russell house as well as the flat in Rose Court and found nothing, but then remembered he wasn't supposed to know.

'Where you'd expect. In her bedroom at Mulberry Crescent. Miss Dakers' room, that is. She'd wrapped it up in pretty paper with a tag and tucked it away in her chest of drawers. It looks like she was going to give it to Sylvia as a birthday present.'

The irony struck Jack hard. According to Sylvia, the bracelet had been the proverbial straw, the force that had led to a fatal push. Her cousin had told her to wait. What Polly had meant was that Sylvia must wait for her birthday to be given the piece of jewellery she coveted, but in her anger and bitterness, the girl had interpreted the innocent remark quite differently. It was sobering that on such small moments, a person's fate could hang. There was a further irony, Jack reflected. When Frank Foster had searched, he must have found the present but, seeing the birthday paper and tag, had dismissed it as unimportant.

'Now you tell me something,' Ridley said. 'Did you have a stone through your window recently?'

'Not a stone, a shard of flint,' Jack said cautiously.

'And you didn't report it?'

'I didn't want to waste police time,' he lied. 'I thought it must be one of the local ne'er-do-wells, out on an evening spree.'

'Nothing like that, old chap,' the inspector said complacently. 'It was our friend, Sylvia. She's a strange one, I have to say. Proud of leaving her cousin to drown, proud of slitting her boyfriend's throat. And very proud of smashing your window. She claims she hit you.'

'She did,' Jack admitted. 'I'd never have imagined her as the guilty one.'

'Not usually in a girl's line, is it? But she did it. Told me she was the netball queen at school. Best shooter that Steyning Secondary Modern ever had.'

THIRTY-THREE

It was Saturday afternoon tea and Alice had baked scones and a very large fruit cake for the occasion. The spread had been laid out on one of the Nook's gingham tablecloths, and the café sign changed to Closed.

Kate went behind the counter and opened her larder cupboard, bringing out a pot of strawberry jam and one of clotted cream.

'We have treats,' she announced. 'The jam comes from Elsie, part of a batch she made last summer, and the cream was given to me by Dilys, of all people. Her cousin in Devon sent up two large pots and she decided you deserved one, Flora. The whole village is buzzing with the news. You're a heroine!' She pulled out a chair. 'And Jack's a hero, naturally.'

'I can't think why,' Flora said, taking a seat at the table. 'There's not much heroism in ending up prisoners.'

'But you found out what was happening. And you got Sylvia arrested.'

'That you did.' Alice brought a heavy teapot to the table. 'Is there any more news of her, d'you know?'

'She's in custody,' Jack said heavily, 'charged with a double murder, though Inspector Ridley isn't sure she'll be fit to stand trial. He's hoping not.'

'Whatever's decided, it's a sad end to a young life,' Kate said gently.

'It's nothing but what she deserves.' Alice was a good deal more severe. 'To push her cousin to her death and then kill poor Raymond like that! Barbaric! I'd have her in the dock.'

'I've never really liked Sylvia Russell,' Kate said, handing round the tea plates, 'but I always felt bad about not liking her. I suppose I felt sorry for her, losing her mum so young. Bad enough if the woman had died, but just to go off like that, leaving her daughter to think she wasn't loved.'

'It was a bad beginning, I grant you,' Alice responded. 'Here, Jack, try these sandwiches. My own pickle. Or mebbe a scone. But bad beginning or not, she can't be excused. Plenty have had as bad a start in life and they don't go round murdering.'

'Perhaps they didn't have a Polly Dakers as a cousin,' Kate said. 'Sylvia always seemed so awkward around Polly.'

'She was.' Flora, too, couldn't help feeling sorry for Sylvia. 'She'd convinced herself that her father preferred Polly, just like her mother had preferred the American soldier. And then Raymond capped it all by falling in love with her cousin when he was supposed to fall for her.'

'He certainly paid the price for it,' Jack mumbled through a mouthful of scone.

'You were lucky the police arrived when they did.' Alice rearranged the teacups and poured for them all. 'Or you'd have been next.'

'Seeing those blue uniforms was the best sight ever,' Flora agreed, 'though not for Sylvia.'

The police had arrived in Mulberry Crescent as the girl shut the front door behind her. Sylvia could barely have got to the garden gate before the handcuffs were round her wrists. Her dream of escaping to Canada was over. Whatever was decided, her future was bleak.

Flora glanced across the table at Jack. When he'd called at the cottage yesterday, she'd been shocked to see how drawn he looked and, since they'd arrived at the café, he'd said very little. Reopening the All's Well this morning, it had felt as though a little piece of normality had crept back into her life. Beforehand, all she'd wanted to do was sleep. A way of forgetting the ordeal, she supposed, or trying to. She imagined it was the same for Jack, but his continued silence was making her uneasy.

'You all right, my love?' Alice asked him. She must have noticed the deep lines on his forehead and the white around his mouth.

He gave a brief nod. 'I'm fine, enjoying my tea.'

'It must have been a terrible shock for you both.' Kate's voice was filled with sympathy. 'It's bound to take time to forget.'

An understatement, Flora thought. Finding Raymond had been the worst thing ever, being flung into that room and realising, even as Jack told her not to look, what it contained. That poor, life-less boy, lying amid a pool of his own blood. They couldn't have been prisoners in that room for more than a few minutes, yet it had seemed a lifetime. She hadn't dared to look again at the mangled body lying so close.

'You'll get over it, Jack, soon enough,' Alice said comfortably. 'You bein' a writer an' all.' It was a clumsy attempt to lighten the conversation. 'Crime, you know,' she persisted, when Jack looked bewildered. 'You're used to it, aren't you?'

'I suppose so.' There was a long pause before, stumbling over his words, he suddenly said, 'I'm sorry.'

The three of them looked at him in puzzlement.

'I let Flora down,' he muttered, looking fixedly at his plate. 'I went to the Russell house with her to make sure she came to no harm, and instead she nearly died. Look at the scar on her throat.'

'That's rubbish,' Flora said robustly, pulling up the collar of her blouse to hide her neck. 'If you had tried to wrest that knife from Sylvia, she would have killed me without a second thought. She was like a bomb ready to explode with one false move. You did absolutely the right thing, or we wouldn't both still be alive and eating these wonderful scones.'

Jack's face told her he was unconvinced. What he saw as his failure still gnawed at him.

'If it hadn't been for you ringing Alan Ridley before we left for Mulberry Crescent,' she insisted, 'we'd have been locked in that room with a dead body for days. Maybe until Ted Russell came home from hospital. And Sylvia would have escaped and, by now, be in Toronto.'

Her two friends nodded. 'That's true,' Alice said. 'If it weren't for you, that wicked girl would never have been caught. And think what a horror for Ted to walk into!'

'Do you know how he is?' Flora asked, hoping to change the subject.

She would speak to Jack later, make sure he stopped blaming himself. How could he think in that way? He'd done the right thing. In those harrowing moments when she believed she might die, it was Jack who'd stopped her from breaking down. Knowing he was close by had kept her together, kept her rational in a dreadful situation. And if Sylvia *had* wielded the knife to kill, as she'd threatened, Jack would have acted, overpowering the girl and possibly inflicting serious injury on them both. It was better by far that he'd kept a cool head.

'Ted won't have to go back to the house just yet,' Kate put in. 'Vicar's offered to collect him from St Luke's this afternoon, and take him to stay at the vicarage for a while. Amy Dunmore's his housekeeper and she's a good sort. She's looked after Vicar for years and she'll look after Ted, too – until the poor man can cope with what's happened.'

'I doubt he ever will,' Alice said glumly. 'He'll blame himself, and there's no gettin' away from it, he did spoil that girl. Then Polly came to stay when her folks went to New Zealand, and suddenly she's the centre of attention. He'll definitely blame himself.'

'Think of her family, coming all the way back to bury their daughter.' Kate's lip trembled. But then, reaching across the counter for a knife, she said in a firm voice, 'It should be a celebration today. Shall I cut the cake?' She half-turned to Alice. 'It looks one of your best.'

'I aim to please,' Alice responded. 'That's more than that darn niece of mine. You know, Kate, the one I was tellin' you about in Germany.'

'You have a niece in Germany?' Jack brightened, seeming to shake off his gloom.

'Sally, that's her name. Got a good job in the British embassy there. Decent money and a secure future. Plenty of opportunity to go up the ladder. But you wouldn't believe what she's written to me. She's fed up with the job, she says, fed up with the embassy, fed up with Germany. She's throwin' it all away.'

'That's a big decision.' Flora helped herself to a slice of fruit cake. 'What will she do instead?'

'That's just it. What indeed?' Alice sounded incensed. 'I told her – wrote a long letter – there's not much work goin' here. It's better than it was, but nothin' much for women, even single women. As for the poor souls who were daft enough to get married, pushed back in the home now they're not needed. The war was awful but it had its upsides – for women, leastways. Sally's got a solid career ahead of her if she does well, but she don't want it.'

'You shouldn't worry about her so much,' Kate said, getting up to refresh the pot. 'She's got her head screwed on and she'll land on her feet somewhere.'

'Like a blessed cat,' Alice grumbled.

'Have you heard any more about the sale of the Priory?' It was half in Flora's mind that there might be work for Sally Jenner.

There was a general shaking of heads. 'One of the administrators came by earlier this week,' Kate told them. 'Bought a meat pie for his lunch, but he didn't mention the Priory and I didn't feel I could press him. It won't be sold to Frank Foster now, that's for sure. Hopefully, Abbeymead has seen the last of him. I reckon that when he lied about going back to London and stayed on at the Cross Keys, he was following Polly all the time.' She gave a shudder. 'I knew he was a horrible man.'

'I'm sure you're right. He could well have been in Brighton the day Polly died,' Flora said, 'stalking her that Monday morning. But if he saw there was trouble on the pier, he'd have made himself scarce. The police were out in force and he wouldn't want them taking notice of him.'

'Luckily, they did,' Kate said, sounding unusually firm, 'and now he's going to jail.'

'Which is the one piece of good news to come out of this hideous time.' Flora took a large mouthful of fruit cake.

'There is another.' Alice looked smug. 'I heard, private like, that Harry Barnes is back with his missus.'

'Harry's been forgiven? That's quite something.' Jack's face wore his familiar crooked smile and it did Flora good to see it.

'I don't think she's actually forgiven him,' Alice said cautiously. 'It's more she didn't know what to do with him, the big lummock, if he didn't live at Pelham Lodge.'

'It's still good news,' Jack said. 'And that's what we need.'

Alice nodded vigorously. 'It's been a bad few weeks for Abbeymead, losin' two young people like that. Three, if you count Sylvia.'

There was a brief silence, broken almost immediately by the unexpected ringing of a bell. Jack glanced across at the café door. The blurred figure of a boy appeared through its dimpled glass. 'Here's one young person we won't be losing,' he said, half laughing.

Flora twisted round in her chair. It was a brave customer who disregarded the Closed notice. Then she smiled.

'Come on in, Charlie. Did you smell the scones?'

An hour later, Flora and Jack strolled together along the high street, arms linked.

'We seem to be heading towards the All's Well,' he said, a frown creasing his forehead, 'and I'm not sure why. You're not thinking of opening again?'

Flora shook her head. 'Definitely not. I'm closed until Monday, but I've left some very important papers on my desk. Ones I want to read tomorrow.'

'They must be important.'

'They are. They're yours! Your very latest chapters.'

He ruffled a hand through his hair. 'I'd have thought the first few were enough. You really don't have to read more.'

'I want to – before you finish the book when we're in Cornwall. Why don't you send what you've done to Arthur Bellaby?'

'For my dear agent to tear to pieces, you mean?'

'Nonsense.' She squeezed his arm. 'Arthur is going to love it. I'm halfway through what you gave me and I can tell you the writing is good.' She gave him a sly smile. 'You see what sleuthing does for you? Supercharges your brain.'

'More likely pumps it full of adrenalin – all that dragging you out of the sea, dragging you out of a ditch, dragging you out of the river. Constantly terrified of what you're going to do next.'

'You love our adventures. I know you do.'

His smile was reluctant. 'Well, some of them maybe. Just a little,' he admitted.

They came to a halt at the All's Well's imposing front door and Flora turned to say goodbye, but found a finger being wagged in her face.

'Oh, no. You're not getting rid of me that easily. I'm walking back with you to your cottage.'

'Relax, Jack. I'm safe. We're both safe. We both survived.'

'But only just and that's something I can't forget. When we get to Cornwall, it's strictly work. And the work is writing, not looking out for the local axe man. OK?'

She nodded, still smiling. 'You're the boss.'

'I very much doubt it,' he said ruefully.

She turned to unlock the bookshop door.

'It's been a difficult few weeks,' he said to her back. 'You do still want to come to Cornwall?'

She turned once again and walked back to him, reaching up to put a hand on each shoulder and looking straight into his changeful grey eyes.

'Try and stop me!' she said, and kissed him on the cheek.

A LETTER FROM MERRYN

Dear Reader,

I want to say a huge thank you for choosing to read *Murder on the Pier*. If you enjoyed it and want to keep up to date with all my latest releases, just sign up at the following link. Your email address will never be shared and you can unsubscribe at any time.

www.bookouture.com/merryn-allingham

The 1950s is a fascinating period to write about, outwardly conformist but beneath the surface, there's rebellion brewing, even in Sussex! I've lived in the county for many years now and love it – the small villages, the South Downs, and the sea – and I hope you enjoyed Flora's and Jack's adventures there as much as I loved writing them. If you did, you can follow their fortunes in the next Abbeymead mystery.

If you enjoyed *Murder on the Pier*, I would love a short review. Getting feedback from readers is amazing and it helps new readers to discover one of my books for the first time.

And hearing from readers makes this author's day! So do get in touch on my Facebook page, through Twitter, Goodreads or my website.

Thank you for reading,

Merryn

www.merrynallingham.com

 facebook.com/MerrynWrites
twitter.com/merrynwrites